NEW PENGUIN SHAKESPEARE

GENERAL EDITOR: T. J. B. SPENCER

ASSOCIATE EDITOR: STANLEY WELLS

RICHARDS CHARACTER IS VERY WEEK AND
INDECISIVE. PORTRAYED TO THE AUDIENCE
AS YOUTHFULL WE ALSO HEAR HE HAS
AN EXTRAVAGANT TASTE IN CLOTHES
IMPORTED FROM OTHER COUNTRIES (-QUOTE)
PICK UP ON HIS INDECISIVE WAYS EARLY ON IN
THE PLAY - HE ALLOWS THE DUEL BETWEEN
BOLLINGBROOK AND MOWBRAY TO GO AHEAD
BUT STOPS IT AS IT IS ABOUT TO COMMENCE.
CHARACTERS TAKES EVERYTHING IN HIS
STRIDE HE DOESN'T SEEM TO NOTICE THE
ENVIRONMENT SURROUNDING HIM.
WE ARE MADE AWARE OF THE FACT RICH
DOESN'T LIKE TO BE TOLD WHAT TO DO
HE BELIEVES HE IS THE MOST IMPORTANT
AND THE ONLY ONE WHO MATTERS (DIVINE RIGHT
WE ALSO SEE WITIN THE 1ST ACT THE SHADY
ASPECTS OF THE ICING. WE FIND OUT HE DID
HAVE A PART IN THE MURDER OF HIS
UNCLE THE DUKE OF GLOUSTER THIS IS
WHOSE DEATH TM HAS BEEN ACCUSED OF
by Bol. Rich doesn't own up he just
banishes MOW for life so the truth
doesn't get out. Everyone believes
mowbray did it and has been punished.
All the Characteristics involved in Rich's
character appear negative and in the end
lead to his downfall.

BOLS CHARACTER

- Comes across as an honourable man and is well respected by lots of people including the common people. This last point is proved when he tells Richard of Mowbrays part in the plot to kill the duke of Nolfe he is genuinly trying to protect Ric

- Talked about frequently, especially what a good person he is and wha a good king he would make.

- Obvious people like Bol much more than Rich as he is not stuck up and talks to everyone not just the 1st class people

- He is a very secretive character we don't really know much about him he keeps himself to himself and does let us know much about his charact

- This is where the characters differ so much Rich is much more out going compared to Bol who remain as one big mystery.

WILLIAM SHAKESPEARE

*

KING RICHARD
THE SECOND

EDITED BY
STANLEY WELLS

Views on Kingship.

In those days people believed in Devine
Right of Kings. The king of the country
is appointed by god and only god can
remove him. They couldn't get rid of
him except hope he dies.

Richard believes he has total power
and nobody can go against him

Richard was the last king to rule
under devine right.

PENGUIN BOOKS

PENGUIN BOOKS

Published by the Penguin Group
Penguin Books Ltd, 27 Wrights Lane, London W8 5TZ, England
Penguin Books USA Inc., 375 Hudson Street, New York, New York 10014, USA
Penguin Books Australia Ltd, Ringwood, Victoria, Australia
Penguin Books Canada Ltd, 10 Alcorn Avenue, Toronto, Ontario, Canada M4V 3B2
Penguin Books (NZ) Ltd, 182–190 Wairau Road, Auckland 10, New Zealand

Penguin Books Ltd, Registered Offices: Harmondsworth, Middlesex, England

This edition first published in Penguin Books 1969
Reprinted with revised Further Reading 1997
1 3 5 7 9 10 8 6 4 2

This edition copyright © Penguin Books Ltd, 1969
Introduction and notes copyright © Stanley Wells, 1969
Further Reading copyright © Michael Taylor, 1997
All rights reserved

Printed in England by Clays Ltd, St Ives plc
Set in Monotype Ehrhardt

CONTENTS

INTRODUCTION

Richard II is the most purely lyrical of Shakespeare's histories – perhaps of all his plays – and the role of King Richard is the most lyrical among the tragic heroes. The play is written wholly in verse, which except for occasional irregularities is entirely in ten-syllabled lines, whether rhymed or unrhymed. Considering the metrical virtuosity that Shakespeare had already displayed in *Love's Labour's Lost*, and his masterly use of varied styles of prose in both that play and others written before *Richard II*, we may suspect that he was here deliberately restricting – or concentrating – his resources. True, the verse of *Richard II* encompasses the bluntness of Bolingbroke and Northumberland, the irresolution of the Duke of York, the business-like scheming of the conspirators, and the allegorizing formalities of the Head Gardener, as well as the elegiac lyricism of Richard and his grief-stricken Queen. Yet the mode we feel to be most characteristic of *Richard II* is the elegiac. Our image of the play is primarily an image of Richard himself, a beautiful young man luxuriating in sorrow. We think of him, not as the judicial figure of the opening scenes, nor as the maliciously petulant one revealed in his encounters with John of Gaunt, nor even in the splendid anger of his death, but rather as the man whose suffering we share intensely from the moment he returns from Ireland and is compelled to divest himself of all that he valued most highly.

It is a process that seems to result from inner rather than external compulsion; and while we should perhaps censure him for inflicting punishment upon himself, for the weakness that causes him to renounce responsibility, yet we can forgive his self-indulgence because of the reality of his grief and bewilderment as he feels himself stripped away to a point where he seems no longer to possess a self. We forgive him too because he suffers so articulately, so expressively, and in such melodious and perfectly controlled verse. We think of him as a voice, and a voice with tears in it.

Actors who have succeeded as Richard have inevitably been praised for beauty of speech. One – William Macready – said of another – Edmund Kean – that he could 'never forget the music of the musical passages of Richard II and the sublime melancholy of their delivery'. Ellen Terry regarded Richard as one of the two best roles of Edmund's son, Charles Kean, because in it 'his beautiful diction had full scope'; Walter Pater wrote that when Charles acted in it 'the play became like an exquisite performance on the violin'. Of the American Edwin Booth, William Winter wrote: 'It was luxury merely to listen, with closed eyes, to the voice of Edwin Booth, when he spoke the soliloquies in "Richard II", for his tones were music, and his clear articulation and delicate shading of the words enchanted the ear.' These performances all belong to the nineteenth century, when the play was only moderately popular and was performed in versions that were always severely shortened and sometimes significantly altered. Since the turn of the century the text has been treated with more respect, and perhaps its most influential interpreter has been F. R. Benson, who played it many times in the late nineteenth century and the early years of the twentieth. C. E. Montague wrote a famous review praising him for 'a fine sensibility to beauty in words and situations and a voice that gives this sensibility its due'. Since then the greatest interpreter of the role has understandably been our finest

verse speaker, Sir John Gielgud, who was influenced by a
letter from Harley Granville Barker in which he wrote,
after seeing an early performance, 'my chief grouse is about
the verse. It is a lyrical play. W. S. has not yet learned to
express anything except in speech. There is nothing much,
I mean, in between the lines, as there is in *Macbeth* (for an
extreme example). Therefore – I am preaching; forgive me
– everything the actor does must be done *within the frame* of
the verse. Whatever impression of action or thought he can
get within this frame without disturbance of *cadence* or
flow, he may. But there must be nothing, no trick, no check,
beyond an honest pause or so at the end of a sentence or
speech. And I believe you'll seldom find that the cadence
and emphasis – the mere right scansion of the verse does
not give you the meaning without much of any further
effort on the actor's part. . . . Variety of pace – tone – colour
of speech; yes, as much as possible, but within the *frame*.'
And he complained that Gielgud had been inclined 'to play
more and more astride the verse instead of in it'. This is
valuable less as a final judgement on Gielgud's performance, which matured into one of the best pieces of verse-
speaking imaginable, than as a wise comment on the nature
of the verse in this play and the actor's problems in speaking it.

If we are so conscious of the style of the play, the beauty
of its language, this may be partly because it is deliberately
a play of character, thought, and emotion rather than
action. It is remarkably passive. Events seem to occur of
themselves or by a remote, divine will rather than as the
result of human volition. The play constantly approaches
action only to withdraw before it happens. The third scene
is characteristic: the lists are set up, all is ready for a personal combat between Mowbray and Bolingbroke, yet
violence is averted at the last moment as Richard throws

'his warder down'. Gaunt is held back from taking revenge on Richard for the murder of Gloucester. Bolingbroke, though he returns to England illegally, needs to take no action in order to gain the crown; his mere presence is enough to draw from Richard a submission that seems to satisfy something within himself as well as representing his defeat. Aumerle's conspiracy against Bolingbroke is thwarted in its early stages. Except for the pageant-like *Henry VIII* this is the only history play of Shakespeare that has no battle scenes. The one violent action in the play is the murder of Richard, a deed which its instigator immediately claims to have wished not to happen.

*

When he wrote *Richard II*, Shakespeare had already composed at least four plays about English history. Three are devoted to the long and eventful reign of Henry VI, and are closely linked. They are among his earliest work. Another, written probably after an interval, is *Richard III*, which tells how the warring houses of York and Lancaster were finally reconciled in the person of the Earl of Richmond, later King Henry VII. It is closely related to the early plays, which form a necessary background to it. Its triumphant ending celebrating Henry VII, Elizabeth's grandfather, was a genuine climax, the culmination of what might well have been regarded as a historical process designed by God for the benefit of the English nation. In choosing to write about Richard II Shakespeare went back to an earlier period, though one that could easily be seen in relation to that which he had already dramatized. The reign of Richard II was a real starting-point, for Richard was the last king of England to rule by direct and undisputed succession from William the Conqueror. Bolingbroke's usurpation of his throne set in motion the train of events which was finally expiated only by the union of the houses of York and Lancaster celebrated in the last speech of *Richard III*.

There is thus some appearance of a 'grand design'. Shakespeare might have written a great and closely integrated cycle of plays on English history from Richard II to Richard III. But he did not. He wrote eight plays, each capable of standing by itself, though to varying degrees related to others. He wrote them in two groups of four, the earlier group dealing with the later period. The three concerned with the reign of Henry VI are closely connected. So are the two concerned with Henry IV; and *Henry V* falls easily into place after them. But on the whole Shakespeare seems to have been more concerned to give unity to the individual plays than to subordinate them to an overall design. To consider or perform them together as a national epic may increase our perception of relationships that truly exist. But we are liable to distort each play if we try to force it into too close a relationship with the others. Though, for instance, the events of *1 Henry IV* are foreshadowed in *Richard II*, the two plays differ greatly in style. Historically, Harry Percy is the same character in both; artistically and theatrically, he is not. It is more valuable to attempt to realize the individual design, structure, and mode of each play than to seek for consistency of design from one to another.

It is reasonable, then, to see *Richard II* as a new departure, an attempt to do something different from what Shakespeare had done in his earlier history plays. The story that he chose was one that may well have seemed to have contemporary relevance. He was writing, we believe, about 1595. Queen Elizabeth had been on the throne since 1558, and had never married. The question of the succession was a major political issue. Elizabeth had done much to unify England and increase the country's prosperity. It was important that the next monarch should not throw away what she had won. A weak ruler would have been a national disaster, and there were those who felt that her successor should be chosen and appointed for his merits rather than on hereditary principle. Elizabeth, for all her popularity, was not exempt from criticism, and a charge often brought against her was that she was excessively influenced by favourites. This was one of the reasons why she was liable to be compared to Richard II. And there is good reason to believe that Shakespeare's play had special significance for his politically minded contemporaries. When it was first printed, in 1597, the scene of Richard's abdication was omitted, probably as the result of official censorship directed against the representation of the deposition of a monarch, even though Shakespeare elicits such sympathy for the victim. The scene is absent from the two later editions printed during Elizabeth's lifetime, but was restored in the first edition to appear after her death.

If Elizabeth was often compared to Richard, the most obvious candidate for identification with Bolingbroke was the Earl of Essex, a favourite of the Queen who was himself ambitious for power. In 1599 John Hayward published a book called *The First Part of the Life and Reign of King Henry IV*. It bore an ill-judged dedication to Essex which was considered so inflammatory that within three weeks the Archbishop of Canterbury ordered that it should be cut out, and copies of the book were burnt. Hayward deals almost entirely with the history of Richard II and the reasons for his deposition, and many readers must have been tempted to draw the obvious parallels between Richard and Elizabeth, and Bolingbroke and Essex. Among them was the Queen. When in 1600 Essex was on trial for having returned from Ireland the previous year against the

Queen's orders, Hayward was examined and his book was regarded as potential evidence of Essex's treacherous intentions.

In the following year a play about Richard II, almost certainly Shakespeare's, was used as an instrument in the political struggle. A performance at the Globe Theatre by the company of players to which Shakespeare belonged was arranged and paid for by Essex's supporters, apparently as a gesture of encouragement and defiance. The actors complained that the play was 'so old and so long out of use as that they should have small or no company at it', but they were paid enough to justify their putting it on, and Essex's supporters attended the performance on 7 February 1601. On the following day Essex led his abortive rebellion, and before the month was out he had been tried and executed. The Queen clearly resented the identification of herself with Richard, and disliked contemplating the resemblances. A rather enigmatic conversation has been preserved between her and William Lambarde, the keeper of the records of the Tower. In August 1601 he presented her with some of the archives and she 'fell upon the reign of King Richard II, saying "I am Richard II, know ye not that?"' Lambarde made a diplomatic reply agreeing that Essex, 'the most adorned creature that ever your majesty made', had made the identification, and his sovereign replied 'He that will forget God will also forget his benefactors; this tragedy was played forty times in open streets and houses.' 'This tragedy' is not an undisputable reference to Shakespeare's play, particularly since the actors had complained that the play they performed was 'long out of use' (though it could be that the Queen referred to performances some years previously). But there is no doubt that Elizabeth was peculiarly sensitive about comparisons between Richard and herself, and that some of her subjects felt the comparison was damaging to her.

Still, nothing in Shakespeare's play suggests that he was specially interested in the topical parallels, or that he wrote with any immediate political intent. Nor does he seem to have been suspected of doing so, since he and his fellows were not punished when the play was used as a prologue to Essex's rebellion. Shakespeare was not concerned merely to present a documentary account of the facts. Certainly he was interested in the political aspects of Richard's reign and their bearing on the general topic of the position of a monarch in relation to God and to his people. The play raises many general issues, both political and personal. But Shakespeare does not specifically relate them to the situation at the time he was writing. Nor does he twist the facts so as to force his audience into an awareness of relationships with contemporary politics. This play is closer to history as Shakespeare knew it than most of his other plays about English history.

His main source was Raphael Holinshed's massive *Chronicles*, which had been first published in 1577 and of which Shakespeare used the second edition, of 1587. He may have been directly influenced too by an earlier chronicle, that by Edward Hall, first printed in 1548, which begins at precisely the same point as Shakespeare's play – the quarrel between Bolingbroke and Mowbray. Hall's overall scheme too seems to have influenced Shakespeare. It is revealed by Hall's full title: *The Union of the Two Noble and Illustre Families of Lancaster and York, being long in continual dissension for the crown of this noble realm, with all the acts done in both the times of the princes, both of the one lineage and of the other, beginning at the time of King Henry the Fourth, the first author of this division, and so successively proceeding to the reign of the high and*

*prudent prince King Henry the Eight, the undubitate flower
and very heir of both the said lineages.* If one wanted to produce a simplified description of Shakespeare's history
plays as a group, it might read something like that.

Shakespeare seems to have worked hard to prepare himself to write this play. Oscar Wilde has the pleasant fancy
that he looked carefully at Richard's tomb in Westminster
Abbey where 'we can still discern on the King's robe his
favourite badge – the sun issuing from a cloud'. Certainly
Richard is often associated in the play with the sun. The
correspondence between sun and king was commonplace.
Still, Wilde's suggestion reminds us that more than books
existed to stimulate Shakespeare's imagination. The influence of some writings that have been suggested as
sources is doubtful, and not of the first importance to an
understanding of the play itself. It is, for instance, con-
ceivable that Shakespeare used two French chronicles, one
in verse, Jean Créton's *Histoire du Roi d'Angleterre
Richard II*, and the other an anonymous *Chronique de la
Traison et Mort de Richard Deux roi d'Angleterre*. Both
existed only in manuscript in Shakespeare's time, but they
were known in England. Shakespeare probably read Lord
Berners's great translation of *The Chronicles of Sir John
Froissart*, and may have been distantly influenced by it; he
appears to have known an anonymous play that has survived only in a slightly incomplete manuscript and is
generally known as *Woodstock*; and his last Act in particular seems to be coloured by memories of Samuel
Daniel's long narrative poem *The First Four Books of the
Civil Wars between the Two Houses of Lancaster and York*.
This was published in 1595, and Shakespeare's play must
have been written at about the same time. But unquestion-
ably his main source of information was Holinshed's
Chronicles, a compilation which drew heavily on the

writings of earlier chroniclers and was for Shakespeare the obvious, most up-to-date reference book. The Commentary to this edition draws attention to some of the more interesting features of Shakespeare's use of his source material.

In his plays about British history of the comparatively recent past Shakespeare did not depart so freely from the chroniclers as he did in, for instance, *Macbeth* or *King Lear*. In dramatizing the reign of Richard II he followed Holinshed fairly closely, but even so he chose to use only the final pages of Holinshed's long account of the reign, and with that he took liberties. Harry Percy becomes younger and Prince Hal (who is referred to but does not appear) older than in reality; thus, whether consciously or not, Shakespeare prepares for their rivalry in *1 Henry IV*. Queen Isabel too he transforms from the little girl that she really was at the time of the events of the play to a woman capable of full emotional sympathy with Richard's plight. He invents characters, especially ones whom he requires for symbolic effect such as the Welsh Captain (II.4) and the Gardeners (III.4). The attitudes that he takes towards the characters are not always the orthodox ones; he is more sympathetic with Richard in the later part of the play than most historians were.

Besides omitting much, Shakespeare creates a theatrical and verbal structure which tells its historical story in a manner that transcends particularity. *Richard II* is often spoken of in musical terms. This is an indication of the extent to which Shakespeare has turned actuality into art. There is something operatic about it. Actions are shaped into an intricate pattern, characters engage and conflict in significant ways, and they are given things to say and ways of saying them that create a greatly resonant structure of words and ideas so intricately inter-related that they play against and recall one another like the phrases in a complex piece of music.

*

In the first edition *Richard II*, like most of Shakespeare's plays, is printed continuously. The division into Acts and scenes was made in the Folio (1623), and we have no reason to believe that it has Shakespeare's authority. Structurally the major break comes at the end of what editors have called III.1. The first part of the play thus considered presents Richard rather unfavourably, but also keeps us distanced from him. We watch him performing his kingly functions, but are rarely conscious of him as a man with feelings of his own. In his relationship to John of Gaunt on the one hand, and to his favourites, Bushy, Bagot, and Green, on the other, it is fair to see the influence of the patterned structures of morality drama. All but Bagot are dead at the end of the first part. With their departure Richard emerges into full prominence as a dramatic character.

In the first line Richard addresses 'Old John of Gaunt, time-honoured Lancaster', and this is suggestive of Gaunt's main function. He is to represent values associated with the old order, and Richard is to be judged partly by them. But though Richard is on stage throughout the first scene, and as king must be prominently placed, we are not told much about him. He is only in the chair, as it were, exercising his official, public function. He watches silent while the others speak: a situation later to be notably reversed. When he speaks it is with formality. Coleridge noted the display of 'that feature in Richard's character which is never forgotten throughout the play – his attention to decorum and high feeling of the kingly dignity'. The actor has to decide how far he should try to suggest

Richard's true personality under the kingly exterior. Richard's very inaction can be turned to account. Benson played him here as a luxurious lounger, caressing and feeding his hounds in bored indifference. Gielgud has written that the actor 'must use the early scenes to create an impression of slyness, petty vanity, and callous indifference'. Yet the quarrel between Bolingbroke and Mowbray is about a matter in which the King is deeply implicated – the murder of his uncle, Thomas of Woodstock, Duke of Gloucester. Some actors of Richard have silently conveyed consciousness of guilt, and fear that Mowbray may betray him. It has been argued that the only reason Shakespeare did not write these emotions into the play was that an Elizabethan audience, familiar with history and its representation in *Woodstock*, would have known full well that Richard was guilty; and also that it would not have needed to be told of his extravagant and pleasure-loving nature. This is possible, though it is by no means certain that Shakespeare could reasonably have expected such knowledge in his audience. There is no real evidence that *Woodstock* was ever performed, let alone printed. It is more likely that Shakespeare deliberately left the issue vague so that Richard would not be too much exposed to censure. In any case the accusation that Mowbray 'did plot the Duke of Gloucester's death', which might be interpreted as a covert accusation against the King, is only one of Bolingbroke's charges. The emphasis in this scene is on the quarrel itself, the enmity between Bolingbroke and Mowbray, and the ideas released as a result of it, rather than on the rights and wrongs of the case.

It is not until the second scene that characters in the play assert their belief in Richard's responsibility for the murder; and this scene, invented by Shakespeare, has the important function of consolidating John of Gaunt as a strongly virtuous character. The desire for vengeance expressed by Gloucester's widow is understandable, but her argument turns back upon itself, for the very stress she lays on the sanctity of Edward III's line justifies Gaunt's refusal to act: the King rules by divine authority, so his subjects have no right to judge him. Shakespeare departs from his sources here, for Holinshed records that Gaunt and York made proposals for revenge, and *Woodstock* shows them put into action. The audience is encouraged to sympathize with Bolingbroke, both for his father's sake and because of the apparent justice of his charges against Mowbray as the King's agent, and this bias is maintained in the scene of the lists (I.3), in which again we see only the public side of Richard.

We are given our first glimpse of the private man in I.4. Whereas thus far he has maintained a show of impartiality, seeming if anything to favour Bolingbroke rather than his accomplice Mowbray, now he reveals both scorn and fear of Bolingbroke and also some of the less admirable aspects of his own nature as both man and king. He admits that he has kept 'too great a court', and is cynically callous in his reactions to the news of his uncle Gaunt's illness. The measuring of Richard as a king against the standards represented by Gaunt reaches its climax in the scene in which Gaunt, dying, expresses his wish to counsel him. In Richard's absence his uncle, York, speaks contemptuously of his susceptibility to flattery, his vanity, and his self-will, and is answered by Gaunt in the best-known lines of the play, lines which help to justify the common assertion that England is herself one of the *dramatis personae*. They foretell Richard's impending downfall – 'His rash fierce blaze of riot cannot last' – set up an image of England as Gaunt feels it should be, and deplore what

Richard is doing to his country. Gaunt's speech is a climax, and an eloquent one, giving full expression to one view of what a king should be able to accomplish.

Richard is not present to hear Gaunt; and the implied criticism of him is perhaps softened on his immediately following entry by York's emphasis on his youth. Yet Gaunt is highly critical of Richard to his face. His analogy between himself and Richard, claiming that 'Thy death-bed is no lesser than thy land', will be paralleled later in the play in the Gardener's likening of the land to an ill-tended garden. In a climax of anger Gaunt taxes Richard with Woodstock's murder, and goes off to his death. It is characteristic of the peace-loving York that, having defended Richard to Gaunt on the grounds of his youth, he should now defend Gaunt to Richard on the grounds of his sickness and age. Yet his patience is sorely taxed by Richard's confiscation of Gaunt's possessions, and he utters a dire warning that in violating the principle of inheritance Richard is denying the very principle by which he has come to the throne –

> *how art thou a king*
> *But by fair sequence and succession?*

Bolingbroke uses the same argument later (II.3.122–3).

In this section Shakespeare goes a long way towards alienating the audience's sympathies from Richard, and II.1 ends with severe criticism of him from those who favour Bolingbroke, mitigated only by Northumberland's attribution of some of the blame to Richard's favourites:

> *The King is not himself, but basely led*
> *By flatterers.*

The characterization of the favourites is slight. Either Shakespeare decided to leave much to his actors or he relied on his audience's preconceptions. In *Woodstock* the favourites are much more prominent and more obviously evil in their influence. At this low point in Richard's career the counter-action against him begins, as Bolingbroke's supporters in England learn from Northumberland of his plan to return, and agree to join him when he does so.

From then onwards sympathy with Richard is gradually built up, at first obliquely, in his absence. His Queen's grief and foreboding (II.2) suggest a more attractive side to his character than we have seen so far, and this is balanced by a corresponding demonstration of less-than-admirable characteristics in Bolingbroke. He had left the play declaring himself 'a trueborn Englishman'. He returns accepting Northumberland's egregious flattery of his 'fair discourse' (II.3.2–20), and diplomatically offering rewards in return for support (lines 45–50). York, over-whelmed by a 'tide of woes', epitomizes the moral dilemma out of which Shakespeare is making dramatic capital. York owes duty to both his nephews: to Richard as hereditary king, to Bolingbroke as one whom the King has wronged. In his encounter (II.3) with Bolingbroke he berates him for breaking his exile and declares his own continued allegiance to Richard, saying that if his forces were strong enough he would arrest the rebels and compel them to submit; but in the next line he admits that as he is too weak to do this he will 'remain as neuter', and he follows this by inviting them to stay the night. Thus does the old order yield to the new. II.4 is another scene of foreboding, and III.1, in which Bolingbroke seems already to have assumed royal power in his condemnation of Bushy and Green, throws on them much of the blame for Richard's irresponsibility.

The situation to this point is fully summed up in III.2, a scene of both recapitulation and realignment which marks the full emergence of Richard as the centre of

dramatic attention in his double role of king and man. He
has been off stage for 465 lines – more than one sixth of the
whole play. So far we have seen him largely in his public
role, with very little expression of his private feelings. He
has been tested against a high ideal of kingship, and he has
been found wanting. He has relied on the strength of his
public position to compensate for private weaknesses which
make him ill-fitted to hold that position. The weaknesses
give some justification to the assumption of authority by
Bolingbroke and his followers which we have watched
during Richard's absence in Ireland. As Aumerle puts it:

> *we are too remiss,*
> *Whilst Bolingbroke through our security*
> *Grows strong and great in substance and in power.*
>
> III.2.33–5

Richard has been warned of the danger of his position, but
has seemed confident in the security of his hereditary
kingship. Now he expresses love for his country and confidence that she will take his part against rebellion. Now
too just before the storm breaks he utters his strongest
affirmation of the power of his public office, of the idea of
kingship:

> *Not all the water in the rough rude sea*
> *Can wash the balm off from an anointed king.*
> *The breath of worldly men cannot depose*
> *The deputy elected by the Lord.* III.2.54–7

He is to learn most painfully that the identification suggested here between the kingly office and the holder of that
office is an illusion. Thoughts of the power of his name
console him when Salisbury brings news that the Welshmen, believing him dead, have 'gone to Bolingbroke':

> *Arm, arm, my name! A puny subject strikes*
> *At thy great glory.*

But bad news continues to assail him, and believing himself betrayed by his favourites he compares them to Judas, implicitly initiating a comparison between himself and Christ which is to recur several times. Taking their cue from this, actors have often tried to suggest Christ in their make-up; but this surely is to take Richard too much at his own valuation. Learning that his favourites are dead he launches into the first of his great solo speeches (III.2. 144–77), a meditation on mortality which gives classic expression to the theme of the vanity of human greatness. Richard is beginning to learn that the façade of kingship may offer inadequate shelter to the human being who dwells behind it.

Bestirred for a moment by Carlisle and Aumerle to the optimism of projected action, Richard is rapidly cast down again by Scroop's further revelation that even his uncle York has gone over to Bolingbroke, and he gives up hope of regaining his power:

> Go to Flint Castle. There I'll pine away.
> A king, woe's slave, shall kingly woe obey.
> That power I have, discharge, and let them go
> To ear the land that hath some hope to grow;
> For I have none. Let no man speak again
> To alter this; for counsel is but vain.

Though it is not heavily stressed, this might well be regarded as the true moment of Richard's capitulation. He gives way not to violence, not in direct confrontation with Bolingbroke, but to words; to the news that Scroop brings and his imaginings of what it may mean.

Words are important too at the beginning of the next scene. Bolingbroke receives messages, and this leads into a quibbling episode resulting from Northumberland's omission of the word 'King' in speaking of Richard. The quibbling might be considered trivial, yet it is related to a central concern of the play. On one level kingship is no more than a verbal trick, a distinguishing of one man from his fellows by the addition of a prefix to his name. Yet it can have other attributes too. In the previous scene Richard's faith in the power of the mere idea of kingship was affirmed, then tested, then destroyed. Now on his entry both Bolingbroke and York are impressed by the majestic appearance of kingship that he still retains.

YORK

> Yet looks he like a king. Behold, his eye,
> As bright as is the eagle's, lightens forth
> Controlling majesty.

In appearance the man and his office are still at one. As in the previous scene, Richard is given an affirmation of faith in the power of his office. But now it seems a public statement rather than an expression of personal belief. His actions are at variance with his words. Having instructed Northumberland to tell Bolingbroke

> That every stride he makes upon my land
> Is dangerous treason

he nevertheless capitulates to Bolingbroke's demand that his rights shall be returned to him. An aside to Aumerle shows that, behaving like this, he seems far less kingly to himself than he had to York:

> We do debase ourselves, cousin, do we not,
> To look so poorly and to speak so fair?

Aumerle counsels him still to rely on the power of words:

> Let's fight with gentle words
> Till time lend friends, and friends their helpful swords.

Richard's consciousness of the division within himself between the actor and the role finds expression along with his chagrin that he has had to acquiesce in Bolingbroke's illegal return from banishment:

> *O that I were as great*
> *As is my grief, or lesser than my name.*

And in fearful expectation that he will have to give up the throne he envisages a new role for himself:

> *I'll give my jewels for a set of beads,*
> *My gorgeous palace for a hermitage,*
> *My gay apparel for an almsman's gown,*
> *My figured goblets for a dish of wood,*
> *My sceptre for a palmer's walking-staff,*
> *My subjects for a pair of carvèd saints,*
> *And my large kingdom for a little grave,*
> *A little, little grave, an obscure grave. . . .*

They are marvellous lines, marvellous partly because they express the possibility of consolation as well as the experience of despair. To emphasize the first element of each antithesis falsifies the picture. Richard imagines himself renouncing the kingly way of life, with all its obvious attractions, for another that might be held to be better still. The austerities that he envisages are those associated with the way to the kingdom of heaven. That he will be able to embrace them is unfortunately yet another of his illusions. Sir John Gielgud has demonstrated how moving the speech can be, yet he has written too of Richard's 'utter lack of humour and his constant egotism and self-posturing', qualities that are felt in this speech as he elaborates his fantasy of grief till it is in danger of seeming ludicrous:

> *Well, well, I see*
> *I talk but idly, and you laugh at me.*

He recovers enough to make his splendid comparison of his own descent to that of the falling sun-god, an imaginative vision quite beyond the capacities of his enemies, who think he speaks 'fondly, like a frantic man'. Nevertheless they pay him the homage of their knees, and he ends the scene, as he had begun it, with external dignity but, we feel, greater consciousness of emptiness within.

Our direct view of Richard's progress is interrupted by a scene of comment and expansion which invites us to consider the public implications of his plight. This is the garden scene, invented by Shakespeare and clearly symbolic in function. The Queen's grief maintains an overall emphasis of the play (see page 41). And her personal grief is a prologue to the generalized comments of the Gardeners. These characters are liable to suffer in the theatre from the fact that *Richard II* contains little comedy, some of which is uncertain in execution and as a consequence often omitted in performance. There is a temptation to remedy the deficiency by playing the Gardeners for low comedy, giving them heavily rustic accents and exaggeratedly personal characteristics which put them in the same world as the grave-diggers in *Hamlet*. This is unjustified, and unnecessarily emphasizes Shakespeare's purposeful departure from decorum in giving highly wrought language to characters of lowly rank. The stylization of the action calls for equally stylized presentation. The scene is as obvious in its artifice as the one in *3 Henry VI* when King Henry expresses grief as intense as that of Richard's Queen, and hears the plaints of a father who has killed his son and a son who has killed his father. There, as here, the emblematic predominates over the natural. The fact that these men are gardeners is itself part of the metaphor that Shakespeare employs also in their language, and the absence from their presentation of individualizing characteristics should cause us to respect what they say as general truth rather than idiosyncratic comment. At various points in the play England has been compared to a garden, and now the image is fully extended and developed. The servant's summary of the distressed state of the country resembles John of Gaunt's plaint (II.1.31–68), and again the responsibility is shown to be Richard's. But while Gaunt spoke as a prophet, grieving over what was likely to happen, the Gardeners speak with pitiful regret of an irremediable state of affairs. Richard's 'rash fierce blaze of riot' has burnt itself out, and the Gardener rebukes his man for harshness, demanding sympathy for the King, who though he

> *suffered this disordered spring*
> *Hath now himself met with the fall of leaf.*

His favourites, those 'caterpillars of the commonwealth' (II.3.165), are dead, and

> *Bolingbroke*
> *Hath seized the wasteful King.*

As a king, Richard is blamed for his failure to govern his country as conscientiously as these men tend their garden, and especially for his failure to control his nobles; but as a man he is pitied for his suffering. The Queen's imagery as she rebukes the Gardener for the harshness of his news extends the imaginative scope of the scene still further. As 'old Adam's likeness' (line 73) the Gardener is tending the Garden of Eden, and Richard's fate is 'a second Fall of cursèd man'. Whereas the Queen's grief expresses itself in bitterness, the Gardener, less personally involved, maintains in face of her rebukes the tender compassion that he had expressed for Richard.

The fourth Act begins with one of the play's less satisfactory episodes, though one which has its place in the overall design. Bolingbroke reopens the question of responsibility for Gloucester's death. We may wonder why he should permit suspicion of Aumerle to be entertained considering that he had been so vehement in accusing Mowbray of the same crime. A more serious fault results from the compression that Shakespeare has exercised on his historical material. Events that took place over several months have been conflated and patterned in a manner that is obviously intentional but liable to seem over-stylized. The scene would have most chance of succeeding if it were consciously played as an elaborate ritual; but as one lord after another throws down his gage the situation is in danger of becoming ludicrous. Conceivably the humour is deliberate, suggesting a decline in the dignity of the monarchy as an inevitable consequence of usurpation; but it is not easy to see how this could be conveyed in the theatre. There is a hint that the problem may have arisen in Shakespeare's day in the fact that the final challenge, that of the anonymous lord, was omitted from the Folio text. In performance the episode has generally been omitted or curtailed.

Richard II is at no point a play of clear-cut moral issues. Though we sympathize with Richard, it is not because we feel him to be wholly virtuous; and though we may condemn Bolingbroke, we cannot deny his many good qualities. Bolingbroke, having already declared that he will recall his enemy, Mowbray, from banishment, is allowed another display of magnanimity on the report of Mowbray's death. Shakespeare is careful to give us no excuse for adopting an over-simple attitude. Bolingbroke is moving acceptably towards the throne. He is seen to lack no qualification for the royal office except hereditary right. This, though intangible, seems supremely important to the Bishop of Carlisle, who fiercely demonstrates the strength of his feelings about it (IV.1.114–49), and thus acts as a spokesman for the traditional values. As in the scene of Richard's return from Ireland, and the one at Flint Castle, a strong statement of faith in regality is the prelude to a demonstration of its vulnerability; but this time the statement does not come from the holder of the office. Carlisle speaks with the authority of the Church and the force of one who feels impelled to proclaim his commitment to beliefs so dangerous that he is arrested on a charge of treason immediately after expressing them. As Gaunt prophesied disaster that would result from Richard's folly, so now Carlisle prophesies disaster that will result from Bolingbroke's deposition of Richard. His speech is appropriate here, but looks forward too to the events portrayed in the later plays about Bolingbroke as Henry IV.

The episode of abdication is another one in which action is suspended while a situation is explored in depth, a scene of retrospection, summary, and expansion. The technique is operatic, Richard holding the centre of the stage in what is virtually a solo *scena*. When he enters this time it is his private, not his public self that he struggles to define and assert in a difficult and bitterly painful process of re-education. He is the deviser, director, and central performer in the rite of renunciation which forms an emotional climax to the play. The first formality is his cry of 'God save the King!', to which he receives no reply – understandably, since none of the onlookers can be sure to whom he refers. Then he takes the crown and uses it symbolically to illustrate the reversal of fortunes that has brought about the present situation. Responsibility is being transferred from him to Bolingbroke; yet the passing from Richard of the cares associated with the crown does not leave him free from care. The complications of the situation are expressed in wordplay and paradox ('Ay, no. No, ay . . .') suggestive of a tension created by the opposition of equal pressures. It finds release in the movement from a complex style expressive of dilemma to a fluent series of simple one-line sentences as Richard resolves the situation and gives up the last remnants of regality. His public façade is crumbling away and he fears that soon he will have nothing and be nothing. He can look forward only to 'an earthy pit'. Though he can still accuse his enemies of heinous crime, and again compares himself to Christ by referring to the silent onlookers as Pilates who 'Have here delivered me to my sour cross', yet he acknowledges treachery on his own part, too, when (using an antithesis that occurs frequently in the play) he says:

> *I have given here my soul's consent*
> *To'undeck the pompous body of a king.*

He lacks even a name, and, as another property of the rite, calls for a looking-glass as if to assure himself that his appearance at least still exists. In his grief he acknowledges sin (line 274) and meditates on the discrepancy between his still-glorious appearance and the wretchedness of his state. As he casts the glass down he shatters the last remaining pretensions and unrealities of kingship. The true reality 'lies all within'; his laments are mere reflections of

> *the unseen grief*
> *That swells with silence in the tortured soul.*

'There' (paradoxically) 'lies the substance.' The only boon he seeks is to be permitted to leave Bolingbroke's presence. The episode after his departure forms a structural parallel to that at the end of II.1. There, Richard's harshness to Gaunt provoked plans for rebellion against

him; now Bolingbroke's harshness to him provokes plans
for a rebellion on his behalf.

The Queen's subsequent appearance (V.1) shows the
reluctance of the person most associated with Richard's
private life to accept the change in his public station. She
clings to the idea of Richard as king; unkinged, he is only
a shell – 'tomb' and 'inn' are the images she uses –
housing his grief. But Richard has progressed enough in
self-knowledge to tell her that she is still living a dream:

> *Learn, good soul,*
> *To think our former state a happy dream,*
> *From which awaked the truth of what we are*
> *Shows us but this. I am sworn brother, sweet,*
> *To grim Necessity, and he and I*
> *Will keep a league till death.*

Acknowledging sin, he returns to the imagery of the religious way of life in which he had envisaged his deposition:

> *Our holy lives must win a new world's crown*
> *Which our profane hours here have thrown down.*

He is himself permitted a prophecy. Rebuking Northumberland for his share in the rebellion he prophesies strife
between the allies, and counter-rebellion. In a passage of
great formality, yet also of grace and tenderness, he parts
in grief from his Queen.

The closing episodes emphasize Richard's grief and the
pity that it evokes in others far more strongly than the
faults in his past way of life. Nevertheless the change in the
political situation is one that his countrymen must recognize. The Duke of York, uncle of both Richard and
Bolingbroke, gives a most sympathetic account of
Richard's entry into London, pitying his grief and ad-
miring the patience with which he endured his humilia-

tion. But just as John of Gaunt had refused to try to take vengeance on Richard for the murder of Gloucester – 'God's is the quarrel' (I.2.37) – so York believes that 'heaven hath a hand in these events' (V.2.37), with the result that he now owes duty to the new king. He has accepted the change in the *status quo*. But his son has not. On discovering the conspiracy, in which Aumerle is involved, to assassinate Bolingbroke he does not hesitate to act in accordance with his duty to the new king rather than to his family. Understandably his wife takes the more personal point of view, and the conflict is worked out in a scene which, like that of the gages (IV.1), is uneasily balanced between the serious and the comic. Until recently it has generally been omitted in performance, though it can be defended as having definable functions in the play's economy.

York is the nearest approach to a comic character in *Richard II*. He is potentially amusing because of his vacillations, his inability in the early part of the play to reconcile his disapproval of Richard's conduct with his respect for the office of king, his feeling of the injustice done to Bolingbroke with condemnation of the wrong he has committed in usurping the throne. In the later scenes the completeness of York's transference of loyalty to the usurper, which prompts him not simply to inform on his own son but actively to plead against Bolingbroke's offer to forgive Aumerle, also has within it the seeds of comedy. Yet he is the mouthpiece of serious thoughts and the upholder of high ideals, touching in his refusal to be shaken when he feels himself to be in the right. Undoubtedly Shakespeare was aware of the possibility of comic effect, and at times deliberately cultivated it. But it is difficult to feel that he has completely succeeded in fusing the serious and the comic so that they emerge as different aspects of

32

the same, rounded character. Sir John Gielgud has
written: 'The character of York, used by Shakespeare as a
kind of wavering chorus throughout the play, touching yet
sometimes absurd, can be of great value, provided that the
actor and director can contrive between them a tactful
compromise between comedy and dramatic effect.' The
problem is most acute in the episode of Aumerle's conspiracy. The sequence of knockings at Bolingbroke's door
as first Aumerle comes to confess and beg forgiveness,
then York arrives to urge that his son should be punished,
then the Duchess of York to beg that he should be for-
given, becomes ludicrous, as Bolingbroke himself recognizes:

Our scene is altered from a serious thing,
And now changed to 'The Beggar and the King'. V.3.78–9

The kneeling competition that follows, as each visitor
presses his case, has the same kind of mechanistic over-
patterning as afflicts the episode of the gages. Even Bolingbroke is apt to seem comically ineffective as he fails on
three separate attempts to persuade his aunt to rise from
her knees.

Nevertheless, there are good reasons for performing the
scene if actors can find a satisfactory mode of playing it.
As early as 1773 George Steevens wrote to Garrick: 'If
you revive King Richard, I beg that proper regard may be
paid to old *puss in boots*, who arrives so hastily in the fifth
act.' Why he was so anxious to see him he does not make
clear. Granville Barker disapproved of Gielgud's omission
of the episode, 'the dramatic point of which is merely that
it is a swift and excited interlude between the *slow* . . .
farewell between Richard and the Queen and the slow,
philosophical death scene'. The Duchess's assertions that
her husband's 'words come from his mouth, ours from our

<blockquote>33</blockquote>

breast' (V.3.101), and her emphasis on the power of a king's words, though they may seem like trivial quibbling, maintain a recurrent concern of the play (see page 42). And the actor playing Bolingbroke may well be anxious for the scene to be retained, since even if it does put the character in danger of seeming ridiculously ineffective in his dealings with his cousin, his uncle, and his aunt, at a more public level he is eventually given the opportunity to behave mercifully to Aumerle and to voice his determination to have the other rebels killed.

Though Richard speaks often and at length about himself during the course of the play, it is not until his final appearance (V.5) that we see him alone. So far his meditations have all been conducted in public, and with at least some consciousness of his audience. Now, in the imposed solitude of his prison cell, stripped of his office and all its trappings, he utters his only real soliloquy. With no audience, he has no role to play. Only he has to try to define his real self. He has thoughts of religious salvation, but counter-thoughts of the difficulty of attaining it. He thinks of escape, but recognizes his folly. He considers resignation to his fate, and in this thought finds 'a kind of ease'. Bolingbroke, going into exile, had refused even to try to use his imagination to lighten his suffering; Richard makes a great effort to do so. Yet none of the roles in which he casts himself can content him, for each carries its anti-type along with it. The discovery that even the role of king is one from which he could be dislodged has made him feel that contentment can come only with oblivion:

> *But whate'er I be,*
> *Nor I, nor any man that but man is,*
> *With nothing shall be pleased till he be eased*
> *With being nothing.*

These lines suggest a hard-won acceptance of the fact of death, and this, along with the process of painful self-investigation that has led up to it, is characteristic of Shakespeare's tragic heroes. Richard II is sometimes said not to be truly 'tragic'. No one would deny that he is pathetic, but some find him ultimately inadequate in stature. Admittedly he lacks the grandeur revealed by Macbeth in his final defiance of his fate, or the sublimity of King Lear in the last stages of his purgatorial journey. It may be felt that he has not learned enough as the result of his sufferings. But perhaps there is something about the manner in which he faces death that may justly increase our respect for him. Shakespeare was limited by history. Our feelings about Richard's stature are likely to depend not so much on what he does as on sentiments such as those he expresses in his parting with his Queen (see page 31), and still more on our response to the style of his final speeches and the relationship of this style to that which he has employed previously. It is a concentrated style, luxuriant no longer. It suggests a man facing up to reality, trying to encompass it with his imagination, even though he is powerless to change it. There is a toughness about Richard's language in his last scene; he speaks like one who has come through suffering rather than been overcome by it.

Nevertheless, in Richard's soliloquy, as in so much of the play, Shakespeare is working in a heavily stylized mode. The cast of the speech itself is consciously artificial. Its opening lines draw attention to the metaphorical technique – 'I have been studying how I may compare ...'. The style is not wholly externalized, for mental effort on Richard's part is strongly suggested – 'Yet I'll hammer it out'; but he does not speak with the approach to real speech patterns characteristic of Hamlet's soliloquies and adumbrated in, for instance, the Nurse's speech of recollection in *Romeo and Juliet* (I.3.17–49). Unrealistic too is the interruption of Richard's meditation by the sound of music. Clearly we are here in the world of imagination and symbol rather than reality. The music is part of the dramatic metaphor just as the garden has been. For Shakespeare's audience the music was perhaps more obviously symbolic of the kind of order violated both by Richard's irresponsibility and by his deposition than it is liable to be for us. Hearing it Richard immediately puts it to metaphorical use, meditating on the paradox that he can discern harmonic inequalities though he was unable to notice the discrepancy between his behaviour and his office. Retrospectively he remarks and laments his own failure. Once, shortening the period of Bolingbroke's exile, he had seemed to have time under his command:

BOLINGBROKE
How long a time lies in one little word!
Four lagging winters and four wanton springs
End in a word – such is the breath of kings.   I.3.213–15

Even then, in response to his 'Why, uncle, thou hast many years to live', Gaunt had replied 'But not a minute, King, that thou canst give' (I.3.225–6). Now time is catching up with him. 'I wasted time, and now doth time waste me –' (V.5.49). Bolingbroke has taken over from him, usurping his time, and 'I stand fooling here, his jack of the clock' (line 60). The idea seems to be that when a man is in tune with his office, when the actor is fulfilling his role, when the public and the private functions coincide, then he is in tune with his time; otherwise 'The time is out of joint' (*Hamlet*, I.5.189) and life runs to waste.

But consolations remain. Richard explains away the music as a sign of love to him. (Could Shakespeare have been recalling Richard I's minstrel, Blondel, singing to his imprisoned master?) The final twist of pathos occurs with the entrance of the Groom, who has with difficulty got permission to visit his former master, but who saddens him with the tale of how Richard's horse carried Bolingbroke to his coronation. Life goes on. The horse has changed allegiance as York has. Barbary too is made to carry symbolic significance as Richard compares himself to an animal, 'Spurred, galled, and tired by jauncing Bolingbroke' (V.5.94). The end is near, and comes in the play's solitary episode of violence as Richard resists his attackers, kills some of them, but dies with a last assertion of regality and a commitment to the values of the soul over the body:

> Exton, thy fierce hand
> Hath with the King's blood stained the King's own land.
> Mount, mount, my soul. Thy seat is up on high,
> Whilst my gross flesh sinks downward here to die.

In the last scene Shakespeare seems simply to be conscientiously tidying things up. The rebellion against Bolingbroke is quelled, he is established in the throne, promises rewards to his helpers, is merciful to the Bishop of Carlisle, and expresses regret at the death of his chief enemy. The tone at the end is one of grief, not triumph. Bolingbroke is, as Richard had prophesied, assuming the cares of kingship, and his last lines foreshadow the care-laden and penitent usurper who is to be at the centre of the next two plays of the history cycle.

*

So far we have been concerned mainly with the characters of *Richard II* and their actions. Even so, comment on their language has been unavoidable. We cannot finally distinguish between what someone is and what he says, since it is largely through what he says that we receive our impression of what he is. And in this play nuances of speech, the vocabulary, syntax, and imagery through which the characters express themselves, are of unusual importance. So too are the sentiments that they voice over and above the statements required to delineate the situation. From time to time action is suspended to allow for verbal expansion of the situation. This happens in the deposition scene, the play's most generally admired episode. Its omission from the early quartos, usually attributed to censorship, has also been defended on the grounds that it is dramatically redundant. But this is mistaken; the technique Shakespeare adopted is not, in his hands, undramatic. Movement can be of the mind as well as of the body. The actor playing Richard can hold and sway his audience as effectively in his meditations as in his more active moments.

The fact that Richard talks so eloquently about himself has caused him frequently to be spoken of as a poet. If one is a poet because one speaks verse, then all the characters in this play are poets. The poetry Richard speaks is of course Shakespeare's, not Richard's. Yet it is fair to call him poetic in temperament in that he is portrayed as a man of strong imagination who needs to put suffering into words, and who is intensely conscious of the power of words, though also of their ultimate inadequacy. In this he is strongly contrasted with Bolingbroke, who throughout is seen more than heard, and whose realistic attitude towards the imagination is made explicit in the scene of his banishment (I.3.294–303). Verbally *Richard II* is both immensely complex and unusually self-conscious. Its complexity might fairly be called inexhaustible. Many studies have

Introduction

been written of the patterns formed by the inter-relation-
ships and echoes of words and the ideas that they express,
but even the subtlest and fullest of them do not succeed in
capturing all the play's elusive harmonies and revealing all
the strains in its counterpoint. There are too many overtones, too many latent patterns of sense and sound in what
has been called the play's 'symphonic imagery'. But it may
be worth drawing attention to a few of the dominant
images, and suggesting a view of their functions.

Richard II is about men. Women are shown only in
relation to them. And the men are seen almost exclusively
in relation to public life. Almost all are noblemen, deeply
concerned with affairs of state. We hear something of the
common people, see practically nothing of them. The
Queen's ladies are lay figures; the Gardeners, highly
symbolic. The Groom (V.5) gives a hint of the loyalty that
some of the common people felt for their King, but his role
is tiny. There is no attempt to give a sense of the ordinary
life of the country through figures such as the frequenters
of the Boar's Head Tavern in the *Henry IV* plays. Neither
Richard nor Bolingbroke feels such concern for his
meanest subjects as Henry V evinces in especially the night
scene before Agincourt. This may represent a deliberate
design on Shakespeare's part, *Richard II* looking back to a
formal, medieval class structure. However this may be,
England is not absent from *Richard II*. Richard is conscious of responsibility to his country, and others (notably
Gaunt in his great panegyric) blame him for neglecting it;
but the country, instead of being represented by a variety
of members of the commonwealth, is brought to our consciousness rather through references to it as a living being,
or as something of natural purity which is in danger of
being stained, most horribly by the blood of those who
have been brought up in it. Richard speaks thus of it before

banishing Bolingbroke and Mowbray (I.3.125-43). Bolingbroke, in the challenge he sends to Richard through
Northumberland, threatens the bloodstains that Richard
tried to avert (III.3.42-50). Richard threatens the same
result if Bolingbroke persists in his insurrection (III.3.
93-100). Carlisle prophesies similar horror in later times
as the result of the deposition (IV.1.136-47). The image
finds forceful use in Richard's dying speech:

> *Exton, thy fierce hand*
> *Hath with the King's blood stained the King's own land.*

And finally Bolingbroke regrets that 'blood should
sprinkle me to make me grow' (V.6.46) – an image which
he is to recall in the fifth and sixth lines of *1 Henry IV*:

> *No more the thirsty entrance of this soil*
> *Shall daub her lips with her own children's blood.*

Richard's feeling for his land as a sentient being,
capable of taking his part against his enemies, is fully expressed on his return from Ireland (III.2.4-26). In the
great speech in which he envisages his own overthrow
(III.3.143-75) the land is the source of his glory, his 'large
kingdom', and also one day will easily swallow him up into
'a little grave'. The tension created between an imaginative man's awareness of his possibilities and the knowledge
that sooner or later he will be no more than dust is a source
of great poetic power, and the image of the land over
which Richard now holds sway but in which before long
he will be buried while the subjects 'hourly trample on
their sovereign's head' embraces both the glory and the
pathos of kingship, elsewhere polarized in images such as
the crown and the skull, the soul and the body. The land
has continuity; so does the nation; so does the office of
king; but the King himself is a mortal man.

In the speech just referred to, Richard says that Aumerle and he will weep themselves graves. As the land receives the blood of those who fight on it, so it receives also the tears of those who grieve. Tears are another recurrent image, and the vocabulary of grief helps to form the play's dominant emotional tone. Indeed the language almost creates of grief a dramatic character associated especially, though by no means exclusively, with the women. The Duchess of Gloucester initiates this emphasis in I.2 as she speaks of 'her companion, grief' (line 55), discourses on grief and sorrow, creates an image of herself as a desolate person in a derelict building, and departs weeping. This is the first of the play's many sad partings. The next, between Gaunt and his exiled son, also makes much of the grief of the parted. Bolingbroke will be able to

> *boast of nothing else*
> *But that I was a journeyman to grief.* I.3.273-4

Dying, Gaunt complains:

> *Within me grief hath kept a tedious fast.* II.1.75

The first episode in which the Queen is prominent (II.2. 1-76) is an extended meditation on the grief that she entertains as the result of parting from Richard and the sorrow she feels to be approaching. Indeed, the imagery here goes through a process of bringing grief to birth: Isabel imagines an 'unborn sorrow' in 'fortune's womb', speaks of a grief which 'nothing hath begot', and, hearing that Bolingbroke has landed, gives birth to her woe. Green, the bringer of the news, is the midwife, and Bolingbroke the offspring of her sorrow (II.2.62-6). Thus, for her, grief is firmly identified with Bolingbroke's usurpation of her husband's place.

Shakespeare is labouring to create a sense of foreboding

and imminent tragedy, increased by the bad news that the
Queen receives of the desertion of Richard's supporters.
When York hears of the Duchess of Gloucester's death he
justly exclaims:

> *what a tide of woes*
> *Comes rushing on this woeful land at once!* II.2.98–9

Richard's reunion with his country releases tears that are
for once of joy (III.2.4), but the sequence of bad news that
he receives culminates in his great expression of grief
(lines 144–77). The Queen sustains the tone in the episode
with her ladies and the Gardeners, and Richard's grief
reaches its eloquent climax in the deposition scene,
through which chime the words 'tears', 'sorrow', 'grief',
and 'woe', as they do through the subsequent parting of
Richard from his Queen. The scenes of Aumerle's conspiracy give some respite from the prevailing woefulness,
and although Richard in prison is undoubtedly a grieving
figure, speaking of his sighs, tears, and groans (V.5.51–8),
he is far less indulgent in his grief than he had previously
been. The effort at intellectual control displayed in his
soliloquy may help us to feel that he has passed through
the lachrymose to a more stoical and a nobler frame of
mind. At the end of the play it is Bolingbroke's soul that is
'full of woe' (V.6.45), and he is grieving that (in another of
the play's dominant images) 'blood should sprinkle me to
make me grow'.

Richard's awareness of the power of words, and of his
own dependence on them, is one of the many manifestations in this play of a direct concern with the functions of
language. It was remarked earlier (page 23) that Richard
capitulates to words, not deeds. This aspect of the action
finds correspondences in details of the language. In the
episode of Mowbray's banishment the emphasis on words

is so strong that the word 'sentence' acquires the force of a pun, referring equally to the banishment and the fact that it is expressed in words. Mowbray's reaction takes the form of a lament that his native language and his skill in it are now of no use to him. Richard's 'sentence' means, paradoxically, 'speechless death' – Mowbray will be as good as dead because deprived of the use of his tongue. Just as he sees himself, in a country whose language he does not speak, as 'an unstringèd viol or a harp' (I.3.162), so Northumberland reporting Gaunt's death says 'His tongue is now a stringless instrument' (II.1.149). 'Tongue' becomes a key-word, and is often paired with 'heart' in references to the possible disjunction between what men mean and what they say. Aumerle in his account of his parting from Bolingbroke says that his heart prevented his tongue from profaning the word 'farewell' (though he admits to having acted the hypocrite by assuming a false appearance of grief); however, if the word had had power to lengthen Bolingbroke's exile he would have used 'a volume of farewells' (I.4.18). Ross, doubtful whether to reveal his opinion of Richard's actions, fears that his heart

> *must break with silence*
> *Ere't be disburdened with a liberal tongue....* II.1.228–9

The Duchess of York, trying to defend her son against her husband's accusations, claims that York's 'words come from his mouth, ours from our breast' (V.3.101). And Richard's faithful Groom, as he leaves his master, declares 'What my tongue dares not, that my heart shall say' (V.5.97). The truest sympathy may find no expression.

Aumerle's rebellious regret that his words could not lengthen Bolingbroke's exile recalls and sets in relief Bolingbroke's exclamation at the moment when Richard shortened the period of his exile:

> *How long a time lies in one little word!*
> *Four lagging winters and four wanton springs*
> *End in a word – such is the breath of kings.*   I.3.213–15

Yet even then the limitations of the King's power had been pointed out. Though Richard can shorten Bolingbroke's exile, and Gaunt's lifetime, he cannot give life; he may urge time on, but cannot stop its progress:

> *Thou canst help time to furrow me with age,*
> *But stop no wrinkle in his pilgrimage.*   I.3.229–30

And though the King's words are powerful, they may be constrained, so that before long Richard is regretting

> *that e'er this tongue of mine,*
> *That laid the sentence of dread banishment*
> *On yon proud man, should take it off again*
> *With words of sooth!*   III.3.133–6

He himself has to rely on other men's words, such as the oaths that Mowbray and Bolingbroke swear on their banishment (I.3.178–92); and oaths may be broken. So Richard complains bitterly of Northumberland's 'cracking the strong warrant of an oath', an offence that is 'Marked with a blot, damned in the book of heaven' (IV.1.234–5). And he may be deceived by false words, the flattery of his favourites, the 'praises', 'lascivious metres', 'report of fashions' which, York complains, are 'buzzed into his ears' (II.1.17–26).

It is easy – and fashionable – to claim of many works of literature that they are in some sense 'about' language, that the true concern of the artefact is the art that has created it rather than the events and ideas that form its ostensible subject matter. We may be sceptical of the more extreme manifestations of this tendency, but it is hard to deny that within the texture of *Richard II* there lies a sense of life as a fiction which, while it may be regarded on one level as a natural metaphor for the characters to employ, is likely also to make us reflect upon the relationship between reality and art, and thus to distance us somewhat from the events of the play, expanding them from the representational to the emblematic. The dying John of Gaunt hopes that his 'death's sad tale' may convey more of the truth to Richard than his 'life's counsel' has done. In his despair, Richard wishes to

> *sit upon the ground*
> *And tell sad stories of the death of kings.* III.2.155–6

In the examples that he gives he recalls the chronicled lives and deaths of earlier kings, so that we have a sense of him, too, as one of the many who have receded from life into history or – like him – into a play, with his 'little scene' in which to monarchize. It is a speech which (like some of Shakespeare's epilogues) might almost be spoken by the actor in his own person rather than the character he is representing.

In the abdication scene Richard speaks of himself as

> *the very book indeed*
> *Where all my sins are writ*   IV.1.273–4

and after his fall he envisages himself as the central figure of a 'lamentable tale' that his Queen will tell by the fireside 'In winter's tedious nights' (V.1.40). His tale will be sadder than all the others that have been told, so that even the

> *senseless brands will sympathize*
> *The heavy accent of thy moving tongue,*
> *And in compassion weep the fire out;*
> *And some will mourn in ashes, some coal-black,*
> *For the deposing of a rightful king.*

And just after he has died his murderer admits that 'this deed is chronicled in hell' (V.5.116). The notion of Richard's life as a tale in a chronicle – where Shakespeare found it – does something to lessen the pain of the story, and may relate too to the old, poignant, but consoling notion that the life of this world is a fiction, heavenly life the only reality. In a famous lyric which is part of his play *Summer's Last Will and Testament*, performed at about the same date as *Richard II*, Thomas Nashe wrote:

> *Heaven is our heritage,*
> *Earth but a player's stage.*

Shakespeare lays less emphasis on the reality of the heavenly life; but Richard, in renouncing his kingdom for 'a little grave', in seeing his life as 'a little scene' from which the figure of Death, like a character in a morality play, will soon remove him, and in his final declaration that his soul's 'seat is up on high', gives expression to the old enduring theme of the transience of human glory and worldly beauty, a theme which pervades the whole play, linking it in subject matter as well as manner to a central tradition of lyrical verse.

FURTHER READING

The two major editions of *Richard II*, Peter Ure's Arden edition (1956) and Andrew Gurr's New Cambridge edition (1984), base their texts on the 1597 First Quarto rather than on the 1623 Folio on the principle, in Gurr's words, 'that the author's text is in the main preferable to the play-house text'. The principle is not an unchallengeable one and in fact seems to have been overturned by Gurr himself in his New Cambridge edition of *Henry V* (1992). Gurr notes that Shakespeare dramatized all three usurpations in English history after William the Conqueror: King John, Richard II and Henry VI. Shakespeare, he believes, was obviously fascinated by the problem of the unjust king and the difficulty of belling the cat. Matthew Black's New Variorum edition (1955) gives us extensive quotation from the commentary of previous centuries on this and other matters.

As Black's edition indicates, *Richard II* has traditionally been the site chiefly of character analysis (Richard's and Bolingbroke's or, as Gurr claims, Bullingbrook's) and of the play's poetic accomplishment. Recent criticism, responding perhaps as much to the pressures of our own time as anything else, has become fascinated with the politics of the play, especially with its stance towards the phenomenon of kingship. Alexander Leggatt's *Shakespeare's Political Drama: The History Plays and the Roman Plays* (1988) argues that 'In no other play of Shakespeare's is the office of kingship subjected to such intense scrutiny, from such a wide variety of angles.' H. M. Richmond's *Shakespeare's Political Plays* (1977), as its title proclaims, shifts the emphasis from the tragic story of Richard to the political drama going on around him. Michael Manheim's *The Weak King Dilemma in the*

Shakespearean History Play (1973) discusses *Richard II*, Marlowe's *Edward II* and the anonymous *Woodstock*. What links these plays is 'an articulation of public reaction to the burden of monarchy'. Christopher Pye, in *The Regal Phantasm: Shakespeare and the Politics of Spectacle* (1990), believes that what we get in this and the other Histories is the representation of the absolutism of the sovereign in an attempt to preserve a feudal power structure in centralized form against 'the gradual emergence of mobile free labour'. Of *Richard II* in particular, 'The central question ... is whether sovereignty can prove itself absolute in mastering its own subversion.' Leonard Tennenhouse in *Power on Display: The Politics of Shakespeare's Genres* (1979) puts it more straightforwardly: what's plaguing the state in *Richard II*, he says, is 'its failure to exercise force'.

Of course what constitutes the play's politics is as open to interpretation as any other investigative procedure. E. M. W. Tillyard's highly influential (balefully so, some say) *Shakespeare's History Plays* (1944) and Lily B. Campbell's *Shakespeare's 'Histories': Mirrors of Elizabethan Policy* (1965) argue for what Campbell calls 'a dominant political pattern characteristic of the political philosophy of his age', in which events are providentially determined. Providentiality has been called strongly into question, most cogently by H. A. Kelly's *Divine Providence in the England of Shakespeare's Histories* (1978), and more recently by Jonathan Hart in his *Theater and World: The Problematics of Shakespeare's History* (1992): 'In the second tetralogy Shakespeare represents something akin to what in *The History of the World* Walter Raleigh calls the realm of secondary causes, a fallen world in which the search for meaning in the relation of cause and effect remains for ever uncertain.' Are the politics then those of Shakespeare's time or Richard II's? Most commentators think they are of Shakespeare's. Tillyard didn't, and his position has gained support in an unexpected quarter. Graham Holderness in *Shakespeare Recycled: The Making of Historical Drama* (1992) and in *Shakespeare: The Play of History* (1987) (with Nick

Potter and John Turner) argues that in *Richard II* and the other plays of the tetralogy Shakespeare reveals 'a historically informed apprehension of the struggles of later mediaeval society; in particular the long struggle between monarchy and nobility which developed out of the contradictory nature of the feudal order, and was arrested by the accession of the Tudors'. (See also his compilation of essays in *Shakespeare's History Plays: 'Richard II' to 'Henry V'* in the New Casebooks Series (1992) – 'New' because of its concern with modern critical theory.) Some light is thrown on all this by Peter Saccio's *Shakespeare's English Kings: History, Chronicle, and Drama* (1977), which examines the differences between medieval history as we now understand it and Shakespeare's versions of that history. Barbara Hodgdon's *The End Crowns All: Closure and Contradiction in Shakespeare's History* (1991) proves that the other historical emphasis continues to flourish as it explores the connections between the privately commissioned *Richard II* in February 1601 and Essex's rebellion and the manner in which Richard II reflects Essex himself.

An interest in the language of the play has undergone a similar political modification. We might contrast, say, James Winny's *The Player King: A Theme of Shakespeare's Histories* (1968), which describes how characters in the play are hedged in by ritual and rhetoric, or Winifred Nowottny's examination of Richard's soliloquy in *The Language Poets Use* (1962), with W. F. Bolton's *Shakespeare's English Language in the History Plays* (1992), Joseph A. Porter's *The Drama of Speech Acts: Shakespeare's Lancastrian Tetralogy* (1979) and, perhaps most profitably, Harry Berger's *Imaginary Audition: Shakespeare on Stage and Page* (1989), whose second part consists of a 'decelerated microanalysis' of what Richard says in Act 3, Scene 2 in terms of the politics of speech rather than of the manifestation of a dominantly narcissistic, lyrical and aestheticizing sensibility. The moral Berger draws is sound if not terribly original, namely that the page can't do without the stage, nor the stage without the page. These works might be read in the light of James L. Calderwood's *Metadrama in Shakespeare's Henriad: 'Richard II' to 'Henry V'* (1979).

Good introductions to some of the themes already discussed can be found first of all in a number of essay collections: Nicholas Brooke's Casebook (1973), Paul Cubeta's Twentieth Century Interpretations (1971), R. J. Dorius's *Discussions of Shakespeare's Histories: 'Richard II' to 'Henry V'* (1964) and Eugene Waith's *Shakespeare the Histories*, Twentieth Century Views (1965). Other works that should be consulted include: Larry Champion's *Perspective in Shakespeare's English Histories* (1980), A. R. Humphreys' *Shakespeare: 'Richard II'* (1967), Robert C. Jones's *The Valiant Dead: Renewing the Past in Shakespeare's Histories* (1991), Robert Ornstein's *A Kingdom for a Stage: The Achievement of Shakespeare's History Plays* (1972), E. Pearlman's *William Shakespeare: The History Plays* (1992) and Moody Prior's *The Drama of Power: Studies in Shakespeare's History Plays* (1973).

Michael Taylor, 1997

KING RICHARD THE SECOND

THE CHARACTERS IN THE PLAY

KING RICHARD the Second

JOHN OF GAUNT, Duke of Lancaster, King Richard's uncle (Powerful uncle)

Edmund of Langley, DUKE OF YORK, King Richard's uncle

HENRY BOLINGBROKE, Duke of Hereford; John of Gaunt's son; afterwards KING HENRY the Fourth

DUKE OF AUMERLE, Earl of Rutland; the Duke of York's son

THOMAS MOWBRAY, Duke of Norfolk

EARL OF SALISBURY

LORD BERKELEY

BAGOT
BUSHY } followers of King Richard
GREEN

Henry Percy, EARL OF NORTHUMBERLAND

HARRY PERCY (Hotspur), the Earl of Northumberland's son

LORD ROSS

LORD WILLOUGHBY

} of Bolingbroke's party

BISHOP OF CARLISLE

SIR STEPHEN SCROOP

LORD FITZWATER

DUKE OF SURREY

ABBOT OF WESTMINSTER

SIR PIERS OF EXTON

LORD MARSHAL
CAPTAIN of the Welsh army

Q

QUEEN ISABEL, King Richard's wife
DUCHESS OF YORK
DUCHESS OF GLOUCESTER, widow of Thomas of Wood-
    stock, Duke of Gloucester (King Richard's uncle)
LADIES attending Queen Isabel

Important Scene

GARDENER
TWO GARDENER'S MEN
KEEPER of the prison at Pomfret
SERVINGMAN
GROOM to King Richard

Lords, two Heralds, officers, soldiers, and other
    attendants

*Q does the Queen come across as
    a real person.*

Enter King Richard and John of Gaunt, with other **I.1**
nobles, including the Lord Marshal, and attendants

KING RICHARD

Old John of Gaunt, time-honoured Lancaster,
Hast thou according to thy oath and band
Brought hither Henry Hereford, thy bold son,
Here to make good the boisterous late appeal –
Which then our leisure would not let us hear –
Against the Duke of Norfolk, Thomas Mowbray?

JOHN OF GAUNT

I have, my liege.

KING RICHARD

Tell me, moreover, hast thou sounded him
If he appeal the Duke on ancient malice,
Or worthily, as a good subject should,
On some known ground of treachery in him?   10

JOHN OF GAUNT

As near as I could sift him on that argument,
On some apparent danger seen in him
Aimed at your highness; no inveterate malice.

KING RICHARD

Then call them to our presence.   *Exit Attendant*
                                        Face to face,
And frowning brow to brow, ourselves will hear
The accuser and the accusèd freely speak.
High-stomached are they both, and full of ire;
In rage, deaf as the sea, hasty as fire.
          Enter Bolingbroke and Mowbray

55

I.1

BOLINGBROKE

20 Many years of happy days befall
    My gracious sovereign, my most loving liege!

MOWBRAY

    Each day still better other's happiness
    Until the heavens, envying earth's good hap,
    Add an immortal title to your crown!

KING RICHARD

    We thank you both. Yet one but flatters us,
    As well appeareth by the cause you come,
    Namely, to appeal each other of high treason.
    Cousin of Hereford, what dost thou object
    Against the Duke of Norfolk, Thomas Mowbray?

BOLINGBROKE

30 First, heaven be the record to my speech!
    In the devotion of a subject's love,
    Tendering the precious safety of my prince,
    And free from other, misbegotten hate
    Come I appellant to this princely presence.
    Now, Thomas Mowbray, do I turn to thee;
    And mark my greeting well, for what I speak
    My body shall make good upon this earth
    Or my divine soul answer it in heaven.
    Thou art a traitor and a miscreant,
40 Too good to be so, and too bad to live,
    Since the more fair and crystal is the sky,
    The uglier seem the clouds that in it fly.
    Once more, the more to aggravate the note,
    With a foul traitor's name stuff I thy throat,
    And wish – so please my sovereign – ere I move
    What my tongue speaks my right-drawn sword may
          prove.

MOWBRAY

    Let not my cold words here accuse my zeal.

56

(handwritten margin annotations:)
Bolingbroke accusing mowbray
both sucking up
all overdone flattery
Royal plural
→ whats the pro...
love of his kin is what is bringing him here.
God is my witness
– you are a liar and a cheat, you deserve to die.
Hatred for the man
I am ready to prove that I am right.

Th restraing themselves really all they want to do is beat each other up but they know they can't.

'Tis not the trial of a woman's war,
The bitter clamour of two eager tongues, *arguing is*
Can arbitrate this cause betwixt us twain. *the womans*
The blood is hot that must be cooled for this. *way of*
Yet can I not of such tame patience boast *fighting.*
As to be hushed, and naught at all to say. *cant keep quiet on this*
First, the fair reverence of your highness curbs me
From giving reins and spurs to my free speech, *cant say*
Which else would post until it had returned *exactly what*
These terms of treason doubled down his throat. *his feeling (to rude)*
Setting aside his high blood's royalty,
And let him be no kinsman to my liege, *If he wasnt the*
I do defy him, and I spit at him, *Kingrelation he would*
Call him a slanderous coward, and a villain; *spit at him.*
Which to maintain I would allow him odds,
And meet him, were I tied to run afoot *What he says*
Even to the frozen ridges of the Alps, *is all lies.*
Or any other ground inhabitable
Where ever Englishman durst set his foot.
Meantime, let this defend my loyalty:
By all my hopes most falsely doth he lie. *challenged*
BOLINGBROKE (*throws down his gage*) *him to a dual*
Pale, trembling coward, there I throw my gage,
Disclaiming here the kindred of the King,
And lay aside my high blood's royalty, *70*
Which fear, not reverence, makes thee to except. *You are scared of me.*
If guilty dread have left thee so much strength
As to take up mine honour's pawn, then stoop.
By that, and all the rites of knighthood else,
Will I make good against thee, arm to arm,
What I have spoke or thou canst worse devise.
MOWBRAY (*takes up the gage*)
I take it up; and by that sword I swear
Which gently laid my knighthood on my shoulder,

57

I.1

80 I'll answer thee in any fair degree
Or <u>chivalrous</u> design of knightly trial;
And when I mount, alive may I not light
If I be traitor or unjustly fight!

KING RICHARD

What doth our cousin lay to Mowbray's charge?
It must be great that can inherit us
So much as of a thought of ill in him.

BOLINGBROKE

Look what I speak, my life shall prove it true: *means*
That Mowbray hath received eight thousand nobles   *money*
In name of lendings for your highness' soldiers,
90 The which he hath detained for lewd employments,
Like a false traitor and injurious villain.
mowbray Besides I say, and will in battle prove
has been Or here or elsewhere to the furthest verge
plotting That ever was surveyed by English eye,
against That all the treasons for these eighteen years,
the king Complotted and contrivèd in this land
for 18 Fetch from false Mowbray, their first head and spring.
years. Further I say, and further will maintain   *Killing duke*
Upon his bad life to make all this good,   *of glouster.*
100 That he did plot the Duke of Gloucester's death,
accusing Suggest his soon-believing adversaries,
mowbery And consequently, like a traitor coward,
of Sluiced out his innocent soul through streams of blood;
plotting Which blood, like sacrificing Abel's, cries
death. Even from the tongueless caverns of the earth
To me for justice and rough chastisement.
And, by the glorious worth of my descent,
This arm shall do it, or this life be spent.

KING RICHARD

How high a pitch his resolution soars!
110 Thomas of Norfolk, what sayst thou to this?

Bollingbrook / King Richard = different reactions.

MOWBRAY

O, let my sovereign turn away his face
And bid his ears a little while be deaf
Till I have told this slander of his blood
How God and good men hate so foul a liar!

[handwritten note: → Turn away as I don't want you to hear this (King)]

KING RICHARD

Mowbray, impartial are our eyes and ears. *[handwritten: I am impartial]*
Were he my brother – nay, my kingdom's heir –
As he is but my father's brother's son,
Now by my sceptre's awe I make a vow *[handwritten: Promise]*
Such neighbour nearness to our sacred blood *[handwritten: I swear blood]*
Should nothing privilege him, nor partialize *[handwritten: with not]* 120
The unstooping firmness of my upright soul. *[handwritten: alter my judgement.]*
He is our subject, Mowbray. So art thou.
Free speech and fearless I to thee allow.

MOWBRAY

Then, Bolingbroke, as low as to thy heart
Through the false passage of thy throat thou liest!
Three parts of that receipt I had for Calais *[handwritten: 3/4 he gave to]*
Disbursed I duly to his highness' soldiers. *[handwritten: the soldiers and kept the remainder]*
The other part reserved I by consent *[handwritten: as it was owed to him.]*
For that my sovereign liege was in my debt
Upon remainder of a dear account 130
Since last I went to France to fetch his queen.
Now swallow down that lie! For Gloucester's death,
I slew him not, but to my own disgrace *[handwritten: I didn't kill him]*
Neglected my sworn duty in that case. *[handwritten: but I did plot]*
(*To John of Gaunt*) *[handwritten: to kill John of]*
For you, my noble lord of Lancaster, *[handwritten: gaunt! I regret]*
The honourable father to my foe, *[handwritten: that now.]*
Once did I lay an ambush for your life,
A trespass that doth vex my grievèd soul.
But ere I last received the sacrament *[handwritten: – communion]*
I did confess it, and exactly begged 140

59

King Richard tries to Calm them down.

Your grace's pardon; and I hope I had it.
This is my fault. As for the rest appealed,
It issues from the rancour of a villain,
A recreant and most degenerate traitor,
Which in myself I boldly will defend,
And interchangeably hurl down my gage
Upon this overweening traitor's foot,
To prove myself a loyal gentleman
Even in the best blood chambered in his bosom.

      He throws down his gage

150 In haste whereof most heartily I pray
Your highness to assign our trial day.

KING RICHARD
Wrath-kindled gentlemen, be ruled by me:
Let's purge this choler without letting blood.
This we prescribe, though no physician;
Deep malice makes too deep incision.
Forget, forgive, conclude, and be agreed;
Our doctors say this is no month to bleed.
(To John of Gaunt)
Good uncle, let this end where it begun.
We'll calm the Duke of Norfolk, you your son.

JOHN OF GAUNT
160 To be a make-peace shall become my age.
Throw down, my son, the Duke of Norfolk's gage.

KING RICHARD
And, Norfolk, throw down his.

JOHN OF GAUNT   When, Harry, when?
Obedience bids I should not bid again.

KING RICHARD
Norfolk, throw down! We bid: there is no boot.

MOWBRAY *(kneels)*
Myself I throw, dread sovereign, at thy foot.
My life thou shalt command, but not my shame.

Hatred cuts like a Knife.

getting rid of their hot temp.

60

The one my duty owes, but my fair name,
Despite of death that lives upon my grave,
To dark dishonour's use thou shalt not have.
I am disgraced, impeached, and baffled here,   170
Pierced to the soul with slander's venomed spear,
The which no balm can cure but his heart-blood
Which breathed this poison.

KING RICHARD   Rage must be withstood.
Give me his gage. <u>Lions make leopards tame.</u> *Coat of arms.*

MOWBRAY
Yea, but not change his spots. Take but my shame
And I resign my gage. My dear dear lord,
The purest treasure mortal times afford
Is spotless reputation. That away,
Men are but gilded loam, or painted clay.
A jewel in a ten-times barred-up chest   180
Is a bold spirit in a loyal breast.
Mine honour is my life. Both grow in one.
Take honour from me, and my life is done.
Then, dear my liege, mine honour let me try.
In that I live, and for that will I die.

KING RICHARD (*to Bolingbroke*)
Cousin, throw up your gage. Do you begin.

BOLINGBROKE
O God defend my soul from such deep sin!
Shall I seem crest-fallen in my father's sight?
Or with pale beggar-fear impeach my height
Before this outdared dastard? Ere my tongue   190
Shall wound my honour with such feeble wrong,
Or sound so base a parle, my teeth shall tear
The slavish motive of recanting fear
And spit it bleeding in his high disgrace
Where shame doth harbour, even in Mowbray's face.
                                        Exit John of Gaunt

KING RICHARD

> We were not born to sue, but to command;
> Which since we cannot do to make you friends,
> Be ready as your lives shall answer it
> At Coventry upon Saint Lambert's Day.
> 200 There shall your swords and lances arbitrate
> The swelling difference of your settled hate.
> Since we cannot atone you, we shall see
> Justice design the victor's chivalry.
> Lord Marshal, command our officers-at-arms
> Be ready to direct these home alarms.   *Exeunt*

I.2   *Enter John of Gaunt with the Duchess of Gloucester*

JOHN OF GAUNT

> Alas, the part I had in Woodstock's blood
> Doth more solicit me than your exclaims
> To stir against the butchers of his life.
> But since correction lieth in those hands
> Which made the fault that we cannot correct,
> Put we our quarrel to the will of heaven
> Who, when they see the hours ripe on earth,
> Will rain hot vengeance on offenders' heads.

DUCHESS OF GLOUCESTER

> Finds brotherhood in thee no sharper spur?
> 10 Hath love in thy old blood no living fire?
> Edward's seven sons, whereof thyself art one,
> Were as seven vials of his sacred blood,
> Or seven fair branches springing from one root.
> Some of those seven are dried by nature's course,
> Some of those branches by the destinies cut.
> But Thomas, my dear lord, my life, my Gloucester,
> One vial full of Edward's sacred blood,
> One flourishing branch of his most royal root,

62

y allowing your brother to be
murded it will happen again. to you
this time.

I.2

Is cracked, and all the precious liquor spilt;
Is hacked down, and his summer leaves all faded,   20
By envy's hand, and murder's bloody axe.
Ah, Gaunt, his blood was thine! That bed, that womb,
*That mettle, that self mould, that fashioned thee
Made him a man; and though thou livest and breathest
Yet art thou slain in him. Thou dost consent
In some large measure to thy father's death
In that thou seest thy wretched brother die,
Who was the model of thy father's life.
Call it not patience, Gaunt. It is despair.
In suffering thus thy brother to be slaughtered   30
Thou showest the naked pathway to thy life,
Teaching stern murder how to butcher thee.
That which in mean men we entitle patience
Is pale cold cowardice in noble breasts.
What shall I say? To safeguard thine own life
The best way is to venge my Gloucester's death.

JOHN OF GAUNT

God's is the quarrel; for God's substitute,
His deputy anointed in His sight,
Hath caused his death; the which if wrongfully,
Let heaven revenge, for I may never lift   40
An angry arm against His minister.

DUCHESS OF GLOUCESTER

Where then, alas, may I complain myself?

JOHN OF GAUNT

To God, the widow's champion and defence.

DUCHESS OF GLOUCESTER

Why then, I will. Farewell, old Gaunt.
Thou goest to Coventry, there to behold
Our cousin Hereford and fell Mowbray fight.
O, sit my husband's wrongs on Hereford's spear
That it may enter butcher Mowbray's breast!

63

Duchess in angry because nothing has been done, to avenge her husbands death.

Or if misfortune miss the first career,
Be Mowbray's sins so heavy in his bosom
That they may break his foaming courser's back

She is convinced that Mowbray is guilty

And throw the rider headlong in the lists,
A caitiff recreant to my cousin Hereford!
Farewell, old Gaunt! Thy sometimes brother's wife
With her companion, grief, must end her life.

JOHN OF GAUNT
Sister, farewell! I must to Coventry.
As much good stay with thee as go with me!

DUCHESS OF GLOUCESTER
Yet one word more. Grief boundeth where it falls,
Not with the empty hollowness, but weight.

WARNING

60 I take my leave before I have begun;
For sorrow ends not when it seemeth done.
Commend me to thy brother, Edmund York.
Lo, this is all. — Nay, yet depart not so.
Though this be all, do not so quickly go.
I shall remember more. Bid him – ah, what? –
With all good speed at Pleshey visit me.
Alack, and what shall good old York there see
But empty lodgings and unfurnished walls,
Unpeopled offices, untrodden stones,
70 And what hear there for welcome but my groans?
Therefore commend me. Let him not come there
To seek out sorrow that dwells everywhere.
Desolate, desolate will I hence and die.
The last leave of thee takes my weeping eye.

Exeunt

I.3   *Enter the Lord Marshal and the Duke of Aumerle*
LORD MARSHAL
My Lord Aumerle, is Harry Hereford armed?

[handwritten at top: umerle - duke of yoaks son. cousin of Richard and Henry]

AUMERLE

Yea, at all points, and longs to enter in.

LORD MARSHAL

The Duke of Norfolk, sprightfully and bold,
Stays but the summons of the appellant's trumpet.

AUMERLE

Why then, the champions are prepared, and stay
For nothing but his majesty's approach.

> *The trumpets sound and the King enters with his
> nobles, including Gaunt, and Bushy, Bagot, and
> Green. When they are set, enter Mowbray, Duke of
> Norfolk, in arms, defendant; and a Herald*

KING RICHARD

Marshal, demand of yonder champion
The cause of his arrival here in arms.
Ask him his name, and orderly proceed
To swear him in the justice of his cause.   10

LORD MARSHAL (*to Mowbray*)

In God's name and the King's, say who thou art
And why thou comest thus knightly-clad in arms,
Against what man thou comest, and what thy quarrel.
Speak truly on thy knighthood and thy oath,
As so defend thee heaven and thy valour!

MOWBRAY

My name is Thomas Mowbray, Duke of Norfolk,
Who hither come engagèd by my oath, –
Which God defend a knight should violate! –
Both to defend my loyalty and truth
To God, my King, and my succeeding issue   20
Against the Duke of Hereford that appeals me;
And by the grace of God and this mine arm
To prove him, in defending of myself,
A traitor to my God, my King, and me.
And as I truly fight, defend me heaven!

The trumpets sound. Enter Bolingbroke, Duke of
Hereford, appellant, in armour; and a Herald

KING RICHARD

Marshal, ask yonder knight in arms
Both who he is, and why he cometh hither
Thus plated in habiliments of war;
And formally, according to our law,
30   Depose him in the justice of his cause.

LORD MARSHAL (*to Bolingbroke*)

What is thy name? And wherefore comest thou hither
Before King Richard in his royal lists?
Against whom comest thou? And what's thy quarrel?
Speak like a true knight, so defend thee heaven!

BOLINGBROKE

Harry of Hereford, Lancaster, and Derby
Am I, who ready here do stand in arms
To prove by God's grace and my body's valour
In lists on Thomas Mowbray, Duke of Norfolk,
That he is a traitor foul and dangerous
40   To God of heaven, King Richard, and to me;
And as I truly fight, defend me heaven!

LORD MARSHAL

On pain of death, no person be so bold
Or daring-hardy as to touch the lists
Except the Marshal and such officers
Appointed to direct these fair designs.

BOLINGBROKE

Lord Marshal, let me kiss my sovereign's hand
And bow my knee before his majesty;
For Mowbray and myself are like two men
That vow a long and weary pilgrimage.
50   Then let us take a ceremonious leave
And loving farewell of our several friends.

66

LORD MARSHAL (*to King Richard*)

   The appellant in all duty greets your highness
   And craves to kiss your hand, and take his leave.

KING RICHARD

   We will descend and fold him in our arms.
      He leaves his throne
   Cousin of Hereford, as thy cause is right,
   So be thy fortune in this royal fight!
   Farewell, my blood – which if today thou shed,
   Lament we may, but not revenge thee dead.

BOLINGBROKE

   O, let no noble eye profane a tear
   For me, if I be gored with Mowbray's spear!   60
   As confident as is the falcon's flight
   Against a bird, do I with Mowbray fight.
   (*To Lord Marshal*)
   My loving lord, I take my leave of you;
   (*to Aumerle*)
   Of you, my noble cousin, Lord Aumerle;
   Not sick, although I have to do with death,
   But lusty, young, and cheerly drawing breath.
   Lo, as at English feasts, so I regreet
   The daintiest last, to make the end most sweet.
   (*To John of Gaunt*)
   O thou, the earthly author of my blood,
   Whose youthful spirit in me regenerate   70
   Doth with a two-fold vigour lift me up
   To reach at victory above my head,
   Add proof unto mine armour with thy prayers,
   And with thy blessings steel my lance's point
   That it may enter Mowbray's waxen coat
   And furbish new the name of John o' Gaunt
   Even in the lusty haviour of his son!

JOHN OF GAUNT

God in thy good cause make thee prosperous!
Be swift like lightning in the execution,
80   And let thy blows, doubly redoubled,
Fall like amazing thunder on the casque
Of thy adverse pernicious enemy!
Rouse up thy youthful blood, be valiant, and live.

BOLINGBROKE

Mine innocence and Saint George to thrive!

MOWBRAY

However God or fortune cast my lot
There lives or dies true to King Richard's throne
A loyal, just, and upright gentleman.
Never did captive with a freer heart
Cast off his chains of bondage and embrace
90   His golden uncontrolled enfranchisement
More than my dancing soul doth celebrate
This feast of battle with mine adversary.
Most mighty liege, and my companion peers,
Take from my mouth the wish of happy years.
As gentle and as jocund as to jest
Go I to fight. Truth hath a quiet breast.

KING RICHARD

Farewell, my lord. Securely I espy
Virtue with valour couchèd in thine eye.
Order the trial, Marshal, and begin.

LORD MARSHAL

100   Harry of Hereford, Lancaster, and Derby,
Receive thy lance; and God defend the right.

BOLINGBROKE

Strong as a tower in hope, I cry 'Amen!'

LORD MARSHAL (*to an officer*)

Go bear this lance to Thomas, Duke of Norfolk.

FIRST HERALD

    Harry of Hereford, Lancaster, and Derby
    Stands here for God, his sovereign, and himself,
    On pain to be found false and recreant,
    To prove the Duke of Norfolk, Thomas Mowbray,
    A traitor to his God, his king, and him,
    And dares him to set forward to the fight.

SECOND HERALD

    Here standeth Thomas Mowbray, Duke of Norfolk,   110
    On pain to be found false and recreant,
    Both to defend himself and to approve
    Henry of Hereford, Lancaster, and Derby
    To God, his sovereign, and to him disloyal,
    Courageously and with a free desire
    Attending but the signal to begin.

LORD MARSHAL

    Sound, trumpets; and set forward, combatants!
        A charge sounded. King Richard throws his warder
        into the lists
    Stay! The King hath thrown his warder down.

KING RICHARD

    Let them lay by their helmets and their spears
    And both return back to their chairs again.   120
    (*To his counsellors*)
    Withdraw with us, and let the trumpets sound
    While we return these dukes what we decree.
        A long flourish. King Richard consults his nobles, then
        addresses the combatants
    Draw near,
    And list what with our council we have done.
    For that our kingdom's earth should not be soiled
    With that dear blood which it hath fosterèd,
    And for our eyes do hate the dire aspect

Richard is inconsistant with his excuses about his relatives fighting.

Of civil wounds ploughed up with neighbours' sword,
And for we think the eagle-wingèd pride
130   Of sky-aspiring and ambitious thoughts
With rival-hating envy set on you
To wake our peace, which in our country's cradle
Draws the sweet infant-breath of gentle sleep,
Which so roused up with boisterous untuned drums,
With harsh-resounding trumpets' dreadful bray,
And grating shock of wrathful iron arms,
Might from our quiet confines fright fair peace
And make us wade even in our kindred's blood:
Therefore we banish you our territories.
140   You, cousin Hereford, upon pain of life
Till twice five summers have enriched our fields
Shall not regreet our fair dominions,
But tread the stranger paths of banishment.

BOLINGBROKE
Your will be done. This must my comfort be:
That sun that warms you here shall shine on me,
And those his golden beams to you here lent
Shall point on me, and gild my banishment.

KING RICHARD
Norfolk, for thee remains a heavier doom,
Which I with some unwillingness pronounce.
150   The sly slow hours shall not determinate
The dateless limit of thy dear exile.
The hopeless word of 'never to return'
Breathe I against thee upon pain of life.

MOWBRAY
A heavy sentence, my most sovereign liege,
And all unlooked-for from your highness' mouth.
A dearer merit, not so deep a maim
As to be cast forth in the common air
Have I deservèd at your highness' hands.

Anachronism, most of the knights were bilingual, they could speak french aswell as english.

The language I have learnt these forty years,   *He cannot —*
My native English, now I must forgo,   *speak english again*   160
And now my tongue's use is to me no more
Than an unstringèd viol or a harp,   *He feels like a musical instrument with-*
Or like a cunning instrument cased up —   *out any strings*
Or being open, put into his hands   *or in the hands of*
That knows no touch to tune the harmony.   *someone who*
Within my mouth you have engaoled my tongue,   *cant play it*
Doubly portcullised with my teeth and lips,   *Gate on a*
And dull unfeeling barren ignorance   *castle*
Is made my gaoler to attend on me.
I am too old to fawn upon a nurse,   170
Too far in years to be a pupil now.
What is thy sentence then but speechless death,
Which robs my tongue from breathing native breath?

KING RICHARD

It boots thee not to be compassionate.   *Richard is getting*
After our sentence plaining comes too late.   *sick of an empathy*

MOWBRAY   *who knows too much.*

Then thus I turn me from my country's light,
To dwell in solemn shades of endless night.

KING RICHARD (*to Bolingbroke and Mowbray*)

Return again, and take an oath with thee.
Lay on our royal sword your banished hands.
Swear by the duty that you owe to God –   180
Our part therein we banish with yourselves –
To keep the oath that we administer:
You never shall, so help you truth and God,
Embrace each other's love in banishment,
Nor never look upon each other's face,
Nor never write, regreet, nor reconcile
This lowering tempest of your home-bred hate,
Nor never by advisèd purpose meet
To plot, contrive, or complot any ill

71

190　'Gainst us, our state, our subjects, or our land.

BOLINGBROKE

　I swear.

MOWBRAY

　And I, to keep all this.

BOLINGBROKE

　Norfolk, so far as to mine enemy:
　By this time, had the King permitted us,
　One of our souls had wandered in the air,
　Banished this frail sepulchre of our flesh,
　As now our flesh is banished from this land.
　Confess thy treasons ere thou fly the realm.
　Since thou hast far to go, bear not along
200　The clogging burden of a guilty soul.

MOWBRAY

　No, Bolingbroke, if ever I were traitor
　My name be blotted from the book of life,
　And I from heaven banished as from hence!
　But what thou art, God, thou, and I do know,
　And all too soon, I fear, the King shall rue.
　Farewell, my liege. Now no way can I stray;
　Save back to England, all the world's my way.　　*Exit*

KING RICHARD (*to John of Gaunt*)

　Uncle, even in the glasses of thine eyes
　I see thy grievèd heart. Thy sad aspect
210　Hath from the number of his banished years
　Plucked four away. (*To Bolingbroke*) Six frozen winters
　　　　spent,
　Return with welcome home from banishment.

down to 6 years

BOLINGBROKE

　How long a time lies in one little word!
　Four lagging winters and four wanton springs
　End in a word – such is the breath of kings.

look at the power the King has he can change it all

73

JOHN OF GAUNT

I thank my liege that in regard of me
He shortens four years of my son's exile.
But little vantage shall I reap thereby;
For ere the six years that he hath to spend
Can change their moons, and bring their times about,   220
My oil-dried lamp and time-bewasted light
Shall be extinct with age and endless night.
My inch of taper will be burnt and done,
And blindfold death not let me see my son.

KING RICHARD

Why, uncle, thou hast many years to live.

dont be silly.

JOHN OF GAUNT

But not a minute, King, that thou canst give.
Shorten my days thou canst with sullen sorrow,
And pluck nights from me, but not lend a morrow.
Thou canst help time to furrow me with age,
But stop no wrinkle in his pilgrimage.   230
Thy word is current with him for my death,
But dead, thy kingdom cannot buy my breath.

you may be king but you cant bring back my life.

KING RICHARD

Thy son is banished upon good advice
Whereto thy tongue a party-verdict gave.
Why at our justice seemest thou then to lour?

JOHN OF GAUNT

Things sweet to taste prove in digestion sour.
You urged me as a judge, but I had rather
You would have bid me argue like a father.
O, had it been a stranger, not my child,
To smooth his fault I should have been more mild.   240
A partial slander sought I to avoid,
And in the sentence my own life destroyed.
Alas, I looked when some of you should say

after effect is unpleasant

I was too strict, to make mine own away.
But you gave leave to my unwilling tongue
Against my will to do myself this wrong.

KING RICHARD

Cousin, farewell – and, uncle, bid him so.
Six years we banish him, and he shall go.

Flourish. Exit King Richard with his train

AUMERLE

Cousin, farewell! What presence must not know,
250 From where you do remain let paper show.

LORD MARSHAL

My lord, no leave take I; for I will ride
As far as land will let me by your side.

JOHN OF GAUNT

O, to what purpose dost thou hoard thy words,
That thou returnest no greeting to thy friends?

BOLINGBROKE

I have too few to take my leave of you,
When the tongue's office should be prodigal
To breathe the abundant dolour of the heart.

JOHN OF GAUNT

Thy grief is but thy absence for a time.

BOLINGBROKE

Joy absent, grief is present for that time.

JOHN OF GAUNT

260 What is six winters? They are quickly gone.

BOLINGBROKE

To men in joy; but grief makes one hour ten.

JOHN OF GAUNT

Call it a travel that thou takest for pleasure.

BOLINGBROKE

My heart will sigh when I miscall it so,
Which finds it an enforcèd pilgrimage.

74

JOHN OF GAUNT

  The sullen passage of thy weary steps
  Esteem as foil wherein thou art to set
  The precious jewel of thy home return.

BOLINGBROKE

  Nay, rather every tedious stride I make
  Will but remember me what a deal of world
  I wander from the jewels that I love.   270
  Must I not serve a long apprenticehood
  To foreign passages, and in the end,
  Having my freedom, boast of nothing else
  But that I was a journeyman to grief?

JOHN OF GAUNT

  All places that the eye of heaven visits
  Are to a wise man ports and happy havens.
  Teach thy necessity to reason thus:
  There is no virtue like necessity.
  Think not the King did banish thee,
  But thou the King. Woe doth the heavier sit   280
  Where it perceives it is but faintly borne.
  Go, say I sent thee forth to purchase honour,
  And not the King exiled thee; or suppose
  Devouring pestilence hangs in our air
  And thou art flying to a fresher clime.
  Look what thy soul holds dear, imagine it
  To lie that way thou goest, not whence thou comest.
  Suppose the singing birds musicians,
  The grass whereon thou treadest the presence strewed,
  The flowers fair ladies, and thy steps no more   290
  Than a delightful measure or a dance;
  For gnarling sorrow hath less power to bite
  The man that mocks at it and sets it light.

BOLINGBROKE

  O, who can hold a fire in his hand

Bolingbrook is see as proud and stuck up

I.3-4

By thinking on the frosty Caucasus,
Or cloy the hungry edge of appetite
By bare imagination of a feast,
Or wallow naked in December snow
By thinking on fantastic summer's heat?

300   O no, the apprehension of the good
Gives but the greater feeling to the worse.
Fell sorrow's tooth doth never rankle more
Than when he bites, but lanceth not the sore.

JOHN OF GAUNT

Come, come, my son, I'll bring thee on thy way.
Had I thy youth and cause I would not stay.

BOLINGBROKE

Then, England's ground, farewell! Sweet soil, adieu,
My mother and my nurse that bears me yet!
Where'er I wander, boast of this I can:
Though banished, yet a trueborn Englishman! *Exeunt*

*more   ~~Politic~~ Patriotic imagery as he leaves
                              the country*

I.4   *Enter the King with Bagot and Green at one door,
           and the Lord Aumerle at another*

KING RICHARD

We did observe. Cousin Aumerle,
How far brought you high Hereford on his way?

AUMERLE *- doesn't like bolingbrook.*

I brought high Hereford, if you call him so,
But to the next highway; and there I left him.

KING RICHARD

And say, what store of parting tears were shed?

AUMERLE

Faith, none for me, except the north-east wind,
Which then blew bitterly against our faces,
Awaked the sleeping rheum, and so by chance
Did grace our hollow parting with a tear.

76

Bollingbrooke is good at Communicating with the country Richard is not.

KING RICHARD

What said our cousin when you parted with him? 10

AUMERLE

'Farewell' –
And, for my heart disdainèd that my tongue
Should so profane the word, that taught me craft
To counterfeit oppression of such grief
That words seemed buried in my sorrow's grave.
Marry, would the word 'farewell' have lengthened hours
And added years to his short banishment,
He should have had a volume of farewells;
But since it would not, he had none of me.

KING RICHARD – *Snob.*

He is our cousin, cousin; but 'tis doubt, 20
When time shall call him home from banishment,
Whether our kinsman come to see his friends.
Ourself and Bushy
Observed his courtship to the common people,
How he did seem to dive into their hearts
With humble and familiar courtesy;
What reverence he did throw away on slaves,
Wooing poor craftsmen with the craft of smiles
And patient underbearing of his fortune,
As 'twere to banish their affects with him. 30
Off goes his bonnet to an oyster-wench.
A brace of draymen bid God speed him well,
And had the tribute of his supple knee,
With 'Thanks, my countrymen, my loving friends',
As were our England in reversion his,
And he our subjects' next degree in hope.

GREEN

Well, he is gone; and with him go these thoughts.
Now, for the rebels which stand out in Ireland,
Expedient manage must be made, my liege,

Richard doesn't like Bollingbrooke he is jelous

Common people - slaves. Richard doesn't mix with common people.

Bollingbrook is Like a good Politician good at getting people on his side.

B talks to the man on his own Level.

nice to play down himself to make it look good.

Bollingbrook attitude with the common people. Richard doesn't believe it should be done.

why does B do this because he is nice or to get popularity.

40   Ere further leisure yield them further means
  For their advantage and your highness' loss.

KING RICHARD

  We will ourself in person to this war;

[handwritten: forget about that!]

  And, for our coffers with too great a court
  And liberal largess are grown somewhat light,
  We are enforced to farm our royal realm,
  The revenue whereof shall furnish us
  For our affairs in hand. If that come short
  Our substitutes at home shall have blank charters
  Whereto, when they shall know what men are rich,
50   They shall subscribe them for large sums of gold
  And send them after to supply our wants;
  For we will make for Ireland presently.

    Enter Bushy

  Bushy, what news?

BUSHY

  Old John of Gaunt is grievous sick, my lord,
  Suddenly taken, and hath sent post-haste
  To entreat your majesty to visit him.

KING RICHARD   *[handwritten: news of joblessness.]*

  Where lies he?

BUSHY

  At Ely House.

KING RICHARD

  Now put it, God, in the physician's mind
60   To help him to his grave immediately!
  The lining of his coffers shall make coats
  To deck our soldiers for these Irish wars.
  Come, gentlemen, let's all go visit him.
  Pray God we may make haste and come too late!

ALL

  Amen!   *Exeunt*

*

[handwritten left margin: Richard decides to go to Ireland to fight the war himself when could be suicide as he leaves the door open for his uncle]

[handwritten right margin: Richard rents all the land to people for a fixed sum which he then uses to fight the war.]

[handwritten bottom: H/W FINISHES HERE.]

is the King comming as with my last
breath i want to give him advice

Enter John of Gaunt sick, with the Duke of York, the **II.1**
Earl of Northumberland, attendants, and others

JOHN OF GAUNT
Will the King come, that I may breathe my last
In wholesome counsel to his unstaid youth?

not a good
thing to say.

YORK   not a viable propsition.

Vex not yourself, nor strive not with your breath;
For all in vain comes counsel to his ear.

— he wont listen to
you so dont
bother.

JOHN OF GAUNT
O, but they say the tongues of dying men
Enforce attention like deep harmony.
Where words are scarce they are seldom spent in vain,
For they breathe truth that breathe their words in pain.
He that no more must say is listened more
    Than they whom youth and ease have taught to glose.   10
More are men's ends marked than their lives before.
    The setting sun, and music at the close,
As the last taste of sweets, is sweetest last,
Writ in remembrance more than things long past.
Though Richard my life's counsel would not hear,
My death's sad tale may yet undeaf his ear.

But he will listen to me as i am dying. People who are dying speak

They talk round the subject

YORK — old man - views different to Richards.

He wont listen to

No, it is stopped with other, flattering sounds,
As praises, of whose taste the wise are fond;
Lascivious metres, to whose venom sound

Evidence for
Rich's character.

h likes   The open ear of youth doth always listen
  fashion   Report of fashions in proud Italy,
Whose manners still our tardy-apish nation
Limps after in base imitation.

Youth will always
listen to things that
appeal to them most

new fad rich will pick up on it.

Where doth the world thrust forth a vanity –
So it be new there's no respect how vile –
That is not quickly buzzed into his ears?
Then all too late comes counsel to be heard
Where will doth mutiny with wit's regard.

Rich needs to grow up, his partying has
to stop,

Direct not him whose way himself will choose.

30 'Tis breath thou lackest, and that breath wilt thou lose.

JOHN OF GAUNT *I have something important to say.*

Methinks I am a prophet new-inspired,

And thus, expiring, do foretell of him:

His rash fierce blaze of riot cannot last; *he needs to grow up.*

For violent fires soon burn out themselves.

Small showers last long, but sudden storms are short.

eventually things will come to a head and he wait cerze
He tires betimes that spurs too fast betimes.

With eager feeding food doth choke the feeder. *- to much*

Light vanity, insatiate cormorant, *(Bird eats fish in one go*

Consuming means, soon preys upon itself.

40 This royal throne of kings, this sceptred isle, *He relates England to*

This earth of majesty, this seat of Mars, *(WAR)* *Eden,*

This other Eden – demi-paradise –

This fortress built by nature for herself *England is the best.*

Against infection and the hand of war,

This happy breed of men, this little world,

This precious stone set in the silver sea, *England = Jewel*

Which serves it in the office of a wall, *in the sea.*

Or as a moat defensive to a house

Against the envy of less happier lands; *famous crusader black prince*

50 This blessèd plot, this earth, this realm, this England,

England = Royal Mother.
This nurse, this teeming womb of royal kings, *up holding*

Feared by their breed, and famous by their birth, *Royalty.*

Renownèd for their deeds as far from home

For Christian service and true chivalry

As is the sepulchre in stubborn Jewry

Of the world's ransom, blessèd Mary's son;

This land of such dear souls, this dear dear land,

Dear for her reputation through the world,

Is now leased out – I die pronouncing it –

60 Like to a tenement or pelting farm.

England, bound in with the triumphant sea,

Whose rocky shore beats back the envious siege
Of watery Neptune, is now bound in with shame,
With inky blots and rotten parchment bonds.
That England that was wont to conquer others
Hath made a shameful conquest of itself.
Ah, would the scandal vanish with my life,
How happy then were my ensuing death!

> *Enter King Richard, Queen Isabel, Aumerle, Bushy,*
> *Green, Bagot, Ross, and Willoughby*

YORK

    The King is come. Deal mildly with his youth;
    For young hot colts being raged do rage the more.   70

QUEEN ISABEL

    How fares our noble uncle Lancaster?

KING RICHARD

    What comfort, man? How is't with agèd Gaunt?

JOHN OF GAUNT

    O, how that name befits my composition!
    Old Gaunt indeed, and gaunt in being old.
    Within me grief hath kept a tedious fast;
    And who abstains from meat that is not gaunt?
    For sleeping England long time have I watched.
    Watching breeds leanness; leanness is all gaunt.
    The pleasure that some fathers feed upon
    Is my strict fast – I mean my children's looks;   80
    And therein fasting hast thou made me gaunt.
    Gaunt am I for the grave, gaunt as a grave,
    Whose hollow womb inherits naught but bones.

KING RICHARD

    Can sick men play so nicely with their names?

JOHN OF GAUNT

    No, misery makes sport to mock itself.
    Since thou dost seek to kill my name in me,
    I mock my name, great King, to flatter thee.

KING RICHARD

Should dying men flatter with those that live?

JOHN OF GAUNT

No, no. Men living flatter those that die.

KING RICHARD

90 Thou now a-dying sayst thou flatterest me.

JOHN OF GAUNT

O, no. Thou diest, though I the sicker be.

KING RICHARD

I am in health. I breathe, and see thee ill.

JOHN OF GAUNT

Now he that made me knows I see thee ill;
Ill in myself to see, and in thee seeing ill.
Thy deathbed is no lesser than thy land,
Wherein thou liest in reputation sick;
And thou, too careless patient as thou art,
Committest thy anointed body to the cure
Of those 'physicians' that first wounded thee.
100 A thousand flatterers sit within thy crown,
Whose compass is no bigger than thy head,
And yet, encagèd in so small a verge,
The waste is no whit lesser than thy land.
O, had thy grandsire with a prophet's eye
Seen how his son's son should destroy his sons,
From forth thy reach he would have laid thy shame,
Deposing thee before thou wert possessed,
Which art possessed now to depose thyself.
Why, cousin, wert thou regent of the world
110 It were a shame to let this land by lease.
But for thy world enjoying but this land,
Is it not more than shame to shame it so?
Landlord of England art thou now, not king.
Thy state of law is bondslave to the law,
And thou –

KING RICHARD

            – a lunatic lean-witted fool,
Presuming on an ague's privilege,
Darest with thy frozen admonition
Make pale our cheek, chasing the royal blood
With fury from his native residence.
Now by my seat's right royal majesty,   120
Wert thou not brother to great Edward's son,
This tongue that runs so roundly in thy head
Should run thy head from thy unreverent shoulders.

JOHN OF GAUNT

O, spare me not, my brother Edward's son,
For that I was his father Edward's son.
That blood already, like the pelican,
Hast thou tapped out and drunkenly caroused.
My brother Gloucester, plain well-meaning soul –
Whom fair befall in heaven 'mongst happy souls –
May be a precedent and witness good   130
That thou respectest not spilling Edward's blood.
Join with the present sickness that I have,
And thy unkindness be like crookèd age,
To crop at once a too-long withered flower.
Live in thy shame, but die not shame with thee!
These words hereafter thy tormentors be!
Convey me to my bed, then to my grave.
Love they to live that love and honour have.

Exit with Northumberland and attendants

KING RICHARD

And let them die that age and sullens have;
For both hast thou, and both become the grave.   140

YORK

I do beseech your majesty, impute his words
To wayward sickliness and age in him.
He loves you, on my life, and holds you dear

As Harry, Duke of Hereford, were he here.

KING RICHARD

Right, you say true. As Hereford's love, so his.
As theirs, so mine; and all be as it is.

Enter Northumberland

NORTHUMBERLAND

My liege, old Gaunt commends him to your majesty.

KING RICHARD

What says he?

NORTHUMBERLAND

          Nay, nothing. All is said.
His tongue is now a stringless instrument.
150 Words, life, and all, old Lancaster hath spent.

YORK

Be York the next that must be bankrupt so!
Though death be poor, it ends a mortal woe.

KING RICHARD

The ripest fruit first falls, and so doth he.
His time is spent, our pilgrimage must be.
So much for that. Now for our Irish wars.
We must supplant those rough rug-headed kerns
Which live like venom where no venom else
But only they have privilege to live.
And for these great affairs do ask some charge,
160 Towards our assistance we do seize to us
The plate, coin, revenues, and moveables
Whereof our uncle Gaunt did stand possessed.

YORK

How long shall I be patient? Ah, how long
Shall tender duty make me suffer wrong?
Not Gloucester's death, nor Hereford's banishment,
Nor Gaunt's rebukes, nor England's private wrongs,
Nor the prevention of poor Bolingbroke
About his marriage, nor my own disgrace,

Have ever made me sour my patient cheek
Or bend one wrinkle on my sovereign's face.   170
I am the last of noble Edward's sons,
Of whom thy father, Prince of Wales, was first.
In war was never lion raged more fierce,
In peace was never gentle lamb more mild
Than was that young and princely gentleman.
His face thou hast; for even so looked he
Accomplished with the number of thy hours;
But when he frowned it was against the French,
And not against his friends. His noble hand
Did win what he did spend, and spent not that   180
Which his triumphant father's hand had won.
His hands were guilty of no kindred blood,
But bloody with the enemies of his kin.
O, Richard! York is too far gone with grief,
Or else he never would compare between.

KING RICHARD
  Why, uncle, what's the matter?
YORK   O, my liege,
  Pardon me if you please. If not, I, pleased
Not to be pardoned, am content withal.
Seek you to seize and grip into your hands
The royalties and rights of banished Hereford?   190
Is not Gaunt dead? And doth not Hereford live?
Was not Gaunt just? And is not Harry true?
Did not the one deserve to have an heir?
Is not his heir a well-deserving son?
Take Hereford's rights away, and take from Time
His charters and his customary rights.
Let not tomorrow then ensue today.
Be not thyself; for how art thou a king
But by fair sequence and succession?
Now afore God – God forbid I say true –   200

85

If you do wrongfully seize Hereford's rights,
Call in the letters patents that he hath
By his attorneys general to sue
His livery, and deny his offered homage,
You pluck a thousand dangers on your head,
You lose a thousand well-disposèd hearts,
And prick my tender patience to those thoughts
Which honour and allegiance cannot think.

KING RICHARD

Think what you will, we seize into our hands
His plate, his goods, his money, and his lands.

YORK

I'll not be by the while. My liege, farewell.
What will ensue hereof there's none can tell;
But by bad courses may be understood
That their events can never fall out good.   *Exit*

KING RICHARD

Go, Bushy, to the Earl of Wiltshire straight,
Bid him repair to us to Ely House
To see this business. Tomorrow next
We will for Ireland, and 'tis time I trow.
And we create in absence of ourself
Our uncle York Lord Governor of England;
For he is just, and always loved us well.
Come on, our Queen; tomorrow must we part.
Be merry; for our time of stay is short.

> *Flourish. Exeunt King Richard and Queen Isabel.*
> *Northumberland, Willoughby, and Ross remain*

NORTHUMBERLAND

Well, lords, the Duke of Lancaster is dead.

ROSS

And living too; for now his son is duke.

WILLOUGHBY

Barely in title, not in revenues.

NORTHUMBERLAND

Richly in both if justice had her right.

ROSS

My heart is great, but it must break with silence
Ere't be disburdened with a liberal tongue.

NORTHUMBERLAND

Nay, speak thy mind; and let him ne'er speak more   230
That speaks thy words again to do thee harm.

WILLOUGHBY

Tends that thou wouldst speak to the Duke of Hereford?
If it be so, out with it boldly, man!
Quick is mine ear to hear of good towards him.

ROSS

No good at all that I can do for him,
Unless you call it good to pity him,
Bereft and gelded of his patrimony.

NORTHUMBERLAND

Now, afore God, 'tis shame such wrongs are borne
In him, a royal prince, and many more
Of noble blood in this declining land.   240
The King is not himself, but basely led
By flatterers; and what they will inform
Merely in hate 'gainst any of us all,
That will the King severely prosecute
'Gainst us, our lives, our children, and our heirs.

ROSS

The commons hath he pilled with grievous taxes,
And quite lost their hearts. The nobles hath he fined
For ancient quarrels, and quite lost their hearts.

WILLOUGHBY

And daily new exactions are devised,
As blanks, benevolences, and I wot not what.   250
But what o' God's name doth become of this?

87

NORTHUMBERLAND

Wars hath not wasted it; for warred he hath not,
But basely yielded upon compromise
That which his noble ancestors achieved with blows.
More hath he spent in peace than they in wars.

ROSS

The Earl of Wiltshire hath the realm in farm.

WILLOUGHBY

The King's grown bankrupt like a broken man.

NORTHUMBERLAND

Reproach and dissolution hangeth over him.

ROSS

He hath not money for these Irish wars –
260 His burdenous taxations notwithstanding –
But by the robbing of the banished Duke.

NORTHUMBERLAND

His noble kinsman! – most degenerate King!
But, lords, we hear this fearful tempest sing
Yet seek no shelter to avoid the storm.
We see the wind sit sore upon our sails
And yet we strike not, but securely perish.

ROSS

We see the very wrack that we must suffer,
And unavoided is the danger now
For suffering so the causes of our wrack.

NORTHUMBERLAND

270 Not so. Even through the hollow eyes of death
I spy life peering; but I dare not say
How near the tidings of our comfort is.

WILLOUGHBY

Nay, let us share thy thoughts, as thou dost ours.

ROSS

Be confident to speak, Northumberland.
We three are but thyself; and speaking so

Thy words are but as thoughts. Therefore be bold.

NORTHUMBERLAND

Then thus: I have from Le Port Blanc,
A bay in Brittaine, received intelligence
That Harry Duke of Hereford, Rainold Lord Cobham,
The son of Richard Earl of Arundel   280
That late broke from the Duke of Exeter,
His brother, Archbishop late of Canterbury,
Sir Thomas Erpingham, Sir John Ramston,
Sir John Norbery, Sir Robert Waterton, and Francis
     Coint,

All these well-furnished by the Duke of Brittaine
With eight tall ships, three thousand men of war,
Are making hither with all due expedience,
And shortly mean to touch our northern shore.
Perhaps they had ere this, but that they stay
The first departing of the King for Ireland.   290
If then we shall shake off our slavish yoke,
Imp out our drooping country's broken wing,
Redeem from broking pawn the blemished crown,
Wipe off the dust that hides our sceptre's gilt,
And make high majesty look like itself,
Away with me in post to Ravenspurgh.
But if you faint, as fearing to do so,
Stay, and be secret; and myself will go.

ROSS

To horse, to horse. Urge doubts to them that fear.

WILLOUGHBY

Hold out my horse, and I will first be there.   *Exeunt* 300

Enter the Queen, Bushy, and Bagot   II.2

BUSHY

Madam, your majesty is too much sad.

You promised when you parted with the King
To lay aside life-harming heaviness,
And entertain a cheerful disposition.

QUEEN ISABEL

To please the King I did. To please myself
I cannot do it. Yet I know no cause
Why I should welcome such a guest as grief
Save bidding farewell to so sweet a guest
As my sweet Richard. Yet again methinks
10   Some unborn sorrow ripe in fortune's womb
Is coming towards me, and my inward soul
With nothing trembles. At something it grieves
More than with parting from my lord the King.

BUSHY

Each substance of a grief hath twenty shadows
Which shows like grief itself, but is not so.
For sorrow's eye, glazèd with blinding tears,
Divides one thing entire to many objects,
Like perspectives which, rightly gazed upon,
Show nothing but confusion; eyed awry,
20   Distinguish form. So your sweet majesty,
Looking awry upon your lord's departure,
Find shapes of grief more than himself to wail,
Which looked on as it is, is naught but shadows
Of what it is not. Then, thrice-gracious Queen,
More than your lord's departure weep not – more is not
            seen,
Or if it be, 'tis with false sorrow's eye,
Which for things true weeps things imaginary.

QUEEN ISABEL

It may be so; but yet my inward soul
Persuades me it is otherwise. Howe'er it be
30   I cannot but be sad – so heavy-sad
As, though on thinking on no thought I think,

Makes me with heavy nothing faint and shrink.

BUSHY

'Tis nothing but conceit, my gracious lady.

QUEEN ISABEL

'Tis nothing less. Conceit is still derived
From some forefather grief. Mine is not so,
For nothing hath begot my something grief,
Or something hath the nothing that I grieve –
'Tis in reversion that I do possess –
But what it is that is not yet known what,
I cannot name; 'tis nameless woe, I wot.   40

    Enter Green

GREEN

God save your majesty, and well met, gentlemen.
I hope the King is not yet shipped for Ireland.

QUEEN ISABEL

Why hopest thou so? 'Tis better hope he is,
For his designs crave haste, his haste good hope.
Then wherefore dost thou hope he is not shipped?

GREEN

That he, our hope, might have retired his power,
And driven into despair an enemy's hope,
Who strongly hath set footing in this land.
The banished Bolingbroke repeals himself,
And with uplifted arms is safe arrived   50
At Ravenspurgh.

QUEEN ISABEL   Now God in heaven forbid!

GREEN

Ah, madam, 'tis too true! And, that is worse,
The Lord Northumberland, his son young Henry Percy,
The Lords of Ross, Beaumont, and Willoughby,
With all their powerful friends are fled to him.

BUSHY

Why have you not proclaimed Northumberland

And all the rest, revolted faction, traitors?

GREEN

We have; whereupon the Earl of Worcester
Hath broken his staff, resigned his stewardship,
60   And all the household servants fled with him
To Bolingbroke.

QUEEN ISABEL

So, Green, thou art the midwife to my woe,
And Bolingbroke my sorrow's dismal heir.
Now hath my soul brought forth her prodigy,
And I, a gasping new-delivered mother,
Have woe to woe, sorrow to sorrow joined.

BUSHY

Despair not, madam.

QUEEN ISABEL   Who shall hinder me?
I will despair and be at enmity
With cozening hope. He is a flatterer,
70   A parasite, a keeper-back of death
Who gently would dissolve the bands of life
Which false hope lingers in extremity.
     Enter York

GREEN

Here comes the Duke of York.

QUEEN ISABEL

With signs of war about his agèd neck.
O, full of careful business are his looks!
Uncle, for God's sake speak comfortable words.

YORK

Should I do so I should belie my thoughts.
Comfort's in heaven, and we are on the earth,
Where nothing lives but crosses, cares, and grief.
80   Your husband, he is gone to save far off,
Whilst others come to make him lose at home.
Here am I left to underprop his land,

Who weak with age cannot support myself.
Now comes the sick hour that his surfeit made.
Now shall he try his friends that flattered him.
    Enter a Servingman

SERVINGMAN

My lord, your son was gone before I came.

YORK

He was? – why, so. Go all which way it will.
The nobles they are fled. The commons they are cold,
And will, I fear, revolt on Hereford's side.
Sirrah, get thee to Pleshey to my sister Gloucester.   90
Bid her send me presently a thousand pound –
Hold: take my ring.

SERVINGMAN

My lord, I had forgot to tell your lordship –
Today as I came by I callèd there –
But I shall grieve you to report the rest.

YORK

What is't, knave?

SERVINGMAN

An hour before I came the Duchess died.

YORK

God for his mercy, what a tide of woes
Comes rushing on this woeful land at once!
I know not what to do. I would to God –   100
So my untruth had not provoked him to it –
The King had cut off my head with my brother's.
What, are there no posts dispatched for Ireland?
How shall we do for money for these wars?
Come, sister – cousin, I would say – pray pardon me.
Go, fellow, get thee home, provide some carts,
And bring away the armour that is there.
Gentlemen, will you go muster men?
If I know how or which way to order these affairs

110 Thus disorderly thrust into my hands,
Never believe me. Both are my kinsmen.
T'one is my sovereign, whom both my oath
And duty bids defend. T'other again
Is my kinsman, whom the King hath wronged,
Whom conscience and my kindred bids to right.
Well, somewhat we must do. (*To the Queen*) Come,
    cousin,
I'll dispose of you. Gentlemen, go muster up your men,
And meet me presently at Berkeley.
I should to Pleshey, too,
120 But time will not permit. All is uneven,
And everything is left at six and seven.

              Exeunt York and the Queen
    Bushy, Bagot, and Green remain

BUSHY
The wind sits fair for news to go for Ireland,
But none returns. For us to levy power
Proportionable to the enemy
Is all unpossible.

GREEN
Besides, our nearness to the King in love
Is near the hate of those love not the King.

BAGOT
And that is the wavering commons; for their love
Lies in their purses, and whoso empties them
130 By so much fills their hearts with deadly hate.

BUSHY
Wherein the King stands generally condemned.

BAGOT
If judgement lie in them, then so do we,
Because we ever have been near the King.

GREEN
Well, I will for refuge straight to Bristol Castle.

The Earl of Wiltshire is already there.

BUSHY

Thither will I with you; for little office
Will the hateful commons perform for us –
Except like curs to tear us all to pieces.
Will you go along with us?

BAGOT

No, I will to Ireland to his majesty.   140
Farewell. If heart's presages be not vain,
We three here part that ne'er shall meet again.

BUSHY

That's as York thrives to beat back Bolingbroke.

GREEN

Alas, poor Duke! The task he undertakes
Is numbering sands and drinking oceans dry.
Where one on his side fights, thousands will fly.

BAGOT

Farewell at once, for once, for all, and ever.

BUSHY

Well, we may meet again.

BAGOT   I fear me, never.   *Exeunt*

Enter Bolingbroke and Northumberland   II.3

BOLINGBROKE

How far is it, my lord, to Berkeley now?

NORTHUMBERLAND

Believe me, noble lord,
I am a stranger here in Gloucestershire.
These high wild hills and rough uneven ways
Draws out our miles and makes them wearisome.
And yet your fair discourse hath been as sugar,
Making the hard way sweet and delectable.
But I bethink me what a weary way

From Ravenspurgh to Cotswold will be found
10 In Ross and Willoughby, wanting your company,
Which I protest hath very much beguiled
The tediousness and process of my travel.
But theirs is sweetened with the hope to have
The present benefit which I possess;
And hope to joy is little less in joy
Than hope enjoyed. By this the weary lords
Shall make their way seem short as mine hath done
By sight of what I have – your noble company.

BOLINGBROKE
Of much less value is my company
20 Than your good words. But who comes here?
   Enter Harry Percy

NORTHUMBERLAND
It is my son, young Harry Percy,
Sent from my brother Worcester whencesoever.
Harry, how fares your uncle?

PERCY
I had thought, my lord, to have learned his health of you.

NORTHUMBERLAND
Why, is he not with the Queen?

PERCY
No, my good lord, he hath forsook the court,
Broken his staff of office, and dispersed
The household of the King.

NORTHUMBERLAND   What was his reason?
He was not so resolved when last we spake together.

PERCY
30 Because your lordship was proclaimèd traitor.
But he, my lord, is gone to Ravenspurgh
To offer service to the Duke of Hereford,
And sent me over by Berkeley to discover
What power the Duke of York had levied there,

Then with directions to repair to Ravenspurgh.

NORTHUMBERLAND

Have you forgot the Duke of Hereford, boy?

PERCY

No, my good lord; for that is not forgot
Which ne'er I did remember. To my knowledge
I never in my life did look on him.

NORTHUMBERLAND

Then learn to know him now – this is the Duke.   40

PERCY

My gracious lord, I tender you my service,
Such as it is, being tender, raw, and young,
Which elder days shall ripen and confirm
To more approvèd service and desert.

BOLINGBROKE

I thank thee, gentle Percy; and be sure
I count myself in nothing else so happy
As in a soul remembering my good friends;
And as my fortune ripens with thy love
It shall be still thy true love's recompense.
My heart this covenant makes, my hand thus seals it.   50

NORTHUMBERLAND

How far is it to Berkeley, and what stir
Keeps good old York there with his men of war?

PERCY

There stands the castle by yon tuft of trees,
Manned with three hundred men as I have heard,
And in it are the Lords of York, Berkeley, and Seymour,
None else of name and noble estimate.
      Enter Ross and Willoughby

NORTHUMBERLAND

Here come the Lords of Ross and Willoughby,
Bloody with spurring, fiery red with haste.

BOLINGBROKE

    Welcome, my lords. I wot your love pursues
60   A banished traitor. All my treasury
    Is yet but unfelt thanks, which, more enriched,
    Shall be your love and labour's recompense.

ROSS

    Your presence makes us rich, most noble lord.

WILLOUGHBY

    And far surmounts our labour to attain it.

BOLINGBROKE

    Evermore thank's the exchequer of the poor,
    Which till my infant fortune comes to years
    Stands for my bounty. But who comes here?
        Enter Berkeley

NORTHUMBERLAND

    It is my Lord of Berkeley, as I guess.

BERKELEY

    My Lord of Hereford, my message is to you.

BOLINGBROKE

70   My lord, my answer is to 'Lancaster'.
    And I am come to seek that name in England,
    And I must find that title in your tongue
    Before I make reply to aught you say.

BERKELEY

    Mistake me not, my lord. 'Tis not my meaning
    To raze one title of your honour out.
    To you, my lord, I come – what lord you will –
    From the most gracious regent of this land,
    The Duke of York, to know what pricks you on
    To take advantage of the absent time
80   And fright our native peace with self-borne arms.
        Enter York

BOLINGBROKE

    I shall not need transport my words by you.

Here comes his grace in person. My noble uncle!
    He kneels

YORK

Show me thy humble heart, and not thy knee,
Whose duty is deceivable and false.

BOLINGBROKE

My gracious uncle –

YORK

Tut, tut, grace me no grace, nor uncle me no uncle!
I am no traitor's uncle; and that word 'grace'
In an ungracious mouth is but profane.
Why have those banished and forbidden legs
Dared once to touch a dust of England's ground?   90
But then more 'why' – why have they dared to march
So many miles upon her peaceful bosom,
Frighting her pale-faced villages with war
And ostentation of despisèd arms?
Comest thou because the anointed King is hence?
Why, foolish boy, the King is left behind,
And in my loyal bosom lies his power.
Were I but now lord of such hot youth
As when brave Gaunt, thy father, and myself
Rescued the Black Prince – that young Mars of men –   100
From forth the ranks of many thousand French,
O then how quickly should this arm of mine,
Now prisoner to the palsy, chastise thee
And minister correction to thy fault!

BOLINGBROKE

My gracious uncle, let me know my fault.
On what condition stands it, and wherein?

YORK

Even in condition of the worst degree,
In gross rebellion and detested treason.
Thou art a banished man, and here art come

99

110 Before the expiration of thy time
In braving arms against thy sovereign!

BOLINGBROKE
As I was banished, I was banished Hereford;
But as I come, I come for Lancaster.
And, noble uncle, I beseech your grace
Look on my wrongs with an indifferent eye.
You are my father; for methinks in you
I see old Gaunt alive. O then, my father,
Will you permit that I shall stand condemned
A wandering vagabond, my rights and royalties
120 Plucked from my arms perforce, and given away
To upstart unthrifts? Wherefore was I born?
If that my cousin King be King in England
It must be granted I am Duke of Lancaster.
You have a son, Aumerle, my noble cousin.
Had you first died and he been thus trod down
He should have found his uncle Gaunt a father
To rouse his wrongs and chase them to the bay.
I am denied to sue my livery here,
And yet my letters patents give me leave.
130 My father's goods are all distrained and sold,
And these, and all, are all amiss employed.
What would you have me do? I am a subject,
And I challenge law. Attorneys are denied me,
And therefore personally I lay my claim
To my inheritance of free descent.

NORTHUMBERLAND (to York)
The noble Duke hath been too much abused.

ROSS
It stands your grace upon to do him right.

WILLOUGHBY
Base men by his endowments are made great.

lets then know that he also thinks Rich was wrong

YORK

My lords of England, let me tell you this: *but thinks*
I have had feeling of my cousin's wrongs, *Bol* 140
And laboured all I could to do him right. *shouldn't*
But in this kind to come, in braving arms, *"Right his*
Be his own carver, and cut out his way *wrong"*
To find out right with wrong – it may not be.
And you that do abet him in this kind
Cherish rebellion, and are rebels all.

NORTHUMBERLAND

The noble Duke hath sworn his coming is
But for his own, and for the right of that
We all have strongly sworn to give him aid; *followers*
And let him never see joy that breaks that oath. 150

YORK

Well, well, I see the issue of these arms.
I cannot mend it, I must needs confess,
Because my power is weak and all ill-left.
But if I could, by Him that gave me life,
I would attach you all and make you stoop
Unto the sovereign mercy of the King.
But since I cannot, be it known unto you
I do remain as neuter. So fare you well,
Unless you please to enter in the castle
And there repose you for this night. 160

BOLINGBROKE

An offer, uncle, that we will accept;
But we must win your grace to go with us
To Bristol Castle, which they say is held
By Bushy, Bagot, and their complices,
The caterpillars of the commonwealth,
Which I have sworn to weed and pluck away.

YORK

It may be I will go with you, but yet I'll pause;

For I am loath to break our country's laws.
Nor friends, nor foes, to me welcome you are.
170   Things past redress are now with me past care.

Exeunt

II.4   *Enter Earl of Salisbury and a Welsh Captain*

CAPTAIN

My Lord of Salisbury, we have stayed ten days
And hardly kept our countrymen together,
And yet we hear no tidings from the King.
Therefore we will disperse ourselves. Farewell.

SALISBURY

Stay yet another day, thou trusty Welshman.
The King reposeth all his confidence in thee.

CAPTAIN

'Tis thought the King is dead. We will not stay.
The bay trees in our country are all withered,
And meteors fright the fixèd stars of heaven.
10   The pale-faced moon looks bloody on the earth,
And lean-looked prophets whisper fearful change.
Rich men look sad, and ruffians dance and leap –
The one in fear to lose what they enjoy,
The other to enjoy by rage and war.
These signs forerun the death or fall of kings.
Farewell. Our countrymen are gone and fled,
As well assured Richard their king is dead.   *Exit*

SALISBURY

Ah, Richard! With the eyes of heavy mind
I see thy glory like a shooting star
20   Fall to the base earth from the firmament.
Thy sun sets weeping in the lowly west,
Witnessing storms to come, woe, and unrest.

102

all Richards army have deserted.

Thy friends are fled to wait upon thy foes,
And crossly to thy good all fortune goes. *Exit*

*Your friends have all gone to join up
with your enemys* *

He feels very sad for Richard.

Enter Bolingbroke, York, Northumberland, with III.1
Bushy and Green, prisoners

BOLINGBROKE
Bring forth these men.
Bushy and Green, I will not vex your souls,
Since presently your souls must part your bodies,
With too much urging your pernicious lives,
For 'twere no charity. Yet, to wash your blood
From off my hands, here in the view of men
I will unfold some causes of your deaths.
You have misled a prince, a royal king,
A happy gentleman in blood and lineaments,
By you unhappied and disfigured clean.   10
You have in manner with your sinful hours
Made a divorce betwixt his Queen and him,   *You have broke*
Broke the possession of a royal bed,   *up the King +*
And stained the beauty of a fair queen's cheeks   *queen.*
With tears drawn from her eyes by your foul wrongs.
Myself – a prince by fortune of my birth,
Near to the King in blood, and near in love
Till you did make him misinterpret me –   *You turned the*
Have stooped my neck under your injuries,   *King against*
And sighed my English breath in foreign clouds, 20 *me.*
Eating the bitter bread of banishment   *It was your*
Whilst you have fed upon my signories,   *decision to*
Disparked my parks, and felled my forest woods, *get me*
From my own windows torn my household coat,   *banished*
Razed out my imprese, leaving me no sign   *coat of arms.*

(Homosexuality)

103

Bushy and Green are going to be executed.

Save men's opinions and my living blood
To show the world I am a gentleman.
This and much more, much more than twice all this,
Condemns you to the death. See them delivered over
30   To execution and the hand of death.

BUSHY

More welcome is the stroke of death to me
Than Bolingbroke to England. Lords, farewell.

GREEN

My comfort is that heaven will take our souls
And plague injustice with the pains of hell.

BOLINGBROKE

My Lord Northumberland, see them dispatched.

Exit Northumberland with Bushy and Green

Uncle, you say the Queen is at your house.
For God's sake, fairly let her be intreated.
Tell her I send to her my kind commends.
Take special care my greetings be delivered.

Why is BB doing this, they are just his ministers. It's the Kings decision.

YORK

40   A gentleman of mine I have dispatched
With letters of your love to her at large.

BOLINGBROKE

Thanks, gentle uncle. Come, lords, away,
To fight with Glendower and his complices.
A while to work, and after, holiday.   *Exeunt*

Bolingbrook attends mere.

III.2   *Drums; flourish and colours. Enter King Richard,
               Aumerle, the Bishop of Carlisle, and soldiers*

KING RICHARD

Barkloughly Castle call they this at hand?

AUMERLE

Yea, my lord. How brooks your grace the air
After your late tossing on the breaking seas?

Echo's Bollingbrook

love btween King and queen.

KING RICHARD

  Needs must I like it well. I weep for joy
  To stand upon my kingdom once again.
  Dear earth, I do salute thee with my hand,
  Though rebels wound thee with their horses' hoofs.
  As a long-parted mother with her child
  Plays fondly with her tears and smiles in meeting,
  So weeping, smiling, greet I thee, my earth,   10
  And do thee favours with my royal hands.
  Feed not thy sovereign's foe, my gentle earth,
  Nor with thy sweets comfort his ravenous sense,
  But let thy spiders that suck up thy venom,
  And heavy-gaited toads, lie in their way,
  Doing annoyance to the treacherous feet
  Which with usurping steps do trample thee.
  Yield stinging nettles to mine enemies;
  And when they from thy bosom pluck a flower
  Guard it, I pray thee, with a lurking adder,   20
  Whose double tongue may with a mortal touch
  Throw death upon thy sovereign's enemies.
  Mock not my senseless conjuration, lords.
  This earth shall have a feeling, and these stones
  Prove armèd soldiers ere her native king
  Shall falter under foul rebellion's arms.

BISHOP OF CARLISLE

  Fear not, my lord, that power that made you king
  Hath power to keep you king in spite of all.
  The means that heavens yield must be embraced
  And not neglected; else heaven would,   30
  And we will not – heaven's offer we refuse,
  The proffered means of succour and redress.

AUMERLE

  He means, my lord, that we are too remiss,
  Whilst Bolingbroke through our security

Grows strong and great in substance and in power.

KING RICHARD

Discomfortable cousin, knowest thou not
That when the searching eye of heaven is hid
Behind the globe, that lights the lower world,
Then thieves and robbers range abroad unseen
40   In murders and in outrage boldly here;
But when from under this terrestrial ball
He fires the proud tops of the eastern pines,
And darts his light through every guilty hole,
Then murders, treasons, and detested sins –
The cloak of night being plucked from off their backs –
Stand bare and naked, trembling at themselves?
So when this thief, this traitor Bolingbroke,
Who all this while hath revelled in the night
Whilst we were wandering with the Antipodes,
50   Shall see us rising in our throne, the east,
His treasons will sit blushing in his face,
Not able to endure the sight of day,
But self-affrighted, tremble at his sin.
Not all the water in the rough rude sea
Can wash the balm off from an anointed king.
The breath of worldly men cannot depose
The deputy elected by the Lord.
For every man that Bolingbroke hath pressed
To lift shrewd steel against our golden crown,
60   God for his Richard hath in heavenly pay
A glorious angel. Then if angels fight,
Weak men must fall; for heaven still guards the right.
    Enter Salisbury

KING RICHARD

Welcome, my lord. How far off lies your power?

SALISBURY

Nor nea'er nor farther off, my gracious lord,

Than this weak arm. Discomfort guides my tongue
And bids me speak of nothing but despair.
One day too late, I fear me, noble lord,
Hath clouded all thy happy days on earth.
O, call back yesterday – bid time return,
And thou shalt have twelve thousand fighting men.   70
Today, today, unhappy day too late,
O'erthrows thy joys, friends, fortune, and thy state;
For all the Welshmen, hearing thou wert dead,
Are gone to Bolingbroke – dispersed and fled.

AUMERLE
Comfort, my liege. Why looks your grace so pale?

KING RICHARD
But now the blood of twenty thousand men
    Did triumph in my face; and they are fled.
And till so much blood thither come again
    Have I not reason to look pale and dead?
All souls that will be safe fly from my side,   80
For time hath set a blot upon my pride.

AUMERLE
Comfort, my liege. Remember who you are.

KING RICHARD
I had forgot myself. Am I not King?
Awake, thou coward majesty; thou sleepest.
Is not the King's name twenty thousand names?
Arm, arm, my name! A puny subject strikes
At thy great glory. Look not to the ground,
Ye favourites of a King. Are we not high?
High be our thoughts. I know my uncle York
Hath power enough to serve our turn. But who comes   90
    here?
    Enter Scroop

SCROOP
More health and happiness betide my liege

107

Than can my care-tuned tongue deliver him.

KING RICHARD

Mine ear is open and my heart prepared.
The worst is worldly loss thou canst unfold.
Say, is my kingdom lost? Why, 'twas my care;
And what loss is it to be rid of care?
Strives Bolingbroke to be as great as we?
Greater he shall not be. If he serve God
We'll serve Him too, and be his fellow so.
100   Revolt our subjects? That we cannot mend.
They break their faith to God as well as us.
Cry woe, destruction, ruin, and decay.
The worst is death, and death will have his day.

SCROOP

Glad am I that your highness is so armed
To bear the tidings of calamity.
Like an unseasonable stormy day
Which makes the silver rivers drown their shores
As if the world were all dissolved to tears,
So high above his limits swells the rage
110   Of Bolingbroke, covering your fearful land
With hard bright steel, and hearts harder than steel.
Whitebeards have armed their thin and hairless scalps
Against thy majesty. Boys with women's voices
Strive to speak big and clap their female joints
In stiff unwieldy arms against thy crown.
Thy very beadsmen learn to bend their bows
Of double-fatal yew against thy state.
Yea, distaff-women manage rusty bills
Against thy seat. Both young and old rebel,
120   And all goes worse than I have power to tell.

KING RICHARD

Too well, too well thou tellest a tale so ill.
Where is the Earl of Wiltshire? Where is Bagot?

What is become of Bushy, where is Green,
That they have let the dangerous enemy
Measure our confines with such peaceful steps?
If we prevail, their heads shall pay for it.
I warrant they have made peace with Bolingbroke.

SCROOP

Peace have they made with him indeed, my lord.

KING RICHARD

O, villains, vipers, damned without redemption!
Dogs easily won to fawn on any man!   130
Snakes in my heart-blood warmed, that sting my heart;
Three Judases, each one thrice worse than Judas –
Would they make peace? Terrible hell
Make war upon their spotted souls for this.

SCROOP

Sweet love, I see, changing his property,
Turns to the sourest and most deadly hate.
Again uncurse their souls. Their peace is made
With heads and not with hands. Those whom you curse
Have felt the worst of death's destroying wound,
And lie full low, graved in the hollow ground.   140

AUMERLE

Is Bushy, Green, and the Earl of Wiltshire dead?

SCROOP

Ay. All of them at Bristol lost their heads.

AUMERLE

Where is the Duke, my father, with his power?

KING RICHARD

No matter where. Of comfort no man speak.
Let's talk of graves, of worms, and epitaphs;
Make dust our paper, and with rainy eyes
Write sorrow on the bosom of the earth.
Let's choose executors and talk of wills –
And yet not so; for what can we bequeath

III.2

150 Save our deposèd bodies to the ground?
Our lands, our lives, and all are Bolingbroke's,
And nothing can we call our own but death
And that small model of the barren earth
Which serves as paste and cover to our bones.
For God's sake let us sit upon the ground
And tell sad stories of the death of kings –
How some have been deposed, some slain in war,
Some haunted by the ghosts they have deposed,
Some poisoned by their wives, some sleeping killed,
160 All murdered. For within the hollow crown
That rounds the mortal temples of a king
Keeps death his court; and there the antic sits,
Scoffing his state and grinning at his pomp,
Allowing him a breath, a little scene,
To monarchize, be feared, and kill with looks,
Infusing him with self and vain conceit,
As if this flesh which walls about our life
Were brass impregnable; and humoured thus,
Comes at the last, and with a little pin
170 Bores through his castle wall, and – farewell, king!
Cover your heads, and mock not flesh and blood
With solemn reverence. Throw away respect,
Tradition, form, and ceremonious duty;
For you have but mistook me all this while.
I live with bread, like you; feel want,
Taste grief, need friends. Subjected thus,
How can you say to me I am a king?

BISHOP OF CARLISLE
My lord, wise men ne'er sit and wail their woes,
But presently prevent the ways to wail.
180 To fear the foe, since fear oppresseth strength,
Gives in your weakness strength unto your foe,

110

Bollingbroke keeps cool but richard alway flys of the handle.

And so your follies fight against yourself.
Fear, and be slain. No worse can come to fight;
And fight and die is death destroying death,
Where fearing dying pays death servile breath.

AUMERLE

My father hath a power. Inquire of him,
And learn to make a body of a limb.

KING RICHARD

Thou chidest me well. Proud Bolingbroke, I come
To change blows with thee for our day of doom.
This ague-fit of fear is overblown.   190
An easy task it is to win our own.
Say, Scroop, where lies our uncle with his power?
Speak sweetly, man, although thy looks be sour.

SCROOP

Men judge by the complexion of the sky
    The state and inclination of the day.
So may you by my dull and heavy eye
    My tongue hath but a heavier tale to say.
I play the torturer, by small and small
To lengthen out the worst that must be spoken.
Your uncle York is joined with Bolingbroke,   200
And all your northern castles yielded up,
And all your southern gentlemen in arms
Upon his party.

KING RICHARD   Thou hast said enough.
(To Aumerle)
Beshrew thee, cousin, which didst lead me forth
Of that sweet way I was in to despair.
What say you now? What comfort have we now?
By heaven, I'll hate him everlastingly
That bids me be of comfort any more.
Go to Flint Castle. There I'll pine away.

Aumerle son of york says his father will help them.

210   A king, woe's slave, shall kingly woe obey.
    That power I have, discharge, and let them go
    To ear the land that hath some hope to grow;
    For I have none. Let no man speak again *York has joined up with Bolingbroke*
    To alter this; for counsel is but vain.

AUMERLE
    My liege, one word!

KING RICHARD   He does me double wrong
    That wounds me with the flatteries of his tongue.
    Discharge my followers. Let them hence away:
    From Richard's night to Bolingbroke's fair day. *Exeunt*

III.3   *Enter with drum and colours Bolingbroke, York,*
        Northumberland, attendants, and soldiers

BOLINGBROKE
    So that by this intelligence we learn
    The Welshmen are dispersed, and Salisbury
    Is gone to meet the King, who lately landed
    With some few private friends upon this coast.

NORTHUMBERLAND
    The news is very fair and good, my lord.
    Richard not far from hence hath hid his head.

YORK
    It would beseem the Lord Northumberland
    To say 'King Richard'. Alack the heavy day
    When such a sacred king should hide his head!

NORTHUMBERLAND
10   Your grace mistakes. Only to be brief
    Left I his title out.

YORK   The time hath been,
    Would you have been so brief with him, he would
    Have been so brief with you to shorten you,
    For taking so the head, your whole head's length.

BOLINGBROKE

  Mistake not, uncle, further than you should.

YORK

  Take not, good cousin, further than you should,
  Lest you mistake the heavens are over our heads.

BOLINGBROKE

  I know it, uncle, and oppose not myself
  Against their will. But who comes here?

    Enter Harry Percy

  Welcome, Harry. What, will not this castle yield?   20

PERCY

  The castle royally is manned, my lord,
  Against thy entrance.

BOLINGBROKE

  Royally?
  Why, it contains no king.

PERCY   Yes, my good lord,
  It doth contain a king. King Richard lies
  Within the limits of yon lime and stone,
  And with him are the Lord Aumerle, Lord Salisbury,
  Sir Stephen Scroop, besides a clergyman
  Of holy reverence; who, I cannot learn.

NORTHUMBERLAND

  O, belike it is the Bishop of Carlisle.   30

BOLINGBROKE

  Noble lord,
  Go to the rude ribs of that ancient castle,
  Through brazen trumpet send the breath of parley
  Into his ruined ears, and thus deliver:
  Henry Bolingbroke
  On both his knees doth kiss King Richard's hand,
  And sends allegiance and true faith of heart
  To his most royal person, hither come
  Even at his feet to lay my arms and power,

40 Provided that my banishment repealed
And lands restored again be freely granted.
If not, I'll use the advantage of my power
And lay the summer's dust with showers of blood
Rained from the wounds of slaughtered Englishmen;
The which how far off from the mind of Bolingbroke
It is such crimson tempest should bedrench
The fresh green lap of fair King Richard's land
My stooping duty tenderly shall show.
Go signify as much while here we march
50 Upon the grassy carpet of this plain.
Let's march without the noise of threatening drum,
That from this castle's tattered battlements
Our fair appointments may be well perused.
Methinks King Richard and myself should meet
With no less terror than the elements
Of fire and water when their thundering shock
At meeting tears the cloudy cheeks of heaven.
Be he the fire, I'll be the yielding water;
The rage be his, whilst on the earth I rain
60 My waters – on the earth, and not on him.
March on, and mark King Richard, how he looks.

*The trumpets sound parley without, and answer with-
in; then a flourish. King Richard appeareth on the
walls with the Bishop of Carlisle, Aumerle, Scroop,
and Salisbury*

BOLINGBROKE
See, see, King Richard doth himself appear,
As doth the blushing, discontented sun
From out the fiery portal of the east
When he perceives the envious clouds are bent
To dim his glory and to stain the track
Of his bright passage to the occident.

YORK

    Yet looks he like a king. Behold, his eye,
As bright as is the eagle's, lightens forth
Controlling majesty. Alack, alack for woe   70
That any harm should stain so fair a show!

KING RICHARD

    We are amazed; and thus long have we stood
To watch the fearful bending of thy knee
Because we thought ourself thy lawful king.
And if we be, how dare thy joints forget
To pay their awful duty to our presence?
If we be not, show us the hand of God
That hath dismissed us from our stewardship;
For well we know no hand of blood and bone
Can grip the sacred handle of our sceptre   80
Unless he do profane, steal, or usurp.
And though you think that all, as you have done,
Have torn their souls by turning them from us,
And we are barren and bereft of friends,
Yet know, my master, God omnipotent,
Is mustering in his clouds on our behalf
Armies of pestilence; and they shall strike
Your children yet unborn and unbegot,
That lift your vassal hands against my head
And threat the glory of my precious crown.   90
Tell Bolingbroke – for yon methinks he stands –
That every stride he makes upon my land
Is dangerous treason. He is come to open
The purple testament of bleeding war;
But ere the crown he looks for live in peace
Ten thousand bloody crowns of mothers' sons
Shall ill become the flower of England's face,
Change the complexion of her maid-pale peace

To scarlet indignation, and bedew
100   Her pastor's grass with faithful English blood.

NORTHUMBERLAND

The King of heaven forbid our lord the King
Should so with civil and uncivil arms
Be rushed upon. Thy thrice-noble cousin
Harry Bolingbroke doth humbly kiss thy hand;
And by the honourable tomb he swears
That stands upon your royal grandsire's bones,
And by the royalties of both your bloods,
Currents that spring from one most gracious head,
And by the buried hand of warlike Gaunt,
110   And by the worth and honour of himself,
Comprising all that may be sworn or said,
His coming hither hath no further scope
Than for his lineal royalties, and to beg
Enfranchisement immediate on his knees,
Which on thy royal party granted once
His glittering arms he will commend to rust,
His barbèd steeds to stables, and his heart
To faithful service of your majesty.
This swears he as he is a prince and just,
120   And as I am a gentleman I credit him.

KING RICHARD

Northumberland, say thus. The King returns
His noble cousin is right welcome hither,
And all the number of his fair demands
Shall be accomplished without contradiction.
With all the gracious utterance thou hast
Speak to his gentle hearing kind commends.

(*To Aumerle*)

We do debase ourselves, cousin, do we not,
To look so poorly and to speak so fair?
Shall we call back Northumberland and send

Defiance to the traitor, and so die?   130

AUMERLE

No, good my lord. Let's fight with gentle words
Till time lend friends, and friends their helpful swords.

KING RICHARD

O God, O God, that e'er this tongue of mine,
That laid the sentence of dread banishment
On yon proud man, should take it off again
With words of sooth! O that I were as great
As is my grief, or lesser than my name,
Or that I could forget what I have been,
Or not remember what I must be now!
Swellest thou, proud heart? I'll give thee scope to beat,   140
Since foes have scope to beat both thee and me.

AUMERLE

Northumberland comes back from Bolingbroke.

KING RICHARD

What must the King do now? Must he submit?
The King shall do it. Must he be deposed?
The King shall be contented. Must he lose
The name of king? A God's name, let it go.
I'll give my jewels for a set of beads,
My gorgeous palace for a hermitage,
My gay apparel for an almsman's gown,
My figured goblets for a dish of wood,   150
My sceptre for a palmer's walking-staff,
My subjects for a pair of carvèd saints,
And my large kingdom for a little grave,
A little, little grave, an obscure grave;
Or I'll be buried in the King's highway,
Some way of common trade where subjects' feet
May hourly trample on their sovereign's head,
For on my heart they tread now whilst I live,
And buried once, why not upon my head?

117

160   Aumerle, thou weepest, my tender-hearted cousin.
     We'll make foul weather with despisèd tears.
     Our sighs and they shall lodge the summer corn
     And make a dearth in this revolting land.
     Or shall we play the wantons with our woes,
     And make some pretty match with shedding tears,
     As thus to drop them still upon one place
     Till they have fretted us a pair of graves
     Within the earth, and therein laid there lies
     Two kinsmen digged their graves with weeping eyes.
170   Would not this ill do well? Well, well, I see
     I talk but idly, and you laugh at me.
     Most mighty prince, my Lord Northumberland,
     What says King Bolingbroke? Will his majesty
     Give Richard leave to live till Richard die?
     You make a leg, and Bolingbroke says 'Ay'.

NORTHUMBERLAND
     My lord, in the base-court he doth attend
     To speak with you, may it please you to come down.

KING RICHARD
     Down, down I come like glistering Phaethon,
     Wanting the manage of unruly jades.
180   In the base-court – base-court, where kings grow base
     To come at traitors' calls, and do them grace.
     In the base-court. Come down – down court, down
         King,
     For night-owls shriek where mounting larks should sing.
                          Exeunt from above

BOLINGBROKE
     What says his majesty?

NORTHUMBERLAND   Sorrow and grief of heart
     Makes him speak fondly, like a frantic man.
     Yet he is come.
        Enter King Richard attended, below

BOLINGBROKE

Stand all apart,
And show fair duty to his majesty.
He kneels down
My gracious lord!

KING RICHARD

Fair cousin, you debase your princely knee   190
To make the base earth proud with kissing it.
Me rather had my heart might feel your love
Than my unpleased eye see your courtesy.
Up, cousin, up. Your heart is up, I know,
Thus high at least, although your knee be low.

BOLINGBROKE

My gracious lord, I come but for mine own.

KING RICHARD

Your own is yours, and I am yours and all.

BOLINGBROKE

So far be mine, my most redoubted lord,
As my true service shall deserve your love.

KING RICHARD

Well you deserve. They well deserve to have   200
That know the strongest and surest way to get.
(To York)
Uncle, give me your hands. Nay, dry your eyes.
Tears show their love, but want their remedies.
(To Bolingbroke)
Cousin, I am too young to be your father
Though you are old enough to be my heir.
What you will have, I'll give, and willing too;
For do we must what force will have us do.
Set on towards London, cousin – is it so?

BOLINGBROKE

Yea, my good lord.

119

KING RICHARD   Then I must not say no.

Flourish. Exeunt

III.4   *Enter the Queen with two Ladies, her attendants*

QUEEN ISABEL

What sport shall we devise here in this garden
To drive away the heavy thought of care?

FIRST LADY

Madam, we'll play at bowls.

QUEEN ISABEL

'Twill make me think the world is full of rubs
And that my fortune runs against the bias.

SECOND LADY

Madam, we'll dance.

QUEEN ISABEL

My legs can keep no measure in delight
When my poor heart no measure keeps in grief.
Therefore no dancing, girl. Some other sport.

FIRST LADY

10   Madam, we'll tell tales.

QUEEN ISABEL

Of sorrow or of joy?

FIRST LADY   Of either, madam.

QUEEN ISABEL

Of neither, girl.
For if of joy, being altogether wanting,
It doth remember me the more of sorrow;
Or if of grief, being altogether had,
It adds more sorrow to my want of joy;
For what I have I need not to repeat,
And what I want it boots not to complain.

SECOND LADY

Madam, I'll sing.

ONE OF THE GARDENERS HAS BEEN SENT OFF TO KILL THE WEEDS AS THEY DAMAGE THE OTHER PLANTS

QUEEN ISABEL   'Tis well that thou hast cause;
  But thou shouldst please me better wouldst thou weep. 20
SECOND LADY
  I could weep, madam, would it do you good.
QUEEN ISABEL
  And I could sing would weeping do me good,
  And never borrow any tear of thee.
> *Enter Gardeners, one the master, the other two his men*

  But stay, here come the gardeners.
  Let's step into the shadow of these trees.
  My wretchedness unto a row of pins
  They will talk of state; for everyone doth so
  Against a change. Woe is forerun with woe.
> *The Queen and her Ladies stand apart*

GARDENER *(to one man)*
  Go, bind thou up young dangling apricocks   *GO AND SUPPORT THE TREE.*
  Which, like unruly children, make their sire   30
  Stoop with oppression of their prodigal weight.
  Give some supportance to the bending twigs.
  (To the other)
  Go thou, and like an executioner
  Cut off the heads of too fast-growing sprays
  That look too lofty in our commonwealth.
  All must be even in our government.
  You thus employed, I will go root away
  The noisome weeds which without profit suck
  The soil's fertility from wholesome flowers.
FIRST MAN
  Why should we, in the compass of a pale,   40
  Keep law and form and due proportion,
  Showing as in a model our firm estate,
  When our sea-wallèd garden, the whole land,
  Is full of weeds, her fairest flowers choked up,

    Her fruit trees all unpruned, her hedges ruined,
    Her knots disordered, and her wholesome herbs
    Swarming with caterpillars?

GARDENER   Hold thy peace.
    He that hath suffered this disordered spring
    Hath now himself met with the fall of leaf.
50   The weeds which his broad-spreading leaves did shelter,
    That seemed in eating him to hold him up,
    Are plucked up, root and all, by Bolingbroke –
    I mean the Earl of Wiltshire, Bushy, Green.

SECOND MAN
    What, are they dead?

GARDENER   They are; and Bolingbroke
    Hath seized the wasteful King. O, what pity is it
    That he had not so trimmed and dressed his land
    As we this garden! We at time of year
    Do wound the bark, the skin of our fruit trees,
    Lest being overproud in sap and blood
60   With too much riches it confound itself.
    Had he done so to great and growing men
    They might have lived to bear, and he to taste
    Their fruits of duty. Superfluous branches
    We lop away that bearing boughs may live.
    Had he done so, himself had borne the crown
    Which waste of idle hours hath quite thrown down.

FIRST MAN
    What, think you the King shall be deposed?

GARDENER
    Depressed he is already, and deposed
    'Tis doubt he will be. Letters came last night
70   To a dear friend of the good Duke of York's
    That tell black tidings.

QUEEN ISABEL
    O, I am pressed to death through want of speaking!

She comes forward

Thou, old Adam's likeness, set to dress this garden,
How dares thy harsh rude tongue sound this unpleasing
    news?
What Eve, what serpent hath suggested thee
To make a second Fall of cursèd man?
Why dost thou say King Richard is deposed?
Darest thou, thou little better thing than earth,
Divine his downfall? Say, where, when, and how
Camest thou by this ill tidings? Speak, thou wretch!   80

GARDENER
Pardon me, madam. Little joy have I
To breathe this news. Yet what I say is true.
King Richard he is in the mighty hold
Of Bolingbroke. Their fortunes both are weighed.
In your lord's scale is nothing but himself
And some few vanities that make him light.
But in the balance of great Bolingbroke
Besides himself are all the English peers,
And with that odds he weighs King Richard down.
Post you to London and you will find it so.   90
I speak no more than everyone doth know.

QUEEN ISABEL
Nimble mischance, that art so light of foot,
Doth not thy embassage belong to me,
And am I last that knows it? O, thou thinkest
To serve me last that I may longest keep
Thy sorrow in my breast. Come, ladies, go
To meet at London London's king in woe.
What was I born to this – that my sad look
Should grace the triumph of great Bolingbroke?
Gardener, for telling me these news of woe,   100
Pray God the plants thou graftest may never grow.
                    Exit Queen with her Ladies

GARDENER *shows sympathy not anger*

Poor Queen, so that thy state might be no worse
I would my skill were subject to thy curse.
Here did she fall a tear. Here in this place *He will plant this in memory of*
I'll set a bank of rue, sour herb of grace. *the Queens sorrow.*
Rue even for ruth here shortly shall be seen
In the remembrance of a weeping Queen.   *Exeunt*

* *missed out in film*

IV.1   *Enter Bolingbroke with the Lords Aumerle, Nor-*
              thumberland, Harry Percy, Fitzwater, Surrey, the
              Bishop of Carlisle, the Abbot of Westminster, another
              Lord, Herald, and officer, to Parliament

Aumerle is the Stunnet in the scene however what he is saying is to be contradicted

BOLINGBROKE
     Call forth Bagot.
          Enter Bagot with officers
     Now, Bagot, freely speak thy mind
     What thou dost know of noble Gloucester's death,
     Who wrought it with the King, and who performed
     The bloody office of his timeless end.

BAGOT
     Then set before my face the Lord Aumerle.

BOLINGBROKE
     Cousin, stand forth, and look upon that man.

BAGOT
     My Lord Aumerle, I know your daring tongue
     Scorns to unsay what once it hath delivered.
10   In that dead time when Gloucester's death was plotted
     I heard you say 'Is not my arm of length,   *implies*
     That reacheth from the restful English court   *Aumerle*
     As far as Calais to mine uncle's head?'   *may have plotted to K Gloucster*
     Amongst much other talk that very time

Baggot is the man he is sent Aumerle to getting rilling of

124

Aumerle denies everything
Puts up a defense

I heard you say that you had rather refuse
The offer of an hundred thousand crowns
Than Bolingbroke's return to England,   *A - is Anti*
Adding withal how blest this land would be   *B.*
In this your cousin's death.

AUMERLE   Princes and noble lords,
What answer shall I make to this base man?   20
Shall I so much dishonour my fair stars
On equal terms to give him chastisement?
Either I must, or have mine honour soiled
With the attainder of his slanderous lips.

      He throws down his gage

There is my gage, the manual seal of death,
That marks thee out for hell. I say thou liest,
And will maintain what thou hast said is false
In thy heart-blood, though being all too base
To stain the temper of my knightly sword.

BOLINGBROKE — *shows a difference between*
Bagot, forbear. Thou shalt not take it up.   *Richards*   30
                                                way of
AUMERLE   *thinking and*
Excepting one, I would he were the best   *handling things*
In all this presence that hath moved me so.   *Bol is more*

FITZWATER   *decisive*
If that thy valour stand on sympathy   *(quick thinking)*
There is my gage, Aumerle, in gage to thine.

      He throws down his gage

By that fair sun which shows me where thou standest
I heard thee say, and vauntingly thou spakest it,
That thou wert cause of noble Gloucester's death.
If thou deniest it twenty times, thou liest,
And I will turn thy falsehood to thy heart,
Where it was forgèd, with my rapier's point.   40

AUMERLE
Thou darest not, coward, live to see that day.

IV.1

FITZWATER
Now by my soul, I would it were this hour.

AUMERLE
Fitzwater, thou art damned to hell for this.

PERCY
Aumerle, thou liest. His honour is as true
In this appeal as thou art all unjust;
And that thou art so there I throw my gage
To prove it on thee to the extremest point
Of mortal breathing.
He throws down his gage
                    Seize it if thou darest.

AUMERLE
And if I do not may my hands rot off,
50 And never brandish more revengeful steel
Over the glittering helmet of my foe.

ANOTHER LORD
I task the earth to the like, forsworn Aumerle,
And spur thee on with full as many lies
As may be hollowed in thy treacherous ear
From sun to sun.
He throws down his gage
                    There is my honour's pawn.
Engage it to the trial if thou darest.

AUMERLE
Who sets me else? By heaven, I'll throw at all.
I have a thousand spirits in one breast
To answer twenty thousand such as you.

SURREY
60 My Lord Fitzwater, I do remember well
The very time Aumerle and you did talk.

FITZWATER
'Tis very true. You were in presence then,
And you can witness with me this is true.

126

SURREY
As false, by heaven, as heaven itself is true.

FITZWATER
Surrey, thou liest.

SURREY   Dishonourable boy,
That lie shall lie so heavy on my sword
That it shall render vengeance and revenge
Till thou, the lie-giver, and that lie do lie
In earth as quiet as thy father's skull.
In proof whereof, there is my honour's pawn.   70
        He throws down his gage
Engage it to the trial if thou darest.

FITZWATER
How fondly dost thou spur a forward horse!
If I dare eat, or drink, or breathe, or live,
I dare meet Surrey in a wilderness
And spit upon him whilst I say he lies,
And lies, and lies. There is my bond of faith
To tie thee to my strong correction.
As I intend to thrive in this new world   B - new
Aumerle is guilty of my true appeal.   word
Besides, I heard the banished Norfolk say   80
That thou, Aumerle, didst send two of thy men
To execute the noble Duke at Calais.

AUMERLE
Some honest Christian trust me with a gage.
        He throws down a gage
That Norfolk lies here do I throw down this,
If he may be repealed to try his honour.

BOLINGBROKE
These differences shall all rest under gage
Till Norfolk be repealed. Repealed he shall be,
And, though mine enemy, restored again
To all his lands and signories. When he is returned

90   Against Aumerle we will enforce his trial.

BISHOP OF CARLISLE

That honourable day shall never be seen.
Many a time hath banished Norfolk fought
For Jesu Christ in glorious Christian field,
Streaming the ensign of the Christian cross
Against black pagans, Turks, and Saracens,
And, toiled with works of war, retired himself
To Italy, and there at Venice gave
His body to that pleasant country's earth,
And his pure soul unto his captain, Christ,
100   Under whose colours he had fought so long.

BOLINGBROKE

Why, Bishop, is Norfolk dead?

BISHOP OF CARLISLE

As surely as I live, my lord.

BOLINGBROKE

Sweet peace conduct his sweet soul to the bosom
Of good old Abraham! Lords appellants,
Your differences shall all rest under gage
Till we assign you to your days of trial.
    Enter York

YORK

Great Duke of Lancaster, I come to thee
From plume-plucked Richard, who with willing soul
Adopts thee heir, and his high sceptre yields
110   To the possession of thy royal hand.
Ascend his throne, descending now from him,
And long live Henry, fourth of that name!

BOLINGBROKE

In God's name I'll ascend the regal throne.

BISHOP OF CARLISLE

Marry, God forbid!
Worst in this royal presence may I speak,

128

Yet best beseeming me to speak the truth:
Would God that any in this noble presence
Were enough noble to be upright judge
Of noble Richard. Then true noblesse would
Learn him forbearance from so foul a wrong.   120
What subject can give sentence on his king? –
And who sits here that is not Richard's subject?
Thieves are not judged but they are by to hear
Although apparent guilt be seen in them;
And shall the figure of God's majesty,
His captain, steward, deputy elect,
Anointed, crownèd, planted many years,
Be judged by subject and inferior breath
And he himself not present? O, forfend it God
That in a Christian climate souls refined   130
Should show so heinous, black, obscene a deed!
I speak to subjects, and a subject speaks,
Stirred up by God thus boldly for his king.
My Lord of Hereford here, whom you call king,
Is a foul traitor to proud Hereford's King;
And if you crown him, let me prophesy
The blood of English shall manure the ground,
And future ages groan for this foul act.
Peace shall go sleep with Turks and infidels,
And in this seat of peace tumultuous wars   140
Shall kin with kin, and kind with kind, confound.
Disorder, horror, fear, and mutiny
Shall here inhabit, and this land be called
The field of Golgotha and dead men's skulls.
O, if you raise this house against this house
It will the woefullest division prove
That ever fell upon this cursèd earth.
Prevent it; resist it; let it not be so,
Lest child, child's children, cry against you woe.

NORTHUMBERLAND

150   Well have you argued, sir; and for your pains
    Of capital treason we arrest you here.
    My Lord of Westminster, be it your charge
    To keep him safely till his day of trial.
    May it please you, lords, to grant the commons' suit?

BOLINGBROKE

    Fetch hither Richard, that in common view
    He may surrender. So we shall proceed
    Without suspicion.

YORK   I will be his conduct.   *Exit*

BOLINGBROKE

    Lords, you that here are under our arrest,
    Procure your sureties for your days of answer.
160   Little are we beholding to your love,
    And little looked for at your helping hands.
        Enter Richard and York

RICHARD

    Alack, why am I sent for to a king
    Before I have shook off the regal thoughts
    Wherewith I reigned? I hardly yet have learned
    To insinuate, flatter, bow, and bend my knee.
    Give sorrow leave awhile to tutor me
    To this submission. Yet I well remember
    The favours of these men. Were they not mine?
    Did they not sometime cry 'All hail!' to me?
170   So Judas did to Christ. But He in twelve
    Found truth in all but one; I, in twelve thousand, none.
    God save the King! Will no man say Amen?
    Am I both priest and clerk? Well then, Amen.
    God save the King, although I be not he;
    And yet Amen if Heaven do think him me.
    To do what service am I sent for hither?

YORK

To do that office of thine own good will
Which tired majesty did make thee offer:
The resignation of thy state and crown
To Henry Bolingbroke.

RICHARD   Give me the crown.   180

Here, cousin – seize the crown. Here, cousin –
On this side, my hand; and on that side, thine.
Now is this golden crown like a deep well
That owes two buckets, filling one another,
The emptier ever dancing in the air,
The other down, unseen, and full of water.
That bucket down and full of tears am I,
Drinking my griefs whilst you mount up on high.

BOLINGBROKE

I thought you had been willing to resign.

RICHARD

My crown I am; but still my griefs are mine.   190
You may my glories and my state depose,
But not my griefs. Still am I king of those.

BOLINGBROKE

Part of your cares you give me with your crown.

RICHARD

Your cares set up do not pluck my cares down.
My care is loss of care by old care done;
Your care is gain of care by new care won.
The cares I give, I have, though given away.
They 'tend the crown, yet still with me they stay.

BOLINGBROKE

Are you contented to resign the crown?

RICHARD

Ay, no. No, ay; for I must nothing be.   200
Therefore no no, for I resign to thee.

Now mark me how I will undo myself.
I give this heavy weight from off my head,
And this unwieldy sceptre from my hand,
The pride of kingly sway from out my heart.
With mine own tears I wash away my balm,
With mine own hands I give away my crown,
With mine own tongue deny my sacred state,
With mine own breath release all duteous oaths.
210 All pomp and majesty I do forswear.
My manors, rents, revenues I forgo.
My acts, decrees, and statutes I deny.
God pardon all oaths that are broke to me;
God keep all vows unbroke are made to thee;
Make me, that nothing have, with nothing grieved,
And thou with all pleased, that hast all achieved.
Long mayst thou live in Richard's seat to sit,
And soon lie Richard in an earthy pit.
'God save King Henry,' unkinged Richard says,
220 'And send him many years of sunshine days.'
What more remains?

NORTHUMBERLAND No more but that you read
These accusations and these grievous crimes
Committed by your person and your followers
Against the state and profit of this land,
That by confessing them the souls of men
May deem that you are worthily deposed.

RICHARD
Must I do so? And must I ravel out
My weaved-up follies? Gentle Northumberland,
If thy offences were upon record,
230 Would it not shame thee in so fair a troop
To read a lecture of them? If thou wouldst,
There shouldst thou find one heinous article,
Containing the deposing of a king

132

And cracking the strong warrant of an oath,
Marked with a blot, damned in the book of heaven.
Nay, all of you that stand and look upon me,
Whilst that my wretchedness doth bait myself,
Though some of you – with Pilate – wash your hands,
Showing an outward pity, yet you Pilates
Have here delivered me to my sour cross,   240
And water cannot wash away your sin.

NORTHUMBERLAND
My lord, dispatch. Read o'er these articles.

RICHARD
Mine eyes are full of tears. I cannot see.
And yet salt water blinds them not so much
But they can see a sort of traitors here.
Nay, if I turn mine eyes upon myself
I find myself a traitor with the rest.
For I have given here my soul's consent
To'undeck the pompous body of a king;
Made glory base, and sovereignty a slave;   250
Proud majesty, a subject; state, a peasant.

NORTHUMBERLAND
My lord –

RICHARD
No lord of thine, thou haught, insulting man;
Nor no man's lord. I have no name, no title –
No, not that name was given me at the font –
But 'tis usurped. Alack the heavy day,
That I have worn so many winters out
And know not now what name to call myself!
O that I were a mockery king of snow,
Standing before the sun of Bolingbroke,   260
To melt myself away in water-drops!
Good king; great king – and yet not greatly good –
An if my word be sterling yet in England

Let it command a mirror hither straight
That it may show me what a face I have
Since it is bankrupt of his majesty.

BOLINGBROKE

Go some of you, and fetch a looking-glass.

Exit attendant

NORTHUMBERLAND

Read o'er this paper while the glass doth come.

RICHARD

Fiend, thou torments me ere I come to hell.

BOLINGBROKE

270 Urge it no more, my Lord Northumberland.

NORTHUMBERLAND

The commons will not then be satisfied.

RICHARD

They shall be satisfied. I'll read enough
When I do see the very book indeed
Where all my sins are writ; and that's myself.

Enter attendant with a glass

Give me that glass, and therein will I read.
No deeper wrinkles yet? Hath sorrow struck
So many blows upon this face of mine
And made no deeper wounds? O, flattering glass,
Like to my followers in prosperity,

280 Thou dost beguile me. Was this face the face
That every day under his household roof
Did keep ten thousand men? Was this the face
That like the sun did make beholders wink?
Is this the face which faced so many follies,
That was at last outfaced by Bolingbroke?
A brittle glory shineth in this face.
As brittle as the glory is the face,

(*he throws the glass down*)

For there it is, cracked in an hundred shivers.

Mark, silent King, the moral of this sport:
How soon my sorrow hath destroyed my face. 290
BOLINGBROKE
The shadow of your sorrow hath destroyed
The shadow of your face.
RICHARD   Say that again!
'The shadow of my sorrow' – ha, let's see.
'Tis very true. My grief lies all within,
And these external manner of laments
Are merely shadows to the unseen grief
That swells with silence in the tortured soul.
There lies the substance; and I thank thee, King,
For thy great bounty, that not only givest
Me cause to wail, but teachest me the way 300
How to lament the cause. I'll beg one boon,
And then be gone and trouble you no more.
Shall I obtain it?
BOLINGBROKE   Name it, fair cousin.
RICHARD
'Fair cousin'? I am greater than a king;
For when I was a king my flatterers
Were then but subjects; being now a subject
I have a king here to my flatterer.
Being so great, I have no need to beg.
BOLINGBROKE
Yet ask.
RICHARD
And shall I have? 310
BOLINGBROKE
You shall.
RICHARD
Then give me leave to go.
BOLINGBROKE
Whither?

Richard is now a pauper

IV.1

RICHARD
  Whither you will, so I were from your sights.

BOLINGBROKE
  Go some of you, convey him to the Tower.

RICHARD
  O, good, 'convey!' – Conveyors are you all,
  That rise thus nimbly by a true king's fall.

BOLINGBROKE
  On Wednesday next we solemnly proclaim
  Our coronation. Lords, be ready, all.

                    Exeunt all except the Abbot of Westminster,
                              the Bishop of Carlisle, Aumerle

ABBOT OF WESTMINSTER *ON RICHARDS SIDE.*
320 A woeful pageant have we here beheld.

BISHOP OF CARLISLE
  The woe's to come. The children yet unborn
  Shall feel this day as sharp to them as thorn.

AUMERLE
  You holy clergymen, is there no plot
  To rid the realm of this pernicious blot?

ABBOT OF WESTMINSTER
  My lord,
  Before I freely speak my mind herein
  You shall not only take the Sacrament
  To bury mine intents, but also to effect
  Whatever I shall happen to devise.
330 I see your brows are full of discontent,
  Your hearts of sorrow, and your eyes of tears.
  Come home with me to supper, I will lay
  A plot shall show us all a merry day.   *Exeunt*

*

QUEEN ISABEL

This way the King will come. This is the way
To Julius Caesar's ill-erected Tower,
To whose flint bosom my condemnèd lord
Is doomed a prisoner by proud Bolingbroke.
Here let us rest, if this rebellious earth
Have any resting for her true King's Queen.
   Enter Richard and guard
But soft, but see, or rather do not see,
My fair rose wither. Yet look up, behold,
That you in pity may dissolve to dew
And wash him fresh again with true-love tears.   10
Ah, thou the model where old Troy did stand!
Thou map of honour, thou King Richard's tomb,
And not King Richard! Thou most beauteous inn,
Why should hard-favoured grief be lodged in thee
When triumph is become an alehouse guest?

RICHARD

Join not with grief, fair woman, do not so,
To make my end too sudden. Learn, good soul,
To think our former state a happy dream,
From which awaked the truth of what we are
Shows us but this. I am sworn brother, sweet,   20
To grim Necessity, and he and I
Will keep a league till death. Hie thee to France,
And cloister thee in some religious house.
Our holy lives must win a new world's crown
Which our profane hours here have thrown down.

QUEEN ISABEL

What, is my Richard both in shape and mind
Transformed and weakened? Hath Bolingbroke
Deposed thine intellect? Hath he been in thy heart?
The lion dying thrusteth forth his paw

30 And wounds the earth, if nothing else, with rage
To be o'erpowered. And wilt thou pupil-like
Take the correction, mildly kiss the rod,
And fawn on rage with base humility,
Which art a lion and the king of beasts?

RICHARD

A king of beasts indeed! If aught but beasts
I had been still a happy king of men.
Good sometimes queen, prepare thee hence for France.
Think I am dead, and that even here thou takest
As from my deathbed thy last living leave.
40 In winter's tedious nights sit by the fire
With good old folks, and let them tell thee tales
Of woeful ages long ago betid;
And ere thou bid goodnight, to quite their griefs
Tell thou the lamentable tale of me,
And send the hearers weeping to their beds;
For why the senseless brands will sympathize
The heavy accent of thy moving tongue,
And in compassion weep the fire out;
And some will mourn in ashes, some coal-black,
50 For the deposing of a rightful king.

Enter Northumberland

NORTHUMBERLAND

My lord, the mind of Bolingbroke is changed.
You must to Pomfret, not unto the Tower.
And, madam, there is order ta'en for you:
With all swift speed you must away to France.

RICHARD

Northumberland, thou ladder wherewithal
The mounting Bolingbroke ascends my throne,
The time shall not be many hours of age
More than it is ere foul sin, gathering head,
Shall break into corruption. Thou shalt think,

Northumberland helped bolingbrook become king.

RICH TELLS NORTH THAT BOLING WILL
DO IT TO HIM.

Though he divide the realm and give thee half,   60
It is too little, helping him to all.
He shall think that thou, which knowest the way
To plant unrightful kings, wilt know again,
Being ne'er so little urged another way,
To pluck him headlong from the usurped throne.
The love of wicked men converts to fear,
That fear to hate, and hate turns one or both
To worthy danger and deservèd death.

NORTHUMBERLAND
My guilt be on my head, and there an end.
Take leave and part, for you must part forthwith.   70

RICHARD
Doubly divorced! Bad men, you violate
A two-fold marriage – 'twixt my crown and me,
And then betwixt me and my married wife.
(*To Queen Isabel*)
Let me unkiss the oath 'twixt thee and me;
And yet not so; for with a kiss 'twas made.
– Part us, Northumberland: I towards the north,
Where shivering cold and sickness pines the clime;
My wife to France, from whence set forth in pomp
She came adornèd hither like sweet May,
Sent back like Hallowmas or shortest of day.   80

QUEEN ISABEL → HAS TO GO BACK TO FRANCE.
And must we be divided? Must we part?

RICHARD
Ay, hand from hand, my love, and heart from heart.

QUEEN ISABEL (*to Northumberland*)
Banish us both, and send the King with me.

RICHARD
That were some love, but little policy.

QUEEN ISABEL
Then whither he goes, thither let me go.

139 ISOLATION = MEANS
THAT PEOPLE CAN'T
SEE HIM.

ISABel wants him to fight back and not just give up.

RICHARD

   So two together weeping make one woe.
   Weep thou for me in France, I for thee here.
   Better far off than, near, be ne'er the nea'er.
   Go count thy way with sighs, I mine with groans.

QUEEN ISABEL

90   So longest way shall have the longest moans.

RICHARD

   Twice for one step I'll groan, the way being short,
   And piece the way out with a heavy heart.
   Come, come – in wooing sorrow let's be brief,
   Since wedding it, there is such length in grief.
   One kiss shall stop our mouths, and dumbly part.
   Thus give I mine, and thus take I thy heart.
      They kiss

QUEEN ISABEL

   Give me mine own again. 'Twere no good part
   To take on me to keep and kill thy heart.
      They kiss
   So, now I have mine own again, be gone,
100   That I may strive to kill it with a groan.

RICHARD

   We make woe wanton with this fond delay.
   Once more, adieu. The rest let sorrow say.   *Exeunt*

V.2   *Enter Duke of York and the Duchess*

DUCHESS OF YORK

   My lord, you told me you would tell the rest,
   When weeping made you break the story off,
   Of our two cousins' coming into London.

YORK

   Where did I leave?

DUCHESS OF YORK At that sad stop, my lord,

Where rude misgoverned hands from windows' tops
Threw dust and rubbish on King Richard's head.

YORK

Then, as I said, the Duke, great Bolingbroke,
Mounted upon a hot and fiery steed
Which his aspiring rider seemed to know,
With slow but stately pace kept on his course,   10
Whilst all tongues cried 'God save thee, Bolingbroke!'
You would have thought the very windows spake,
So many greedy looks of young and old
Through casements darted their desiring eyes
Upon his visage, and that all the walls
With painted imagery had said at once
'Jesu preserve thee, welcome Bolingbroke',
Whilst he, from the one side to the other turning,
Bare-headed, lower than his proud steed's neck
Bespake them thus: 'I thank you, countrymen.'   20
And thus still doing, thus he passed along.

DUCHESS OF YORK

Alack, poor Richard! Where rode he the whilst?

YORK

As in a theatre the eyes of men,
After a well graced actor leaves the stage,
Are idly bent on him that enters next,
Thinking his prattle to be tedious:
Even so, or with much more contempt, men's eyes
Did scowl on gentle Richard. No man cried 'God save
          him!'
No joyful tongue gave him his welcome home;
But dust was thrown upon his sacred head,   30
Which with such gentle sorrow he shook off,
His face still combating with tears and smiles,
The badges of his grief and patience,
That had not God for some strong purpose steeled

The hearts of men, they must perforce have melted,
And barbarism itself have pitied him.
But heaven hath a hand in these events,
To whose high will we bound our calm contents.
To Bolingbroke are we sworn subjects now,
40 Whose state and honour I for aye allow.

Enter Aumerle

THEY
ARE
WITH
BOLLINGBROOK
NON.

DUCHESS OF YORK
Here comes my son Aumerle.

YORK   Aumerle that was;
But that is lost for being Richard's friend;
And, madam, you must call him Rutland now.
I am in Parliament pledge for his truth
And lasting fealty to the new-made King.

DUCHESS OF YORK
Welcome, my son! Who are the violets now
That strew the green lap of the new-come spring?

AUMERLE
Madam, I know not, nor I greatly care not.
God knows I had as lief be none as one.

YORK
50 Well, bear you well in this new spring of time,
Lest you be cropped before you come to prime.
What news from Oxford? Do these justs and triumphs
      hold?

AUMERLE
For aught I know, my lord, they do.

YORK
You will be there, I know.

AUMERLE
If God prevent not, I purpose so.

YORK
What seal is that that hangs without thy bosom?
Yea, lookest thou pale? Let me see the writing.

AUMERLE HAS LOST HIS TITLE
AS HE SUPPORTED RICHARD

AUMERLE

My lord, 'tis nothing.

YORK   No matter, then, who see it.

I will be satisfied. Let me see the writing.

AUMERLE

I do beseech your grace to pardon me.   60

It is a matter of small consequence

Which for some reasons I would not have seen.

YORK

Which for some reasons, sir, I mean to see.

I fear – I fear!

DUCHESS OF YORK

What should you fear?

'Tis nothing but some bond that he is entered into

For gay apparel 'gainst the triumph day.

YORK

Bound to himself? What doth he with a bond

That he is bound to? Wife, thou art a fool.

Boy, let me see the writing.

AUMERLE

I do beseech you, pardon me. I may not show it.   70

YORK

I will be satisfied. Let me see it, I say.

He plucks it out of his bosom, and reads it

YORK

Treason! Foul treason! Villain! Traitor! Slave!

DUCHESS OF YORK

What is the matter, my lord?

YORK

Ho, who is within there? Saddle my horse.

God for his mercy! What treachery is here!

DUCHESS OF YORK

Why, what is it, my lord?

Aumerd is in a plot to kill Bollingbrook.
York has given a pledge to stick with his son.

V.2

YORK

Give me my boots, I say. Saddle my horse.
Now, by mine honour, by my life, by my troth,
I will appeach the villain.

DUCHESS OF YORK

80   What is the matter?

YORK   Peace, foolish woman.

DUCHESS OF YORK

I will not peace. What is the matter, Aumerle?

AUMERLE

Good mother, be content. It is no more
Than my poor life must answer.

DUCHESS OF YORK   Thy life answer?

YORK

Bring me my boots. I will unto the King.

    His man enters with his boots

DUCHESS OF YORK

Strike him, Aumerle! Poor boy, thou art amazed.
(*To York's man*)
Hence, villain! Never more come in my sight!

YORK

Give me my boots, I say!

    York's man gives him the boots and goes out

DUCHESS OF YORK

Why, York, what wilt thou do?
Wilt thou not hide the trespass of thine own?
90   Have we more sons? Or are we like to have?
Is not my teeming-date drunk up with time?
And wilt thou pluck my fair son from mine age?
And rob me of a happy mother's name?
Is he not like thee? Is he not thine own?

YORK

Thou fond, mad woman,
Wilt thou conceal this dark conspiracy?

144

A dozen of them here have ta'en the Sacrament
And interchangeably set down their hands
To kill the King at Oxford.

DUCHESS OF YORK   He shall be none.
We'll keep him here. Then what is that to him?   100

YORK
Away, fond woman. Were he twenty times my son
I would appeach him.

DUCHESS OF YORK
Hadst thou groaned for him as I have done
Thou wouldst be more pitiful.
But now I know thy mind. Thou dost suspect
That I have been disloyal to thy bed,
And that he is a bastard, not thy son.
Sweet York, sweet husband, be not of that mind.
He is as like thee as a man may be;
Not like to me, or any of my kin,   110
And yet I love him.

YORK   Make way, unruly woman.   *Exit*

DUCHESS OF YORK
After, Aumerle. Mount thee upon his horse.
Spur, post, and get before him to the King,
And beg thy pardon ere he do accuse thee.
I'll not be long behind – though I be old,
I doubt not but to ride as fast as York;
And never will I rise up from the ground
Till Bolingbroke have pardoned thee. Away, be gone!

        Exeunt

    Enter Bolingbroke, now King Henry, with Harry V.3
    Percy and other lords

KING HENRY
Can no man tell me of my unthrifty son?

'Tis full three months since I did see him last.
If any plague hang over us, 'tis he.
I would to God, my lords, he might be found.
Inquire at London 'mongst the taverns there;
For there, they say, he daily doth frequent
With unrestrainèd loose companions,
Even such, they say, as stand in narrow lanes
And beat our watch, and rob our passengers,
10 Which he – young wanton, and effeminate boy –
Takes on the point of honour to support
So dissolute a crew.

PERCY
My lord, some two days since I saw the Prince,
And told him of those triumphs held at Oxford.

KING HENRY
And what said the gallant?

PERCY
His answer was he would unto the stews,
And from the commonest creature pluck a glove,
And wear it as a favour; and with that
He would unhorse the lustiest challenger.

KING HENRY
20 As dissolute as desperate. Yet through both
I see some sparks of better hope, which elder years
May happily bring forth. But who comes here?
Enter Aumerle, amazed

AUMERLE
Where is the King?

KING HENRY
What means our cousin, that he stares and looks so
wildly?

AUMERLE
God save your grace. I do beseech your majesty
To have some conference with your grace alone.

146

KING HENRY

Withdraw yourselves, and leave us here alone.

Exeunt Harry Percy and the other lords

What is the matter with our cousin now?

AUMERLE

For ever may my knees grow to the earth,
My tongue cleave to my roof within my mouth, 30
Unless a pardon ere I rise or speak.

KING HENRY

Intended or committed was this fault?
If on the first, how heinous e'er it be
To win thy after-love I pardon thee.

AUMERLE

Then give me leave that I may turn the key
That no man enter till my tale be done.

KING HENRY

Have thy desire.

*Aumerle locks the door. The Duke of York knocks at
the door and crieth*

YORK (*within*)

My liege, beware, look to thyself,
Thou hast a traitor in thy presence there.

KING HENRY (*to Aumerle*)

Villain, I'll make thee safe! 40

AUMERLE

Stay thy revengeful hand, thou hast no cause to fear.

YORK

Open the door, secure foolhardy King.
Shall I for love speak treason to thy face?
Open the door, or I will break it open.

King Henry opens the door. Enter York

KING HENRY

What is the matter, uncle? Speak, recover breath,
Tell us how near is danger,

That we may arm us to encounter it.

YORK

Peruse this writing here, and thou shalt know
The treason that my haste forbids me show.

AUMERLE

50   Remember, as thou readest, thy promise passed.
I do repent me. Read not my name there.
My heart is not confederate with my hand.

YORK

It was, villain, ere thy hand did set it down.
I tore it from the traitor's bosom, King.
Fear, and not love, begets his penitence.
Forget to pity him lest thy pity prove
A serpent that will sting thee to the heart.

KING HENRY

O, heinous, strong, and bold conspiracy!
O loyal father of a treacherous son,
60   Thou sheer immaculate and silver fountain
From whence this stream through muddy passages
Hath held his current and defiled himself –
Thy overflow of good converts to bad,
And thy abundant goodness shall excuse
This deadly blot in thy digressing son.

YORK

So shall my virtue be his vice's bawd
An he shall spend mine honour with his shame,
As thriftless sons their scraping fathers' gold.
Mine honour lives when his dishonour dies,
70   Or my shamed life in his dishonour lies.
Thou killest me in his life – giving him breath,
The traitor lives, the true man's put to death.

DUCHESS OF YORK (within)

What ho, my liege, for God's sake let me in!

KING HENRY

What shrill-voiced suppliant makes this eager cry?

DUCHESS OF YORK

A woman, and thy aunt, great King. 'Tis I.
Speak with me, pity me, open the door!
A beggar begs that never begged before.

KING HENRY

Our scene is altered from a serious thing,
And now changed to 'The Beggar and the King'.
My dangerous cousin, let your mother in.   80
I know she is come to pray for your foul sin.

    Aumerle admits the Duchess. She kneels

YORK

If thou do pardon, whosoever pray,
More sins for this forgiveness prosper may.
This festered joint cut off, the rest rest sound;
This let alone will all the rest confound.

DUCHESS OF YORK

O King, believe not this hard-hearted man.
Love loving not itself, none other can.

YORK

Thou frantic woman, what dost thou make here?
Shall thy old dugs once more a traitor rear?

DUCHESS OF YORK

Sweet York, be patient. Hear me, gentle liege.   90

KING HENRY

Rise up, good aunt!

DUCHESS OF YORK   Not yet, I thee beseech.
For ever will I walk upon my knees,
And never see day that the happy sees
Till thou give joy, until thou bid me joy
By pardoning Rutland, my transgressing boy.

AUMERLE

Unto my mother's prayers I bend my knee.

149

He kneels

YORK

Against them both my true joints bended be.

He kneels

Ill mayst thou thrive if thou grant any grace.

DUCHESS OF YORK

Pleads he in earnest? Look upon his face.

100   His eyes do drop no tears, his prayers are in jest;

His words come from his mouth, ours from our breast.

He prays but faintly, and would be denied;

We pray with heart and soul, and all beside.

His weary joints would gladly rise, I know;

Our knees still kneel till to the ground they grow.

His prayers are full of false hypocrisy,

Ours of true zeal and deep integrity.

Our prayers do outpray his: then let them have

That mercy which true prayer ought to have.

KING HENRY

110   Good aunt, stand up!

DUCHESS OF YORK   Nay, do not say 'Stand up!'

Say 'Pardon' first, and afterwards, 'Stand up!'

An if I were thy nurse thy tongue to teach,

'Pardon' should be the first word of thy speech.

I never longed to hear a word till now.

Say 'Pardon', King. Let pity teach thee how.

The word is short, but not so short as sweet.

No word like 'Pardon' for kings' mouths so meet.

YORK

Speak it in French, King: say 'Pardonne-moi.'

DUCHESS OF YORK

Dost thou teach pardon pardon to destroy?

120   Ah, my sour husband, my hard-hearted lord!

That sets the word itself against the word.

Speak 'Pardon' as 'tis current in our land;

The chopping French we do not understand.
Thine eye begins to speak. Set thy tongue there;
Or in thy piteous heart plant thou thine ear,
That hearing how our plaints and prayers do pierce,
Pity may move thee pardon to rehearse.

KING HENRY
Good aunt, stand up.

DUCHESS OF YORK   I do not sue to stand.
Pardon is all the suit I have in hand.

KING HENRY
I pardon him as God shall pardon me.   *as he was a trator to Richard.* 130

DUCHESS OF YORK
O, happy vantage of a kneeling knee!
Yet am I sick for fear. Speak it again.
Twice saying pardon doth not pardon twain,
But makes one pardon strong.

KING HENRY   With all my heart
I pardon him.

DUCHESS OF YORK
                    A god on earth thou art!
    York, Duchess of York, and Aumerle stand

KING HENRY
But for our trusty brother-in-law and the Abbot,
With all the rest of that consorted crew,
Destruction straight shall dog them at the heels.
Good uncle, help to order several powers
To Oxford, or where'er these traitors are.   140
They shall not live within this world, I swear,
But I will have them if I once know where.
Uncle, farewell; and cousin, adieu.
Your mother well hath prayed; and prove you true.

DUCHESS OF YORK
Come, my old son. I pray God make thee new.   *Exeunt*

Enter Sir Piers of Exton and a Man

EXTON

>Didst thou not mark the King, what words he spake?
>'Have I no friend will rid me of this living fear?'
>Was it not so?

MAN   These were his very words.

EXTON

>'Have I no friend?' quoth he. He spake it twice,
>And urged it twice together, did he not?

MAN

>He did.

EXTON

>And speaking it, he wishtly looked on me,
>As who should say 'I would thou wert the man
>That would divorce this terror from my heart' –
10   >Meaning the King at Pomfret. Come, let's go.
>I am the King's friend, and will rid his foe.   *Exeunt*

V.5   *Enter Richard alone*

RICHARD

>I have been studying how I may compare
>This prison where I live unto the world;
>And for because the world is populous,
>And here is not a creature but myself,
>I cannot do it. Yet I'll hammer it out.
>My brain I'll prove the female to my soul,
>My soul the father, and these two beget
>A generation of still-breeding thoughts,
>And these same thoughts people this little world,
10   >In humours like the people of this world.
>For no thought is contented; the better sort,
>As thoughts of things divine, are intermixed
>With scruples, and do set the word itself

Against the word; as thus: 'Come, little ones';
And then again,
'It is as hard to come as for a camel
To thread the postern of a small needle's eye.'
Thoughts tending to ambition, they do plot
Unlikely wonders – how these vain weak nails
May tear a passage through the flinty ribs
Of this hard world, my ragged prison walls,
And for they cannot, die in their own pride.
Thoughts tending to content flatter themselves
That they are not the first of Fortune's slaves,
Nor shall not be the last; like seely beggars,
Who, sitting in the stocks, refuge their shame
That many have, and others must sit there.
And in this thought they find a kind of ease,
Bearing their own misfortunes on the back
Of such as have before endured the like.
Thus play I in one person many people,
And none contented. Sometimes am I king.
Then treasons make me wish myself a beggar;
And so I am. Then crushing penury
Persuades me I was better when a king.
Then am I kinged again; and by and by
Think that I am unkinged by Bolingbroke,
And straight am nothing. But whate'er I be,
Nor I, nor any man that but man is,
With nothing shall be pleased till he be eased
With being nothing. (*The music plays*) Music do I hear.
Ha, ha; keep time! How sour sweet music is
When time is broke, and no proportion kept.
So is it in the music of men's lives;
And here have I the daintiness of ear
To check time broke in a disordered string,
But for the concord of my state and time,

Had not an ear to hear my true time broke.
I wasted time, and now doth time waste me;
50 For now hath time made me his numbering clock.
My thoughts are minutes, and with sighs they jar
Their watches on unto mine eyes, the outward watch
Whereto my finger, like a dial's point,
Is pointing still in cleansing them from tears.
Now, sir, the sound that tells what hour it is
Are clamorous groans which strike upon my heart,
Which is the bell. So sighs, and tears, and groans
Show minutes, times, and hours. But my time
Runs posting on in Bolingbroke's proud joy,
60 While I stand fooling here, his jack of the clock.
This music mads me. Let it sound no more;
For though it have holp madmen to their wits,
In me it seems it will make wise men mad.
Yet blessing on his heart that gives it me;
For 'tis a sign of love, and love to Richard
Is a strange brooch in this all-hating world.

Enter a Groom of the stable

GROOM
Hail, royal prince!
RICHARD   Thanks, noble peer.
The cheapest of us is ten groats too dear.
What art thou, and how comest thou hither
70 Where no man never comes but that sad dog
That brings me food to make misfortune live?
GROOM
I was a poor groom of thy stable, King,
When thou wert king; who travelling towards York
With much ado at length have gotten leave
To look upon my sometimes royal master's face.
O, how it earned my heart when I beheld
In London streets, that coronation day,

When Bolingbroke rode on roan Barbary,
That horse that thou so often hast bestrid,
That horse that I so carefully have dressed!   80

RICHARD
Rode he on Barbary? Tell me, gentle friend,
How went he under him?

GROOM
So proudly as if he disdained the ground.

RICHARD
So proud that Bolingbroke was on his back!
That jade hath eat bread from my royal hand;
This hand hath made him proud with clapping him.
Would he not stumble, would he not fall down –
Since pride must have a fall – and break the neck
Of that proud man that did usurp his back?
Forgiveness, horse! Why do I rail on thee,   90
Since thou, created to be awed by man,
Wast born to bear? I was not made a horse,
And yet I bear a burden like an ass,
Spurred, galled, and tired by jauncing Bolingbroke.

    Enter Keeper to Richard with meat

KEEPER (*to Groom*)
Fellow, give place. Here is no longer stay.

RICHARD (*to Groom*)
If thou love me, 'tis time thou wert away.

GROOM
What my tongue dares not, that my heart shall say.

                                            Exit

KEEPER
My lord, will't please you to fall to?

RICHARD
Taste of it first, as thou art wont to do.

KEEPER
My lord, I dare not. Sir Piers of Exton,   100

155

Who lately came from the King, commands the contrary.

RICHARD (*attacks the Keeper*)

The devil take Henry of Lancaster, and thee.
Patience is stale, and I am weary of it.

KEEPER

Help, help, help!

The murderers, Exton and servants, rush in

RICHARD

How now! What means death in this rude assault?
Villain, thy own hand yields thy death's instrument.

He snatches a weapon from a servant and kills him

Go thou, and fill another room in hell.

He kills another servant. Here Exton strikes him down

RICHARD

That hand shall burn in never-quenching fire
That staggers thus my person. Exton, thy fierce hand
110   Hath with the King's blood stained the King's own land.
Mount, mount, my soul. Thy seat is up on high,
Whilst my gross flesh sinks downward here to die.

He dies

EXTON

As full of valour as of royal blood.
Both have I spilled. O, would the deed were good!
For now the devil, that told me I did well,
Says that this deed is chronicled in hell.
This dead King to the living King I'll bear.
Take hence the rest, and give them burial here.

Exeunt with the bodies

KING HENRY

Kind uncle York, the latest news we hear
Is that the rebels have consumed with fire
Our town of Ciceter in Gloucestershire.
But whether they be ta'en or slain we hear not.
    Enter Northumberland
Welcome, my lord. What is the news?

NORTHUMBERLAND

First, to thy sacred state wish I all happiness.
The next news is, I have to London sent
The heads of Salisbury, Spencer, Blunt, and Kent.
The manner of their taking may appear
At large discoursèd in this paper here.   10

KING HENRY

We thank thee, gentle Percy, for thy pains;
And to thy worth will add right worthy gains.
    Enter Lord Fitzwater

FITZWATER

My lord, I have from Oxford sent to London
The heads of Brocas and Sir Bennet Seely,
Two of the dangerous consorted traitors
That sought at Oxford thy dire overthrow.

KING HENRY

Thy pains, Fitzwater, shall not be forgot.
Right noble is thy merit, well I wot.
    Enter Harry Percy with the Bishop of Carlisle,
    guarded

PERCY

The grand conspirator Abbot of Westminster
With clog of conscience and sour melancholy   20
Hath yielded up his body to the grave;
But here is Carlisle living, to abide

157

Thy kingly doom and sentence of his pride.

KING HENRY

Carlisle, this is your doom:
Choose out some secret place, some reverent room
More than thou hast, and with it joy thy life.
So as thou livest in peace, die free from strife;
For though mine enemy thou hast ever been,
High sparks of honour in thee have I seen.

Enter Exton with the coffin

EXTON

30 Great King, within this coffin I present
Thy buried fear. Herein all breathless lies
The mightiest of thy greatest enemies,
Richard of Bordeaux, by me hither brought.

KING HENRY

Exton, I thank thee not; for thou hast wrought
A deed of slander with thy fatal hand
Upon my head and all this famous land.

EXTON

From your own mouth, my lord, did I this deed.

KING HENRY

They love not poison that do poison need;
Nor do I thee. Though I did wish him dead,
40 I hate the murderer, love him murderèd.
The guilt of conscience take thou for thy labour,
But neither my good word nor princely favour.
With Cain go wander thorough shades of night,
And never show thy head by day nor light.

Exit Exton

Lords, I protest, my soul is full of woe
That blood should sprinkle me to make me grow.
Come mourn with me for what I do lament,
And put on sullen black incontinent.
I'll make a voyage to the Holy Land

To wash this blood off from my guilty hand.   5
March sadly after. Grace my mournings here
In weeping after this untimely bier.   *Exeunt*

COMMENTARY

'Q' here refers to the first Quarto, 1597. Later quartos (see 'An Account of the Text', pages 269–83) are referred to as Q2, Q3, etc. 'F' refers to the text of the play in the first Folio, of 1623.

Biblical quotations are from the Bishops' Bible, the version likely to have been best known to Shakespeare. Quotations from Holinshed's *Chronicles* have been modernized from the second edition, of 1587; those from *Woodstock* are from Rossiter's edition.

Title
The title-page of Q calls the play *The Tragedy of King Richard the Second*. In F the play is *The Life and Death of King Richard the Second*.

I.1   The matter of this scene is adapted and compressed from Holinshed, according to whom the first accusations between Mowbray and Bolingbroke were made at Shrewsbury in spring 1398, followed six weeks later by the formal 'appeal' at Windsor.
Staging
A formal grouping is required, with the King centrally seated.
(stage direction) *King Richard*. He was known as Richard of Bordeaux, was born in 1367, succeeded to the throne in 1377, and died in 1400. The play covers the last two years of his reign. He had an army of 'livery men' who wore the white hart as his badge.
John of Gaunt. The fourth (third surviving) son of Edward III; he lived from 1340 to 1399, and was Duke of Lancaster. *Gaunt* is Ghent, his birthplace.

Lord Marshal. Mowbray himself was the Earl Marshal at the time, but Holinshed says that the Duke of Surrey acted as his deputy on this occasion. Surrey appears later in the play (IV.1), but there is no reason to think that Shakespeare cared about the identity of the Lord Marshal; he is important simply for his function.

1 *Old ... time-honoured.* In 1398 John of Gaunt was fifty-eight. Here and elsewhere Shakespeare contrasts the comparative age of Richard's uncles with the King's own *youth* (II.1.69).

2 *band* (an alternative form of 'bond')

3 *Hereford.* In the play the name usually has two syllables. In the early editions it is frequently spelt 'Herford'.

4 *boisterous* (two syllables; Q has 'boistrous', a common Elizabethan spelling) rough and violent
   late recent
   appeal accusation (of treason)

5 *our ... us.* Richard uses the royal plural, in keeping with the formality of the occasion.
   leisure (that is, lack of leisure)

8 *sounded* inquired of

9 *appeal* accuse
   on ancient malice because of long-standing personal enmity

12 This is an alexandrine. Most lines in the play are pentameters, but short and long lines are not uncommon. Editors have often attempted to regularize them, either by rearrangement or addition of extra words, but some of them can be justified dramatically (a short line may add emphasis). Others may represent an attempt to avoid monotony, or be the result of negligence.
   As near as I could sift him so far as I could discover by examining him
   argument subject

13 *apparent* obvious

15   (stage direction) *Exit Attendant.* This is not marked in
Q; but it seems the most satisfactory way of managing
the stage business.

      presence. Face to face. Q reads 'presence face to face'.
It is possible (though not likely) that the passage
should be interpreted 'Then call them to our presence
face to face, and – [they] frowning brow to brow – ourselves . . .'.

16   *ourselves* we (royal plural) ourself

18–19 These lines are sometimes spoken aside.

18   *High-stomached* proud, haughty

19   *deaf.* That is, to remonstrance; compare *King John*,
II.1.451: 'The sea enragèd is not half so deaf.'

      (stage direction) *Bolingbroke.* Henry Plantagenet,
Gaunt's son by his first wife; he lived from 1367 to
1413. *Bolingbroke* (often pronounced 'Bullingbrooke')
was a nickname, from his birthplace, in Lincolnshire.

      Mowbray. Thomas Mowbray was born about 1366,
and died in 1399 at Venice (IV.1.97–100). It seems
likely that in 1397 he was responsible for the murder of
Richard's uncle, Gloucester, by Richard's command.
Mowbray in *2 Henry IV* is his eldest son.

22   *Each day still better other's happiness* may each day be
happier than the previous one

23–4   *Until ... your crown.* In *Woodstock* (I.1.37–8) it is
said of the Black Prince that 'heaven forestalled his
diadem on earth | To place him with a royal crown in
heaven.' Compare V.1.24–5.

23   *envying.* The accent is probably on the second syllable:
'heav'ns, envỳing'.

      hap fortune

26   *cause you come* cause about which you come

30   *heaven be the record to my speech!* This might be
regarded as a parenthesis.

      record witness

32   *Tendering* watching over, being careful of

34   *appellant* in accusation

36   *greeting* address

38   *divine* immortal

40   *Too good* too high in rank

41–6   Here, as often, the verse moves into rhymed couplets. This has often been objected to, and in the theatre the play's rhyming passages have sometimes been omitted or rewritten. There is of course no justification for this. In general, couplets signalize a higher degree of formality in the action, or a stronger emphasis on what is being said than on what is happening. Coleridge said of this passage: 'the rhymes ... well express the preconcertedness of Bolingbroke's scheme, so beautifully contrasted with the vehemence and sincere irritation of Mowbray'.

41   *crystal* clear (as crystal), bright

43   *note* reproach, mark of disgrace (from the Latin *nota*, a mark of censure)

46   *right-drawn* drawn in a just cause

47   *Let not my cold words here accuse my zeal* do not let my calm language cast doubt upon my ardour (or 'loyalty')

49   *eager* sharp

51   *cooled* (by death)

54   *reverence of* respect for

56   *post* hasten (continuing the riding metaphor of *curbs, reins and spurs*, and, perhaps, *free*)

57   *These terms of treason* (*traitor* and *miscreant* (line 39))

58–9   *his high blood's royalty, | And let him be no kinsman to my liege.* Bolingbroke was Richard's first cousin.

59   *let him be* assuming that he were

63   *tied* bound, obliged

65   *inhabitable* not habitable, uninhabitable. Similar expressions occur elsewhere, as in *Macbeth*, III.4.103: 'And dare me to the desert with thy sword.' A fight to the death is implied.

67   *this* (perhaps his sword; more probably, the affirmation in the following line)

69   (stage direction) *gage* pledge. It was usually a glove or
gauntlet, but according to Holinshed hoods were used
on the occasion when Fitzwater accused Aumerle of
causing Gloucester's death (IV.1). However, the
phrase *manual seal* (IV.1.25) in Shakespeare's version
suggests that he thought of the gage as a glove.

72   *except* set aside (compare line 58)

74   *honour's pawn*. The gage or pledge of line 69; the
phrase recurs at IV.1.55 and 70.

77   *What I have spoke or thou canst worse devise* the accusations that I have made, or any more heinous ones that
you can think of

78   *I take it up* (and thus accept the challenge)

79   *gently* (perhaps 'conferring nobility' rather than 'with
a light touch' or 'in friendly fashion')

80   *answer thee* give you satisfaction

80–81   *in any fair degree | Or chivalrous design of knightly trial*
to any fair measure or any form of combat allowed by
the laws of chivalry

82   *light* dismount, alight

85–6   *inherit us ... of* put us in possession of

87   *Look what* whatever (a usage common in Shakespeare)

88   *nobles*. A noble was a gold coin, worth twenty groats,
or 6s. 8d. in the currency of the time.

89   *lendings* (money paid to Mowbray for distribution to
the soldiers, perhaps as advances when circumstances
would not permit them to be given regular payments.
Holinshed has 'Thomas Mowbray Duke of Norfolk
hath received eight thousand nobles to pay the
soldiers that keep your town of Calais.')

90   *lewd employments* improper use

93   *Or ... or* either ... or

95   *eighteen years*. The phrase is from Holinshed. Its
significance (which Shakespeare did not necessarily
recognize) is that the commons, under Wat Tyler and
others, had risen in 1381.

96   *Complotted* plotted in combination with others

96   *contrivèd* (could mean 'plotted' or 'devised' as well as 'brought about')

97   *Fetch* derive. The metaphor is of drawing water from the *head* of a fountain, or a *spring*.

98-9 *maintain | Upon his bad life to make all this good.* Bolingbroke seems to mean that he undertakes to prove all this by taking Mowbray's *bad life*.

100   *he did plot the Duke of Gloucester's death.* Thomas of Woodstock, Duke of Gloucester, died at Calais in 1397 while in the custody of Mowbray, then captain of Calais. He was probably murdered by Mowbray or his agents at Richard's instigation. This view was commonly held in Shakespeare's time. Holinshed says 'The King sent unto Thomas Mowbray ... to make the Duke secretly away', and reports that Mowbray 'caused his servants to cast featherbeds upon him, and so smother him to death, or otherwise to strangle him with towels (as some write).' Shakespeare leaves the matter open in this first scene but in the next one Gloucester's widow and his brother assert Richard's guilt. The Duke of York, too, implies belief in it (II.2.100–102). In IV.1 Bolingbroke, taking it for granted that Richard was the instigator, inquires 'who performed | The bloody office', and Bagot seems to suggest that Aumerle, not Mowbray, was responsible. This episode, too, is based on Holinshed. The question is left unsettled. In portraying the varying views Shakespeare may have been concerned to suggest the uncertainties in our interpretation of the past; and the reopening of the question later in the play, with Aumerle's vehement denials, helps Richard's cause with the audience just before he makes big demands on their sympathy, in the deposition scene.

101   *Suggest his soon-believing adversaries* (incite Gloucester's enemies, who were predisposed to believe Mowbray. The enemies included Richard.)

102   *consequently* subsequently

104   *sacrificing Abel's.* The allusion is to the biblical story of Abel, who sacrificed 'the firstlings of his sheep' (Genesis 4.4), and to his murder by his brother, Cain. His blood cried from the ground (Genesis 4.10), and, unlike Christ's, called for retribution (Hebrews 12.24). It is echoed, ironically, in Bolingbroke's words to Piers of Exton (V.6.43–4), when he has murdered Richard at Bolingbroke's instigation.

105   *tongueless* dumb (though resonant)

106   *To me* (as his nephew – as Richard also is)

109   *pitch* (highest point of a falcon's flight before it swoops on its prey)

113   *slander of his blood* (disgrace to the blood royal, shared by both Richard and Bolingbroke)

115   *eyes and ears* (replying to *face* and *ears* in Mowbray's speech)

118   *my sceptre's awe* the reverence due to my sceptre

119   *sacred* (a hint of the theme of the divine nature of kingship, emphasized elsewhere)

120   *partialize* make partial, bias

122   *He is our subject, Mowbray. So . . .* We might equally read 'He is our subject. Mowbray, so . . .'.

124–5   *as low as to thy heart | Through the false passage of thy throat thou liest !* This is a heightening of the common expression 'to lie in the throat', used menacingly.

126   *receipt* (sum received when Mowbray was captain of Calais)

        Calais. The early editions use the spelling 'Callice', which represents the Elizabethan pronunciation.

128   *by consent.* Holinshed does not record that Richard agreed that Mowbray should retain any of the money.

129   *For that* because

130   *remainder of a dear account* the balance of a heavy debt. *Dear* has a wide range of meaning, including 'important', 'of great value', and 'serious'. Heavy expenses were incurred in Mowbray's expedition to France to negotiate Richard's marriage.

131   *to fetch his queen.* In fact, Richard himself escorted his
        bride from France to England.

132   *For* as for

133–4 *to my own disgrace | Neglected my sworn duty in that
        case.* What his *sworn duty* was is obscure. He may
        mean that he should have killed Gloucester, but this is
        tantamount to an accusation against Richard. Alter-
        natively his *sworn duty* may have been to guard
        Gloucester. Holinshed reports that he 'prolonged time
        for the executing of the King's commandment,
        though the King would have had it done with all
        expedition, whereby the King conceived no small dis-
        pleasure and sware that it should cost the Earl his life
        if he quickly obeyed not his commandment', and the
        point is repeated later. So probably Mowbray is here
        claiming to have saved Gloucester's life for a time, and
        perhaps taking refuge in the fact that he did not
        personally kill him.

137   *Once did I lay an ambush for your life.* In Holinshed,
        too, Mowbray admits having 'laid an ambush to have
        slain the Duke of Lancaster', and claims that he was
        forgiven. No details are known.

140   *exactly* 'expressly' or 'completely'

142   *appealed* alleged

144   *recreant* (could be an adjective – 'cowardly' – as well
        as a noun)

145   *Which in myself I boldly will defend* the truth of which
        statement I personally shall boldly defend

146   *interchangeably* reciprocally, in turn
        hurl (present, not future, tense; Mowbray throws
        down his gage. Bolingbroke must pick it up at some
        unspecified point, since at line 161 his father tells him
        to throw it down.)

148–9 *prove . . . in* (probably in the sense 'demonstrate . . . by
        shedding')

149   *chambered* enclosed

150   *In haste whereof* to hasten which

153   *purge this choler without letting blood* drain away anger
(*choler*, or bile) without the letting of blood (playing
on the idea of bloodshed)

154   *though no physician.* The notion of a king as his country's physician was common.

156   *conclude* come to terms

157   *doctors* learned men, astrologers
this is no month to bleed. Some seasons were supposed
to be more favourable than others to the medical
practice of blood-letting.

164   *We bid* (that is, 'since I, the King, bid')
boot alternative, help for it

167   *The one my duty owes* my duty as a subject compels me
to put my life at your disposal

167–8   *name, | Despite of death that lives upon my grave* name
that will live on my tomb despite death. The awkward
inversion of the natural word order is presumably a
result of the use of rhyme.

170   *impeached* accused
baffled treated ignominiously, publicly disgraced. To
'baffle' a knight found guilty of cowardice is explained in Hall's Chronicle: 'he was content that the
Scots should baffle him, which is a great reproach
among the Scots, and is used when a man is openly
perjured, and then they make of him an image painted
reversed, with his heels upward, with his name ...'.
Sometimes the knight seems actually to have been
hung up by his heels. Mowbray is not using the word
in its fullest literal sense.

172–3   *his heart-blood | Which* the heart-blood of him who

173   *breathed this poison* uttered this venomous slander

174   *his.* Bolingbroke's; King Richard repeats his demand.
Lions make leopards tame. The analogy between the
king and the lion (the king of beasts) is common. The
lion was part of the royal coat-of-arms, and the crest
of the Norfolks, worn by Mowbray, was a golden
leopard.

175 *Yea, but not change his spots.* The modern proverb 'The leopard cannot change his spots' goes back to the Bible ('May a man of Ind change his skin, and the cat of the mountain her spots?', Jeremiah 13.23) and was probably proverbial by the time Shakespeare was writing. *Spots* has also the sense of 'stains (of shame)'. The line thus connects with line 166.

   Take but my shame simply remove the disgrace

177 *mortal times* human life

182 *in one* inseparably

184 *try* put to the test

186 *throw up your gage.* Richard tells Bolingbroke to relinquish Mowbray's gage, which he is holding. *Throw up* may indicate that Richard is situated at a higher level than the disputants, perhaps on a throne, possibly (on the Elizabethan stage) on the upper stage. F, however, reads 'throw downe', which may represent a method of staging different from that first imagined by Shakespeare.

188 *crest-fallen* humbled

189 *beggar-fear* fear appropriate to a beggar
   impeach my height disgrace my rank

190 *outdared* (both 'excelled in' and 'overcome by' daring)
   dastard coward

191 *such feeble wrong* the wrong of speaking so feebly

192 *sound so base a parle.* The metaphor is, appropriately, from the sounding of trumpets in combat to ask for a truce.

192–5 *my teeth shall tear ... even in Mowbray's face.* The image seems strained and far-fetched. But behind it lies a story of a philosopher who bit off his tongue and spat it in a tyrant's face. This story was reasonably well known; also, neo-Senecan plays popular when *Richard II* was written sometimes required even the staging of such horrific incidents. In Thomas Kyd's *The Spanish Tragedy* (written about 1587), for instance, the chief character, Hieronimo, 'bites out his tongue', provoking the comment 'See, Viceroy, he hath bitten forth his tongue | Rather than to reveal what we required' (IV.4.193-4). And in Shakespeare's own *Titus Andronicus* the idea recurs when Titus, addressing his daughter, Lavinia, whose tongue has been horribly cut out, asks 'Or shall we bite our tongues, and in dumb shows | Pass the remainder of our hateful days?' (III.1.131-2).

193   *motive* instrument, organ (here, the tongue)

194   *in his high disgrace* (in disgrace of the tongue itself. Shakespeare regularly uses 'his' for modern 'its'.)

195   (stage direction) The direction is in F, but not in Q. There is no good reason why Gaunt should leave except that he is to re-enter at the beginning of the following scene. The Folio direction probably represents Elizabethan stage practice, and perhaps Shakespeare here fails to think in fully theatrical terms.

199   *Saint Lambert's Day* (17 September). Shakespeare takes the date from Holinshed, who however said: 'Here writers disagree about the day that was appointed; for some say it was upon a Monday in August; other upon Saint Lambert's day, being the seventeenth of September, other on the eleventh of September.'

202   *atone* reconcile

203   *design the victor's chivalry* indicate the winner in a combat of chivalry. The theory behind trial by combat is that the justice of God will reveal itself by causing the right man to win.

205   *home alarms* troubles at home (distinct from the Irish rebellion referred to later (I.4.38))

I.2   On this scene, see Introduction, page 18. It marks the difference in time between the first and third scenes, set in April and September.

        (stage direction) *Duchess of Gloucester*. She was born

in either 1359 or 1366, and died in 1399; but Shakespeare probably thought of her as an older woman.

1 *the part I had in Woodstock's blood* my blood-relation-
ship to Thomas of Woodstock, Duke of Gloucester
(Gaunt's brother)
Woodstock's. F has 'Gousters', which would be easier
for an audience unaware that they were the same
person.

4-5 *correction lieth in those hands | Which made the fault that
we cannot correct* the power to punish the murder is in
the hands of the man (Richard) who committed the
crime that we cannot undo

6 *Put we our quarrel* let us commit our cause

7 *Who, when they* which, when it. It is not uncommon in Shakespeare for 'heaven' to take a plural
agreement.

11 *Edward* (Edward III)

12-13 *seven vials ... seven fair branches.* Shakespeare preserves throughout the speech the double metaphor
compounded of the medieval genealogical symbol of
the Tree of Jesse, and the figure of the vials of blood.
A typical Elizabethan genealogical table would represent a tree, the founder of a family being at the foot or
root (and not, as in modern custom, at the head).
Thus the sons are *branches springing from one root.*
Altick, in the article referred to on page 48, comments:
'The imposition of the figure involving the word
blood (in its literal and therefore most vivid use) upon
another figure which for centuries embodied the
concept of family descent, thus welds together with
extraordinary tightness the word and its symbolic
significance.'

15 *Some of those branches by the destinies cut.* The line
recalls the epilogue of Marlowe's *Doctor Faustus,*
written only a few years before *Richard II*: 'Cut is
the branch that might have grown full straight.' *The
destinies* are the Fates – Clotho, Lachesis, and Atropos.

21   *envy*. The word was stronger than it is now, and could mean 'malice' or 'hatred'.

23   *mettle* stuff, substance
             self same

28   *model* copy, image

29   *despair* (a sinful as well as pitiable state of mind)

30   *suffering* permitting

31   *naked pathway to thy life* 'undefended way by which your murderers can reach your life'; or perhaps 'that the way to your life is undefended . . .'

33   *mean* ordinary, common, not noble

36   *venge* (an old form of 'avenge')

37–8   *God's substitute,* | *His deputy* (a common way of thinking of the king)

46   *cousin*. The word was often used to mean no more than 'relative'. Hereford was the Duchess's nephew.
             fell fierce, cruel (since she thinks of him as the agent in her husband's murder)

47   *sit*. Q reads 'set'; F 'sit'; but 'set' was a common spelling of 'sit'.

49   *if misfortune miss the first career* if misfortune does not overcome (Mowbray) at the first encounter. To *career* a horse was to run it at full speed and then stop suddenly. In the following lines Mowbray is imagined overbalancing at the stop and being 'thrown'.

53   *caitiff recreant* wretched coward

54   *sometimes* sometime ('wife of him who was your brother' or 'she who was your brother's wife')

58–9   *Grief boundeth where it falls,* | *Not with the empty hollowness, but weight*. The Duchess is apologizing for adding *one word more*. The image is of a bouncing (bounding) tennis ball; but her grief bounces with the force of its weight, not because of its hollow lightness.

66   *Pleshey* (Gloucester's country house, near Dunmow in Essex)

68   *lodgings* rooms
             unfurnished walls (possibly 'walls unhung with

tapestry' which was taken down when the rooms
were out of use; or the phrase may just mean that the
rooms are unfurnished)

69   *offices* servants' rooms

I.3   The events represented in this scene took place at
Coventry in September 1398. Holinshed describes an
occasion of great splendour. The dukes came 'in
great array, accompanied with the lords and gentlemen
of their lineages. The King caused a sumptuous
scaffold or theatre, and royal lists there to be erected
and prepared.' Aumerle and the Marshal (Surrey)
'entered into the lists with a great company of men
apparelled in silk sendal embroidered with silver, both
richly and curiously, every man having a tipped staff
to keep the field in order'. Bolingbroke entered to
them, before the King arrived, accompanied by all the
peers of the realm and 'above ten thousand men in
armour, lest some fray or tumult might rise amongst
his nobles'. Shakespeare makes Richard enter to his
seat, which according to Holinshed was 'richly hanged
and adorned', before the contestants, and then Mowbray before Bolingbroke who, as appellant, should have
entered the lists first. In Holinshed the Dukes arrived
on elaborately costumed horses, dismounted, and sat
on their ceremonial chairs, Bolingbroke's of green
velvet, Mowbray's of crimson 'curtained about with
white and red damask'. After they had received their
lances (lines 100–103) the chairs were removed, and
the combatants were instructed to remount. At the
sound of the trumpet they moved towards each other.
Shakespeare simplifies the setting, though he mentions
the chairs (line 120). It can hardly be supposed that
horses were used, though they have sometimes figured,
more or less prominently, in nineteenth- and twentieth-
century performances. In *2 Henry IV* (IV.1.115–29)

Mowbray's son describes the events of this scene, attributing Richard's downfall to his intervention in the combat.

(stage direction) *Duke of Aumerle*. Edward of York; he lived from about 1373 to 1415, and was York's eldest son. *Aumerle* is Albemarle, a town in France. In fact he became the Duke of York whose noble death at Agincourt is recounted in Shakespeare's *Henry V* (IV.6); but Shakespeare may not have realized this when writing *Richard II*. He is present here in his function as High Constable. See also Commentary to V.2.43.

2   *at all points* completely (that is, he is wearing all the different pieces of his suit of armour)

3   *sprightfully* spiritedly

5   *stay* wait

6   (stage direction) *Bushy*. Sir John Bushy held a number of important offices, and was Speaker of the House of Commons for several years. He was Richard's chief agent in the House, and is said always to have advanced before the King with obeisances, to Richard's pleasure. He was beheaded in 1399.

Bagot. Sir William Bagot, like Bushy, held various offices of state. He escaped to Ireland after Bolingbroke landed, and later was arrested and released. He died in 1407.

Green. Sir Henry Green, a Member of Parliament and follower of King Richard, executed with Bushy at Bristol.

When they are set. . . . . A separate flourish of trumpets should sound for Mowbray's entrance.

set. The King and his nobles seat themselves in state.

9   *orderly* according to the rules

10   *swear him in the justice of his cause*. A knight entering the lists was required to swear that his cause was just. One of them was thus likely to commit perjury, and so deserve defeat.

11   *say who thou art.* This was not a pure formality, as the knight's visor would be down.

13   *quarrel* cause of complaint

18   *defend* forbid

20   *my succeeding issue.* F reads 'his . . .'. Perhaps Mowbray would have been more likely to swear by the King's descendants than his own; but the latter is not impossible and has the generally superior authority of Q to support it.

28   *plated in habiliments* wearing plate-armour

30   *Depose him* swear him, take his sworn statement

42–5   *On pain of death, no person be so bold | Or daring-hardy as to touch the lists | Except the Marshal and such officers | Appointed to direct these fair designs.* According to Holinshed a king-at-arms (that is, a chief herald) 'made open proclamation, prohibiting all men in the name of the King, and of the High Constable and Marshal, to enterprise or attempt to approach or touch any part of the lists upon pain of death, except such as were appointed to order or marshal the field'.

51   *several* 'various' or 'respective'

55   *as* in so far as

58   *Lament we may, but not revenge thee dead.* Bolingbroke's defeat would indicate his guilt, so Richard would not be justified in seeking revenge.

59–60   *profane a tear | For me* misuse a tear in weeping for me

66   *lusty* strong, vigorous

       cheerly in good cheer

67   *as at English feasts.* This is an allusion to the English habit of ending banquets with elaborate sweet confections. The phrase seems to have been current; Bacon wrote: 'Let not this Parliament end, like a Dutch feast, in salt meats; but like an English feast, in sweet meats.'

       regreet greet, salute

70   *regenerate* reborn

73   *proof* power of resistance

75   *waxen coat* (coat of mail as if it were made of wax)

77   *haviour* (an old form of 'behaviour')

81   *amazing* stupefying (the sense was much stronger than now)

       casque helmet

84   *to thrive* I rely on for success

88   *freer* more willing

90   *uncontrolled enfranchisement* liberation from control

93   Mowbray moves into couplets as he approaches the ritual of the combat.

95   *to jest* to go to a sport or entertainment

96   *Truth hath a quiet breast* (related to the proverb 'Truth fears no trial')

97   *Securely* confidently (*couchèd*)

100   *Harry of Hereford ... Duke of Norfolk.* 'The Lord
-103   Marshal viewed their spears to see that they were of equal length, and delivered the one spear himself to the Duke of Hereford, and sent the other unto the Duke of Norfolk by a knight' (Holinshed).

102   *Strong as a tower in hope* (a biblical phrase: 'for thou hast been my hope, and a strong tower for me against the enemy', Psalm 61.3)

117,   (stage directions) 'The Duke of Norfolk was not fully
122   set forward when the King cast down his warder and the heralds cried "Ho Ho!" Then the King caused their spears to be taken from them, and commanded them to repair again to their chairs, where they remained two long hours while the King and his council deliberately consulted what order was best to be had in so weighty a cause' (Holinshed). It is not easy to say precisely what stage action Shakespeare imagined here. Probably Richard descends from his raised throne as he throws down his warder, or just after doing so. *Withdraw with us* would be addressed to his councillors, and they would consult in a cluster while the trumpets sounded their *long flourish*. Richard could then return to his throne to deliver his decision.

117 (stage direction) *warder* (a truncheon or staff to give the signal for the beginning or ending of hostilities)

122 *While we return* until we tell

125 *For that* so that

129–33 These lines were omitted from F, and though the passage does not make very good sense without them it is not surprising that clarification was sought. The problem is that *peace* (line 132), having been aroused, goes on to *fright fair peace* (line 137). There may be some textual fault, but it is just as likely that Shakespeare lost control of his metaphors.

131 *set on you* set you on

142 *regreet* greet again (not merely 'greet', as in line 67)

143 *stranger* foreign (this is not a comparative, but the noun used adjectivally)

145 *That sun that warms you here shall shine on me.* The biblical 'he maketh his sun to rise on the evil and on the good' had acquired proverbial force.

148 *heavier doom* severer punishment

150 *determinate* bring to an end

151 *dateless limit* limitless period
dear dire, grievous

156 *A dearer merit* a better reward

159 *these forty years.* In fact Mowbray was thirty-three in 1398; but 'forty' was sometimes used as a round figure, with no implication of exactness.

162 *Than an unstringèd viol or a harp. Unstringèd* refers to *harp* as well as *viol.* The viol is a stringed instrument played with a bow.

163 *cunning* 'skilfully made' or 'requiring skill to play'

167 *portcullised* fortified (a portcullis is a metal grating in a door)

170 *a nurse.* A nurse might have the responsibility of teaching her charges to speak.

172 *speechless.* The word is subtly chosen. In death, speech is impossible; so Mowbray's exile will be death to him.

174   *boots* serves

      to be compassionate (either 'to be sorry for yourself' or 'to appeal for pity')

175   *plaining* complaining

181   *Our part therein* (that part of the duty you owe to God that belongs to me, as God's deputy)

188   *advisèd* deliberated

193   *so far as to mine enemy*. This is the first time in the scene that either combatant has spoken to the other. These words seem intended as Bolingbroke's preface to what he is about to say, intimating that though he now deigns to address Mowbray, he continues to hold him in enmity. Some editors read 'fare' instead of *far* (Q spells 'fare'), interpreting 'Bolingbroke bids Norfolk make his way ("fare") through the world in a fashion appropriate to an enemy.'

196   *sepulchre* (accented on the second syllable)

202   *My name be blotted from the book of life*. This is a clear echo of Revelation 3.5: 'He that overcometh shall be thus clothed in white array, and I will not blot out his name out of the book of life.' It is appropriate to the solemnity of Mowbray's utterance.

205   *rue* (transitive: 'the King shall rue what thou art')

206–7   *no way can I stray;* | *Save back to England, all the world's my way* I cannot go astray now, since I can go anywhere in the world except England

208   *glasses of thine eyes* your eyes as mirrors (mirroring his feelings)

209   *aspect* (accented on the second syllable)

214   *wanton* luxuriant

220   *bring their times about* accomplish the cycles of their seasons

222   *extinct with* extinguished by

223   *My inch of taper will be burnt and done*. Shakespeare uses the same image elsewhere. The best-known example is *Macbeth*, V.5.23: 'Out, out, brief candle!' Here it links with *oil-dried lamp* (line 221).

224   *blindfold death.* Death is blindfold because there are
no eyes in its traditional emblem, the skull, and also
perhaps by analogy with Atropos, the blindfold
destiny who cuts the threads of life (Milton's 'blind
fury with the abhorrèd shears', *Lycidas*, line 75). The
image is capable of other interpretations, and indeed
may have had multiple associations for Shakespeare.
Death's being blindfolded causes its impartiality.
Dover Wilson ingeniously suggests that the image is of
death wearing a hood which resembles in shape the
extinguisher of a candle or *taper*. And it has also been
suggested that death simply *is* the blindfold that will
prevent Gaunt from seeing his son.

227   *sullen* gloomy, melancholy

230   *his pilgrimage* its journey

231   *current* valid

234   *party-verdict* one person's share of a joint verdict

236   *Things sweet to taste prove in digestion sour.* This is a
proverbial expression deriving from Revelation 10.10,
where it is said of a book that it 'was in my mouth as
sweet as honey; and as soon as I had eaten it, my belly
was bitter'.

240   *To smooth* in glossing over

241   *partial slander* the accusation of partiality

243   *looked when* expected that

249   *What presence must not know* what we shall not be
able to communicate in person. It may be that
Aumerle should depart after this leave-taking,
especially as he enters at the beginning of the next
scene. It is also a little odd that he should take such
formal leave of Bolingbroke, since he accompanies him
to the next highway (I.4.4).

251–2 The Marshal's friendly attitude to Bolingbroke here
is one of the signs that Shakespeare was not concerned
to identify him with the Duke of Surrey, one of
Richard's supporters.

257   *To breathe* in breathing

257 *dolour*. There is a pun on 'dollar', in conjunction with
hoard (line 253) and *prodigal*.

258–9 *grief ... grief* (both 'grievance' and 'cause of sor-
rows')

262 *travel*. 'Travel' and 'travail' were interchangeable in
spelling and closely related in meaning. M. M.
Mahood comments: 'When Gaunt bids him call his
exile "a *trauaile* that thou takst for pleasure" and a
"*foyle* wherein thou art to set, The pretious Iewell of
thy home returne", Bolingbroke takes up *travel* in its
harsher sense of "travail" and *foil* in the meaning
"frustration, obstacle" to fashion the bitter wordplay
of his reply' (*Shakespeare's Wordplay*, page 78).

265 *sullen* melancholy (and 'dull in colour')

269 *remember* remind
deal of world distance

271–4 *Must I not serve a long apprenticehood | To foreign
passages, and in the end, | Having my freedom, boast of
nothing else | But that I was a journeyman to grief?*
Bolingbroke expects to serve a long apprenticeship in
his foreign travels and experiences (*passages*), and
when he gains his freedom, as an apprentice does, in
the rank of *journeyman* (qualified artisan, with a hint
of 'one who goes a journey'), and also his freedom
from exile, he will still be subject to grief. The tense
of the last sentence causes difficulty because the apprentice would normally become a journeyman on
completion of his apprenticeship. It is as if *having my
freedom* meant simultaneously 'having gained this
amount of experience' and 'when, no longer in exile,
I look back upon this period . . .'. The sense would be
easy if we could interpret *was* as 'have become'.

275–8 *All places that the eye of heaven visits | Are to a wise
man ports and happy havens. | Teach thy necessity to
reason thus: | There is no virtue like necessity.* A source
for this passage has been seen in Lyly's *Euphues*
(1578), in which Lyly is translating Plutarch's *De*

Exilio: 'Plato would never account him banished that had the sun, fire, air, water, and earth that he had before, where he felt the winter's blast and the summer's blaze, where the same sun and the same moon shined, whereby he noted that every place was a country to a wise man, and all parts a palace to a quiet mind.' 'A wise man makes every country his own' was proverbial; so was the phrase 'to make a virtue of necessity'.

279–80 *Think not the King did banish thee, | But thou the King.* Again Shakespeare seems to recall Lyly's *Euphues*: 'When it was cast in Diogenes' teeth that the Synoponetes had banished him Pontus, "Yea," said he, "I them of Diogenes." '

281 *faintly* faintheartedly

284 *pestilence* plague

286 *Look what* whatever

289 *presence strewed* (the King's presence chamber, strewed with rushes)

291 *measure* stately dance

292 *gnarling* snarling

294–9 *O, who can hold ... fantastic summer's heat.* Again Shakespeare seems to recall Lyly's *Euphues*: 'he that is cold doth not cover himself with care, but with clothes; he that is washed in the rain drieth himself by the fire, not by his fancy; and thou which art banished oughtest not with tears to bewail thy hap, but with wisdom to heal thy hurt'. This is from the same passage as that quoted in the note to lines 275–8.

295 *Caucasus* (regularly thought of as cold by the Elizabethans, as in Lyly's *Euphues*: 'If thou be as hot as the Mount Etna, feign thyself as cold as the hill Caucasus')

296 *cloy* surfeit

299 *fantastic* imagined

300 *apprehension* conception

302–3 *Fell sorrow's tooth doth never rankle more | Than when he bites, but lanceth not the sore* cruel sorrow, which bites (line 292), makes his most festering wounds when he bites but does not pierce the skin, as does a physician's lance (on a boil or abscess). Bolingbroke seems to imply that Gaunt's consolations blunt a sorrow which it would be better for him to accept at its worst.

304   *bring* accompany
305   *stay* (perhaps 'away from England' – he would not accept banishment; or perhaps 'linger' – he would leave immediately)

I.4   The main facts conveyed in this scene were available in Holinshed. The description of Bolingbroke's departure (lines 23–36) may have been suggested by him: 'A wonder it was to see what number of people ran after him in every town and street where he came before he took the sea, lamenting and bewailing his departure, as who would say that when he departed the only shield, defence, and comfort of the common-wealth was vaded and gone.' Shakespeare may also have derived a hint for Bolingbroke's *courtship to the common people* from Froissart's description of his return to London: 'and always as he rode he inclined his head to the people on every side'. The coolness of Aumerle to Bolingbroke is not in the sources; and the suggestion that Richard's farming of the realm was particularly to provide resources for his Irish campaign seems to be Shakespeare's.

(stage direction) Q's direction reads '*Enter the King with Bushie, &c at one dore, and the Lord Aumarle at another.*' Probably Shakespeare originally intended Bushy to enter with the other favourites, but then decided to bring him on at line 52. F has '*Enter King, Aumerle, Greene, and Bagot.*' See also notes to lines 23 and 52–3.

1   *We did observe.* Richard enters in the midst of a

conversation. We learn from line 24 that what he observed was Bolingbroke's *courtship to the common people*.

2   *high*. As the apparent irony in Aumerle's reply suggests, various shades of meaning, including 'high-ranking', 'proud', and perhaps 'haughty', may be felt.

6   *for me* on my part
     except except that

8   *Awaked the sleeping rheum* made our eyes water (*rheum*, 'watery discharge')

13   *that* (his heart's disdain)

13–15 *taught me craft | To counterfeit oppression of such grief | That words seemed buried in my sorrow's grave* taught me the skill (*craft*) to pretend to be so stricken with grief that words seemed buried in my sorrow as in a grave

20   *cousin, cousin*. Richard, Bolingbroke, and Aumerle were each other's cousins. Q reads 'cousins cousin'; F, 'cousin, cousin'. The Q reading (meaning 'cousin's cousin') may be right, Richard reminding Aumerle of his relationship with Bolingbroke.

23   *Ourself and Bushy*. In F this line reads 'Our selfe, and *Bushy*: heere *Bagot* and *Greene*', which may be what Shakespeare first wrote. But Q's stage direction at the beginning of the scene includes Bushy among those who enter, though he is also required to enter at line 52. Probably Shakespeare originally intended him to enter at the beginning of the scene, but then he or the actors decided to use Bushy as the carrier of news. This may have resulted in the need to alter this line, though the version found in Q seems unsatisfactory. It sounds clumsy; and the absence of the second part of the line has the theatrical disadvantage of leaving Bagot and Green unidentified on this, their first speaking appearance. A harmless fabrication which would seem nearest to Shakespeare's intentions as well as providing a regular verse line would be 'Ourself and Bushy;

Bagot here and Green', which is in fact the reading of
the (unauthoritative) quarto of 1634.

29   *underbearing* enduring

30   *banish their affects with him* take their affections
      (*affects*) into banishment with him

35   *As were our England in reversion his* as if my England
      were his in reversion (that is, would revert to him on
      my death). Richard means it sarcastically but there is a
      deeper irony.

38   *for* as for
      the rebels which stand out in Ireland. Holinshed records
      that 'the King being advertised that the wild Irish
      daily wasted and destroyed the towns and villages
      within the English pale, and had slain many of the
      soldiers which lay there in garrison for defence of that
      country, determined to make eftsoons a voyage
      thither, and prepared all things necessary for his
      passage now against the spring . . . and so in the month
      of April, as divers authors write, he set forward from
      Windsor and finally took shipping at Milford, and from
      thence with two hundred ships and a puissant power
      of men of arms and archers he sailed into Ireland'.
      stand out resist, hold out

39   *Expedient manage must be made* speedy measures must
      be taken

43-4 *for our coffers with too great a court | And liberal largess
      are grown somewhat light.* Richard was notorious for
      extravagance.

43   *for* because

45   *farm our royal realm* let my land by lease. The pro-
      cedure is explained by a passage in *Woodstock*,
      IV.1.180-93: 'These gentlemen here, Sir Henry
      Greene, Sir Edward Bagot, Sir William Bushy, and
      Sir Thomas Scroope, all jointly here stand bound to
      pay your majesty, or your deputy, wherever you re-
      main, seven thousand pounds a month for this your
      kingdom; for which your grace, by these writings,

surrenders to their hands: all your crown lands, lordships: manors, rents: taxes, subsidies, fifteens, imposts; foreign customs, staples for wool, tin, lead and cloth: all forfeitures of goods or lands confiscate; and all other duties that do, shall, or may appertain to the king or crown's revenues; and for non-payment of the sum or sums aforesaid, your majesty to seize the lands and goods of the said gentlemen above named, and their bodies to be imprisoned at your grace's pleasure.'

48   *blank charters.* Holinshed records that, in order to placate the King after he had been displeased with the City of London, 'many blank charters were devised and brought into the city, which many of the substantial and wealthy citizens were fain to seal, to their great charge, as in the end appeared. And the like charters were sent abroad into all shires within the realm, whereby great grudge and murmuring arose among the people; for when they were so sealed, the King's officers wrote in the same what liked them, as well for charging the parties with payment of money as otherwise.' The author of *Woodstock* makes a good deal of this.

50   *subscribe them for* put them down for

51   *them* (the sums of gold)

52   *presently* immediately

52–3   *Enter Bushy | Bushy, what news?* This is F's alteration from Q, which reads '*Enter Bushie with newes*'. Probably the manuscript from which the play was printed gave the passage substantially as it appears here, but without the second *Bushy*, and with *what* abbreviated in such a way that it was mistaken for 'with' and thus was run on with the stage direction. The confusion may be connected with a late decision to use Bushy as the bringer of news – see note to line 23.

58   *Ely House.* This, the palace of the Bishops of Ely, was

at Holborn, near London. It was often rented to noblemen.

59   *put*. This may be imperative, as interpreted here, or subjunctive, in which case the sense would be 'Now if God should put it ...' and a lighter point after *immediately* would be required.

61   *lining* contents

II.1   Richard's visit to the dying John of Gaunt is Shakespeare's invention. The matter of the scene may be indebted to Froissart, who relates that Gaunt was displeased at his son's exile 'for so little a cause, and also because of the evil governing of the realm by his nephew King Richard; for he saw well that if he long persevered and were suffered to continue, the realm was likely to be utterly lost. With these imaginations and other the Duke fell sick, whereon he died; whose death was greatly sorrowed of all his friends and lovers. The King, by that he showed, took no great care for his death, but soon he was forgotten' (Lord Berners's translation). Richard's seizure of Gaunt's belongings comes from Holinshed, as does York's unfavourable reaction. (See note to lines 201–7 below.) The final episode is based on Holinshed's statement that 'divers of the nobility, as well prelates as other and likewise many of the magistrates and rulers of the cities, towns, and commonalty here in England, perceiving daily how the realm drew to utter ruin, not like to be recovered to the former state of wealth whilst King Richard lived and reigned, as they took it, devised with great deliberation and considerate advice to send and signify by letters unto Duke Henry, whom they now called (as he was indeed) Duke of Lancaster and Hereford, requiring him with all convenient speed to convey himself into England, promising him all their aid, power, and assistance if he, expelling

King Richard as a man not meet for the office he bare,
would take upon him the sceptre, rule, and diadem of
his native land and region'.

(stage direction) *Duke of York*. Edmund of Langley,
1341–1402, fifth (fourth surviving) son of Edward
III. The House of York took its name from him.

Earl of Northumberland. Henry Percy, the first Earl,
1342–1408. He does not speak till line 147, but as he
there reports Gaunt's death his presence at the
scene's opening seems likely.

2   *unstaid* unrestrained

5–6   *they say the tongues of dying men | Enforce attention like
       deep harmony*. The notion that last words have an
       oracular quality was common, and Shakespeare
       makes much of it.

9   *listened* listened to, paid attention to

10   *glose* speak flatteringly (like Richárd's favourites)

12   *music at the close* (the cadence, or closing phrase of a
       piece of music)

13   *last taste of sweets* the last taste of sweet things (before
       the taste disappears)

       sweetest last (perhaps 'sweetest in its most recent
       manifestation'; or 'sweetest because it comes last')

18   *the wise are fond* even the wise are fond. Q reads
       'found', and the line may be corrupt.

19   *metres* verses, poems

21   *fashions in proud Italy*. Italy was a traditional source of
       folly and wickedness. *Fashions* may refer to clothes or
       may extend to manners and behaviour. This passage
       is reminiscent of the lines in Act I of Marlowe's
       Edward II in which Gaveston imagines how he will
       win the King's favour:

       Music and poetry is his delight;
       Therefore I'll have Italian masques by night,
       Sweet speeches, comedies, and pleasant shows.

A similar accusation against King Richard and his

favourites is made in *Woodstock*, II.3.88–93:

> They sit in council to devise strange fashions,
> And suit themselves in wild and antic habits
> Such as this kingdom never yet beheld:
> French hose, Italian cloaks, and Spanish hats,
> Polonian shoes with peaks a hand full long,
> Tied to their knees with chains of pearl and gold.

22   *still* always

         tardy-apish ready to ape fashions after they have become stale

25   *there's no respect* no one cares

28   *will doth mutiny with wit's regard* desire conflicts with the claims of intelligence

30–32   *breath ... new-inspired ... expiring.* Having been reminded of his shortage of breath, the fact that he will not breathe much longer, Gaunt imagines himself to be newly inspired (playing on the sense of 'given breath'), and so, expiring – that is, both 'breathing out' and 'dying' – foretells. ... This type of serious wordplay is particularly characteristic of Gaunt.

31   *Methinks I am a prophet new-inspired.* Compare lines 5–6.

34–7   These lines all have a proverbial ring. Behind the first lies the proverb 'Nothing violent can be permanent', on which many writers played variations, as Shakespeare did in *Romeo and Juliet*, II.6.9: 'These violent delights have violent ends.' *He tires betimes that spurs too fast betimes* was an expression comparable to 'More haste, less speed'.

35   *Small showers last long.* The four long syllables show Shakespeare matching the sound to the sense.

36   *betimes* soon, early

38   *cormorant* glutton

41   *This earth of majesty* this land which is the proper seat of majesty

         seat of Mars home of Mars (the god of war)

45   *little world* world in little. Compare *Cymbeline*, III.1.12–13: 'Britain is | A world by itself.'

52   *Feared by* inspiring fear by

55   *stubborn Jewry* (the land of the Jews, obstinate both in refusing Christianity and in resisting the crusaders)

59–60   *leased out ... Like to a tenement or pelting farm.* This may be a reference to *Woodstock*, IV.1.145–7, where Richard fears criticism because, he says, 'we ... to ease our wanton youth | Become a landlord to this warlike realm, | Rent out our kingdom like a pelting farm ...'.

60   *tenement* estate held by a tenant
     pelting paltry

61–3   Shakespeare makes the Duke of Austria speak of England in similar terms in *King John*, II.1.21–30:

        to my home I will no more return
     Till Angiers and the right thou hast in France,
     Together with that pale, that white-faced shore
     Whose foot spurns back the ocean's roaring tides
     And coops from other lands her islanders,
     Even till that England, hedged in with the main,
     That water-wallèd bulwark, still secure
     And confident from foreign purposes,
     Even till that utmost corner of the west
     Salute thee for her king.

     bound in ... bound in surrounded by ... legally restrained by

64   *blots* (the blank charters)

68   (stage direction) If, as F suggests, King Richard's exit (line 223) is marked by a flourish, trumpets should sound too for his entrance here.
     Queen Isabel. At the time of the events of the play King Richard's wife was Isabel, daughter of Charles VI of France, whom he had married in 1396, 'she being as then not past eight years of age' (Holinshed). Shakespeare does not give a name to Richard's Queen,

and it is important to the scheme of the play that she should be presented as a woman who feels more than childlike love for her husband. Isabel was King Richard's second wife. The character in the play is closer to his first, Anne, to whom he had been deeply devoted and with whose portrayal in *Woodstock* Shakespeare's Queen has much in common.

Ross. Lord Ross sat in Parliament from 1394. He died in 1414.

Willoughby. Lord Willoughby sat in Parliament from 1397, and died in 1409. King Richard made him Knight of the Garter, but he joined Bolingbroke. He later married the Duke of York's widow.

73   *composition* state of both mind and body

75   *grief hath kept a tedious fast.* Fasts were sometimes observed as an expression of grief.

77   *watched* stayed awake at night (worrying over England *sleeping* in sloth or ignorance of what is happening)

78   *Watching* sleeplessness

80   *Is my strict fast* I must go without

83   *inherits* 'possesses' or 'will receive (at my death)'

84   *nicely* 'subtly' and 'triflingly'

85   *misery makes sport to mock itself* it is misery (not sickness) which finds amusement in ridiculing itself

86   *to kill my name in me* (by banishing his son)

88   *flatter with* try to please

89   *flatter* (perhaps in the sense of 'try to cheer up')

93   *see thee ill.* The stress is on *thee*.

94   *Ill in myself to see, and in thee seeing ill* myself having poor power of sight, and seeing evil in you

98   *Committest thy anointed body to the cure.* This line appears to be an alexandrine, but probably should be spoken as a pentameter by pronouncing 'commits' and eliding *thy* and *anointed*.

102   *verge.* Three senses are relevant: (1) compass; (2) the sphere of jurisdiction of the king's marshal, twelve

miles round the royal residence; (3) a measure of land of from fifteen to thirty acres.

103   *waste*. The legal meaning of 'a tenant's destruction of his landlord's property' is relevant.

104–5   *had thy grandsire with a prophet's eye | Seen how his son's son should destroy his sons* (that is, had Edward III seen how his grandson, Richard, would destroy his (Edward's) sons – Gloucester and Gaunt)

107–8   *possessed ... possessed* put in possession ... possessed by a devil, mad

109   *regent* ruler

111   *for thy world enjoying but this land* as this land is all the world that you rule

114   *state of law is bondslave to the law* legal status is now that of one who is bound to obey the law (instead of above the law, as a king should be)

115   *– a lunatic. . . .* Richard interrupts Gaunt's sentence, and turns it back on him. It would be up to the actor to make this clear, perhaps by pointing to Gaunt, or even by saying 'thou' simultaneously with him. F gives 'thou' to Richard, not to Gaunt. Q 3 reads 'Ah lunatick . . .', which is plausible but lacks authority.

122   *roundly* 'bluntly' or 'glibly'

123   *unreverent* disrespectful

124–5   *Edward ... his father Edward* (the Black Prince, Richard's father; son of Edward III, who was also Gaunt's father)

126   *pelican* (an allusion to the common belief that the young pelican feeds on its mother's life-blood)

128   *Gloucester, plain well-meaning soul* (possibly influenced by the portrait of Gloucester as 'plain Thomas' in *Woodstock*)

129   *fair befall* may good befall

130   *precedent* example, proof

131   *thou respectest not* you do not scruple to (the verb may be in the past tense – an elliptical form of 're-spectedest')

133   *unkindness.* The word had a stronger sense to the Elizabethans than it has now: 'unnatural behaviour'.

135   *die not shame with thee!* may your ill-reputation live after you!

139   *sullens* sulks

140   *become* are fit for

143–5   *He loves you ... so his.* York means that Gaunt loves Richard as much as he loves his son; but Richard embarrasses him by taking him to mean 'as much as Bolingbroke loves you'.

149   *stringless instrument.* The image recalls that used by Mowbray at I.3.161–2.

152   *death* (the state of being dead)

153   *The ripest fruit first falls* (proverbial)

154   *our pilgrimage must be* our pilgrimage through life lies before us, and it too will come to an end

156   *supplant* get rid of

       rug-headed shaggy-headed. Edmund Spenser in *The Present State of Ireland* (1596) said of the Irish: 'They have another custom from the Scythians, that is the wearing of mantles and long glibs, which is a thick curled bush of hair hanging down over their eyes and monstrously disguising them.' (*Rug* is a shaggy material.)

       kerns light-armed Irish foot-soldiers

157–8   *live like venom where no venom else | But only they have privilege to live.* This is an allusion to the legend that Saint Patrick banished snakes from Ireland.

159   *charge* expense

164   *suffer* tolerate

166   *Gaunt's rebukes* the insults and shames offered to Gaunt (by Richard)

167–8   *the prevention of poor Bolingbroke | About his marriage.* This refers to an event not mentioned elsewhere in the play. It is explained by Holinshed, who writes that when Bolingbroke, during his exile in Paris, was about to marry the French King's cousin, Richard 'sent the Earl of Salisbury with all speed into France, both to surmise by untrue suggestion heinous offences against him, and also to require the French King that in no wise he would suffer his cousin to be matched in marriage with him that was so manifest an offender'.

168   *my own disgrace.* We do not know to what York refers. There may be significance in the fact that in *Woodstock*, III.2.4, Gloucester says to York and Lancaster that Richard has 'Disgraced our names and thrust us from his court'.

170   *bend one wrinkle* 'cause one frown to appear' or 'once frown (at you)'

172–83   This comparison between Richard and his father may owe something to one made by Gaunt in *Woodstock*, I.1.27–45:

> A heavy charge good Woodstock hast thou had
> To be protector to so wild a prince
> So far degenerate from his noble father
> Whom the trembling French the Black Prince called
> Not of a swart and melancholy brow
> (For sweet and lovely was his countenance)
> But that he made so many funeral days
> In mournful France: the warlike battles won
> At Crecy Field, Poitiers, Artoise and Maine
> Made all France groan under his conquering arm.
> But heaven forestalled his diadem on earth
> To place him with a royal crown in heaven.
> Rise may his dust to glory! Ere he'd 'a done
> A deed so base unto his enemy,
> Much less unto the brothers of his father,
> He'd first have lost his royal blood in drops,
> Dissolved the strings of his humanity
> And lost that livelyhood that was preserved
> To make his (unlike) son a wanton king.

173   *lion raged more fierce* (either 'lion raged more fiercely' or 'a fierce (en-)raged lion')

177   *Accomplished with the number of thy hours* at your age (*Accomplished with*, furnished with)

185   *compare between.* Either York breaks down, leaving his sentence incomplete, or this expression is complete in itself, meaning 'draw comparisons between them'.

186   *Why, uncle, what's the matter?* Richard may be callously detached or genuinely bewildered.

188   *withal* none the less

190   *royalties* (rights granted to a subject by the king; royal prerogatives)

192   *Harry* (Bolingbroke, Duke of Hereford). He is *true* in having accepted exile.

195   *Take ... and take* if you take ... you will take

201–7   *If you do wrongfully seize Hereford's rights, | Call in the letters patents that he hath | By his attorneys general to sue | His livery, and deny his offered homage, | You pluck a thousand dangers on your head, | You lose a thousand well-disposèd hearts, | And prick my tender patience....* Holinshed has: 'The death of this duke gave occasion of increasing more hatred in the people of this realm toward the King, for he seized into his hands all the goods that belonged to him, and also received all the rents and revenues of his lands which ought to have descended unto the Duke of Hereford by lawful inheritance, in revoking his letters patents, which he had granted to him before, by virtue whereof he might make his attorneys general to sue livery for him of any manner of inheritances or possessions that might from thenceforth fall unto him, and that his homage might be respited with making reasonable fine; whereby it was evident that the King meant his utter undoing.

    'This hard dealing was much misliked of all the nobility, and cried out against of the meaner sort; but namely, the Duke of York was therewith sore moved....' The letters patent would have allowed Bolingbroke to institute suits to obtain his father's lands, which under feudal law would revert to Richard until it had been proved that the heir, Bolingbroke, was of age. When the lands were restored to the heir he was required to make an act of homage to the king. Richard is said to refuse (*deny*) this, which was to be 'respited with making reasonable fine' (presumably because the exiled Bolingbroke could not pay homage in person).

203–4 *sue | His livery* (institute suits for obtaining Gaunt's lands)

213–14 *But by bad courses may be understood | That their events can never fall out good* (a not very elegant way of saying 'You cannot expect bad courses of action to have good results')

215 *the Earl of Wiltshire.* He was Richard's treasurer. He was executed at Bristol with Bushy and Green (see III.1.1–35), but does not appear in the play.
straight immediately

216 *Ely House* (where Richard now is)

217 *see* see to
Tomorrow next tomorrow ('morrow' originally meant simply 'morning')

218 *trow* believe

220–21 *York ... he is just, and always loved us well.* This appreciation of York seems surprising considering York's immediately preceding criticism of Richard. It is caused at least partly by Shakespeare's telescoping of events. In Holinshed some time passes between Gaunt's death and Richard's decision to go to Ireland.

228 *great* big with sorrow

229 *liberal* unrestrained

231 *speaks thy words again to do thee harm* uses what you say in evidence against you

232 *Tends that thou wouldst speak to* does what you would say refer (favourably) to

243 *Merely* purely

246–8 *The commons ... lost their hearts.* This echoes *Wood-*

stock, V.3.94: 'thou well may'st doubt their loves that lost their hearts'.

246   *pilled* plundered

250   *blanks* blank charters (I.4.48; see Commentary)
      benevolences forced loans
      wot know

252   *Wars hath.* The singular form of the verb with a plural subject is not uncommon in Elizabethan English. It may possibly be a northern dialectal form especially appropriate to Northumberland. He uses it again at II.3.5.

252–4 *warred he hath not, | But basely yielded upon compromise | That which his noble ancestors achieved with blows.* This probably refers to the giving up of Brest to the Duke of Brittany in 1397, which was a cause of dispute between Richard and Gloucester.

254   *noble.* This was omitted by F, and many editors follow suit, explaining it as an accidental anticipation of the same word in line 262. But Shakespeare may have written the alexandrine.

256   *in farm.* The 'farming' of the land is referred to at I.4.45; see Commentary.

257   *The King's grown bankrupt like a broken man.* Q reads 'King'. 'King's' is in all the early editions after Q 2. But Shakespeare may have written 'King', intending Northumberland to complete Willoughby's sentence.

266   *strike* strike sail (perhaps also 'resist')
      securely carelessly, with excessive sense of security

268   *unavoided* unavoidable

269   *suffering* putting up with, doing nothing about

270   *eyes* eye-sockets

275   *are but thyself* share your feelings, are of one mind with you

277–88 This is based on Holinshed: 'there were certain ships rigged and made ready for him at a place in base Brittaine called Le Port Blanc, as we find in the

197

chronicles of Brittaine, and when all his provision was made ready he took the sea together with the said Archbishop of Canterbury and his nephew Thomas Arundel, son and heir to the late Earl of Arundel beheaded at the Tower Hill, as you have heard. There were also with him Reginald Lord Cobham, Sir Thomas Erpingham, and Sir Thomas Ramston, knights, John Norbury, Robert Waterton, and Francis Coint, esquires. Few else were there, for (as some write) he had not past fifteen lances, as they termed them in those days, that is to say men-of-arms, furnished and appointed as the use then was. Yet other write that the Duke of Brittaine delivered unto him three thousand men of war to attend him, and that he had eight ships well furnished for the war, where Froissart yet speaketh but of three.'

27ʀ   *Brittaine* Brittany, or Bretagne. No modernized form of Q's spelling seems wholly satisfactory.

       intelligence information, news

280   *The son of Richard Earl of Arundel.* This line is not in any of the early editions, but was first added by Edmond Malone in 1790. Something like it seems necessary because Holinshed has 'the Earl of Arundel's son, named Thomas, which was kept in the Duke of Exeter's house, escaped out of the realm'. Shakespeare is heavily dependent on Holinshed in this passage.

       The Archbishop of Canterbury (line 282) was Richard Earl of Arundel's brother. He was *late* Archbishop because he had been banished in 1397, when his brother the earl was executed as one of the Lords Appellant. It is possible that the line was deliberately cut because Queen Elizabeth had had Philip Howard Earl of Arundel executed in 1595, and she did her best to deprive his young son of his inheritance as well as his title.

281   *broke* escaped

283   *Sir Thomas Erpingham.* He appears as a character in

Henry V (IV.1). He was one of Richard's active opponents.

283 *Sir John Ramston.* His real name was Thomas. He became Warden of the Tower when Richard was confined there.

284 *Coint.* This is Holinshed's form of the name. Q reads 'Coines'; F, 'Quoint', which Ure takes to be a conscious correction of Q, perhaps based on consultation of the prompt-book. But it might (as Sisson suggests) be simply a variant spelling.

285 *Duke of Brittaine.* John de Montford, who died in 1399 and whose widow, Joan of Navarre, became Bolingbroke's second wife.

286 *tall* large, fine

287 *expedience* speed

289-90 *they stay | The first departing of the King for Ireland.* Holinshed explains that Bolingbroke 'did not straight take land, but lay hovering aloof, and showed himself now in this place and now in that, to see what countenance was made by the people, whether they meant enviously to resist him, or friendly to receive him'.

292 *Imp out* repair (a metaphor from falconry)

293 *broking pawn* (the possession of the King's money-lenders)

294 *gilt* (punningly)

296 *in post* in haste, travelling by relays of horses
     Ravenspurgh (a port on the Humber)

300 *Hold out my horse* if my horse holds out

II.2 The Queen's emotion both creates foreboding and suggests a more sympathetic view of the King. The events of the remainder of the scene are rearranged and developed from Holinshed.

3 *life-harming* (compare Ecclesiasticus 30.23: 'as for sorrow and heaviness, drive it far from thee; for heaviness hath slain many a man, and bringeth no profit')

14   *Each substance of a grief hath twenty shadows* for each
      real cause of grief there are twenty illusory ones. This
      anticipates the imagery used by Richard at IV.1.294–8.

18   *perspectives* (pronounced with stresses on the first and
      third syllables). A perspective in this sense is a painting
      or drawing which from a normal point of view appears
      distorted, but which produces a clear image when
      looked at from a particular, and unusual, angle. There
      is a well-known example in the National Gallery in
      Holbein's portrait *The Ambassadors*, most of which is
      painted normally but which includes a weird object
      which when looked at *awry* is seen to be a skull. It is
      said to have been painted from the reflection of a skull
      in a curved mirror. Lines 16–17 are suggestive also of
      another kind of perspective, a multiplying glass cut
      into a number of facets, each one of which creates a
      distinct image. Queen Isabel's eyes, out of focus as the
      result of her tears, produce a similar effect.

20   *Distinguish form* show distinct forms

21–4 *Looking awry upon your lord's departure, | Find shapes
      of grief more than himself to wail, | Which looked on as
      it is, is naught but shadows | Of what it is not.* Here the
      two types of perspective mentioned in the note to line
      18 become confused. Isabel, looking awry (which with
      the first type would produce a single, true image),
      sees a multiple image, as if she were looking at a
      multiplying glass. If, says Bushy, she looked at it
      from a normal angle (*as it is*), she would see that her
      cause of grief was all an illusion.

21   *Looking awry upon* considering mistakenly

27   *weeps* weeps for

29   This line has twelve syllables, but can be spoken with
      five main stresses: 'Per*suades* me *it* is *oth*erwise.
      Howe'*er* it *be*'.

31   *though on thinking on no thought I think* though I try to
      think about nothing

32   *with heavy nothing.* Isabel returns to the thought of

the *unborn sorrow*, which in a sense is *nothing*, expressed in lines 10–12.

33   *conceit* fancy

34   *nothing less* anything but that

34–40   *Conceit is still derived ... 'tis nameless woe, I wot* a fancied grief always (*still*) derives from a real one. Mine cannot be fancied, because it derives from an unreal one (the *nothing* of line 12); or else the unreal one that afflicts me exists somewhere, and I own it as I might own an object that as yet is in someone else's keeping. But I cannot give a name to this thing whose identity I do not yet know; I think it must be 'Nameless Woe'.

46   *retired his power* withdrawn his army (from Ireland)

49   *repeals* recalls from exile

50   *uplifted arms* brandished weapons

53–4   *Northumberland ... Willoughby.* These are all among the supporters of Bolingbroke mentioned by Holinshed.

53   *Henry.* This is printed as 'H.' in Q; it may be that we should expand to 'Harry'.

57   *the rest, revolted faction, traitors.* The exact interpretation of this line is disputed. Some take 'rest revolted faction' together as 'rest of the revolted faction'. Others interpret 'and all the rest that are revolted, faction-traitors'. The present reading assumes that *revolted faction* is in apposition to *rest*.

58   *the Earl of Worcester.* He was Thomas Percy, the Earl of Northumberland's brother, and steward of the royal household. He becomes an important character in *1 Henry IV*. Holinshed says: 'Sir Thomas Percy, Earl of Worcester, lord steward of the King's house ... brake his white staff, which is the representing sign and token of his office, and without delay went to Duke Henry. When the King's servants of household saw this – for it was done before them all – they dispersed themselves. . . .'.

63   *heir* offspring

64   *prodigy* monstrous birth (the *unborn sorrow ripe in fortune's womb*, line 10)

69   *cozening* cheating

71   *Who* (death)

72   *lingers in extremity* prolongs to the utmost

74   *signs of war about his agèd neck.* York is wearing the piece of armour called a gorget. It could be worn with civilian dress.

75   *careful business* anxious preoccupation

76   *comfortable* comforting

79   *crosses* troubles

85   *try* put to the test (some of the *friends* are of course on stage with York)

86   *your son was gone.* Aumerle was with the King in Ireland.

88   *The nobles they are fled. The commons they are cold.* This is the reading of all the early editions. Some editors emend to 'The nobles they are fled, the commons cold', which may be correct, but long lines are not uncommon in this play.

90   *sister* sister-in-law

91   *presently* immediately

92   *Hold: take my ring.* The signet ring will be proof that he comes from York.

97   *An hour before I came the Duchess died.* Holinshed mentions the Duchess's death, but does not say where or when it happened, and attributes it to grief at her son's death. In fact it appears to have occurred in October 1399, later than the events of this scene. Shakespeare places it here to increase the *tide of woes*.

101   *So* so long as, provided that
       untruth disloyalty

105   *Come, sister – cousin, I would say.* A. C. Sprague comments: 'He is almost a comic character; a pitiful one, by the same token, and very real. "Come, sister ..." his mind turning back, even as he speaks,

to the past; to that final piece of news, which as yet he has scarcely taken in' (*Shakespearian Players and Performances*, 1953, page 168).

108-9, 116-21   The metre is irregular. Rearrangement is sometimes attempted, but a regular rhythm cannot be obtained from these words. The irregularity may reflect York's harassed state of mind. The present edition follows Q except that there lines 119-21 are printed as two lines, the first ending with *permit*. The rhyme demands rearrangement.

117   *dispose of* make arrangements for

118   *Berkeley*. F reads 'Barkley Castle'. 'Castle' may have been added in performance.

122   The remainder of the scene is based on Holinshed's 'The Lord Treasurer, Bushy, Bagot, and Green, perceiving that the commons would cleave unto and take part with the Duke, slipped away, leaving the Lord Governor of the realm and the Lord Chancellor to make what shift they could for themselves. Bagot got him to Chester, and so escaped into Ireland. The other fled to the castle of Bristol, in hope there to be in safety.'

122-3   *The wind sits fair for news to go for Ireland,* | *But none returns* the wind is favourable for news to go to Ireland, but not for it to come from there

126-7   *our nearness to the King in love* | *Is near the hate of those love not the King* the King's affection for us makes us hated by those who oppose the King

127   *those love* those who love

132   *If judgement lie in them* if our fate depends on them ('the commons' or 'the commons' hearts')

133   *ever* constantly

136   *office* service

140   *No, I will to Ireland to his majesty*. According to Holinshed, Bagot 'got him to Chester, and so escaped into Ireland, the other [Bushy and Green] fled to the castle of Bristol'. Shakespeare follows this here.

However, in II.3.164 Bagot, not Green, is rumoured to be at Bristol with Bushy. In III.1 Bushy and Green are executed at Bristol. It looks as if Shakespeare were rather confused or careless. The discrepancies would probably not be noticed in performance.

141–2 *If heart's presages be not vain, | We three here part that ne'er shall meet again.* Thomas of Woodstock takes leave of his brothers in similar words (*Woodstock*, III.2.102–6):

> Adieu, good York and Gaunt, farewell for ever.
> I have a sad presage comes suddenly
> That I shall never see these brothers more:
> On earth, I fear, we never more shall meet.
> Of Edward the Third's seven sons we three are
>   left. . . .

141 *presages.* The accent is on the second syllable.

143 *That's as York thrives to beat* that's according to how far York succeeds in beating

145 *numbering sands and drinking oceans dry* (proverbial expressions for attempting the impossible)

II.3 In its fluidity of setting this scene is characteristic of the Elizabethan stage. It begins somewhere in Gloucestershire, on the way to Berkeley Castle where, according to Holinshed, Bolingbroke went from Doncaster, and where York had halted on his way to meet the King on his return from Ireland. At line 53 the action localizes itself outside the castle. The material of the scene is created by Shakespeare from facts given by Holinshed.

4 *high wild hills.* Northumberland is referring to the Cotswolds. He, of course, comes from the north of England.

5 *Draws . . . makes.* For the grammar, see Commentary to II.1.252.

7 *delectable* (accented on the first and third syllables)

9   *Cotswold.* Q reads 'Cotshall', an old form of the name of the Gloucestershire hills. In *The Merry Wives of Windsor* it is spelt 'Cotsall', and in *2 Henry IV* 'Cotsole'. Shakespeare's pronunciation was probably something like 'Cotsul'.

11   *beguiled* passed pleasantly

12   *tediousness and process* tedious process

16   *By this* by this hope (of enjoying Bolingbroke's company)

20   (stage direction) *Harry Percy.* He lived from 1364 to 1403, when he was killed at the Battle of Shrewsbury. He was known as Hotspur because of his daring in battle against the border clans. He is vividly characterized in *1 Henry IV*. There is no proof in *Richard II* that Shakespeare had yet conceived the idiosyncrasies of the character as he later portrayed it.

22   *whencesoever* from somewhere or other; wherever he may be

26–8   (as reported at II.2.58–61)

36   *Have you forgot the Duke of Hereford, boy?* (a rebuke to Harry Percy for not greeting Bolingbroke. *Boy* is unhistorical, as in fact 'young' Percy was two years older than Bolingbroke. In *1 Henry IV* Hotspur is of the same generation as Prince Hal – he was actually twenty-two years older.)

38   *To my knowledge* so far as I know; to the best of my knowledge

43–4   *Which elder days shall ripen and confirm | To more approvèd service and desert* (ironical, considering what happened later, portrayed by Shakespeare in *1 Henry IV*)

45–50   *I thank thee . . . thus seals it.* Hotspur recalls this conversation with disgust at Bolingbroke's treachery in *1 Henry IV*, I.3.236–51.

45   *gentle* noble, 'gentlemanly'

47   *As in a soul remembering* as having a heart which remembers

49   *still* continually, all the time

50   *my hand thus seals it*. They shake hands.

51-2   *what stir | Keeps* 'what event detains' or 'what is [he] doing'

56   (stage direction) *Enter Ross and Willoughby*. They actually joined Bolingbroke when he landed at Ravenspurgh, not at Berkeley.

61   *unfelt* intangible

        which (refers to *treasury*)

65   *Evermore thank's the exchequer* 'thank you' is always (or 'always will be') the exchequer. . . . F has 'Euermore thankes, th'Exchequer of the poor', which many editors follow; but 'thank' as an expression of gratitude is an authenticated usage. *Thank* is the antecedent of *Which* in the following line.

66   *to years* to years of discretion, into its own

67   *Stands for* represents, does duty for

        (stage direction) *Berkeley*. He was a baron, and sat in Parliament from 1381 till 1417, when he died.

70   *my answer is to 'Lancaster'*. Berkeley has addressed him by his former title of 'Hereford'. He replies that he answers only to the title of 'Lancaster', which he has inherited from his father. It may be that he begins to reply with 'my answer is', and then interjects 'to "Lancaster"', meaning that this is the only title to which he will reply; or perhaps he says simply 'I reply only in the name of Lancaster.' Northumberland referred to him as 'Hereford' without rebuke at line 36.

75   *raze one title of your honour out* (Q has 'race', a variant form). The title is imagined as an inscription, as at III.1.25 where Bolingbroke complains that his enemies have *Razed out my imprese*. There is probably also a pun on 'tittle', meaning 'any part of'.

79   *absent time* time of (King Richard's) absence

80   *self-borne*. This may mean 'born of' or 'originating in' yourself, or 'carried for your own cause', or

'carried by yourself', or may be a quibble on these meanings: 'begotten and carried on your own initiative and for your own ends'.

84   *duty* (the act of kneeling)
      deceivable deceptive

86   *Tut, tut.* This extra-metrical exclamation has been suspected of being an actor's interpolation.
      grace me no grace, nor uncle me no uncle! Shakespeare uses a similar contemptuous refusal of courtesy in *Romeo and Juliet*, III.5.152: 'Thank me no thankings, nor proud me no prouds.'

87–8 *'grace' ... profane* (alluding to the religious connotations of 'grace', which would have been felt more strongly by Shakespeare's than by a modern audience)

88   *ungracious* wicked. The word was much stronger in Shakespeare's time than it is at present.

90   *dust* grain of dust

91   *But then more 'why'* but even if that can be answered there are more questions (and, perhaps, ones even more indicative of astonishment) to be asked

94   *ostentation* display

98   *lord.* F reads 'the lord', which may be correct; but the irregular metre has strength.

98–101 There is no clear source of this incident.

100   *the Black Prince* (King Richard's father)

102–3 *arm of mine, | Now prisoner to the palsy.* Palsy is a paralytic condition. This may be no more than a general reference to York's advanced years, but it has been said that there is historical warrant for the statement.

103   *chastise.* The accent is on the first syllable.

106–7 *condition ... condition.* In its first use, the word refers to Bolingbroke's personal qualities; in its second, to the circumstances of the rebellion.

111   *braving* defiant, daring (adjectival rather than verbal)

113   *for* 'in the character of', 'as'; or 'to assume the title and rights of'

115   *indifferent* impartial

118–19   *condemned* | *A* condemned as a

119   *royalties* (rights granted to a subject by the king, as at II.1.190)

120   *arms.* The sense 'coat-of-arms' is felt.

121   *unthrifts* spendthrifts, prodigals (such as the King's favourites)

122–3   *If that my cousin King . . . Duke of Lancaster.* Compare York's argument to Richard on Bolingbroke's behalf, II.1.191–9.

122   *cousin King* cousin who is king; kingly cousin

125   *thus* (as I have)

127   *rouse . . . wrongs . . . bay.* The metaphor is from hunting. *Rouse*, startle from the lair. The *wrongs* (presumably 'wrongdoers') are the quarry. *Bay*, last stand.

128   *denied* refused the right

128–9   *sue my livery . . . letters patents* (see Commentary to II.1.203–4)

130   *distrained* seized, taken possession of by crown officers

131   *and all* and everything else

132–5   Holinshed writes that when Bolingbroke arrived at Doncaster he swore 'that he would demand no more but the lands that were to him descended by inheritance from his father and in right of his wife'.

133   *challenge law* demand my rights

135   *of free descent* free from flaw; direct

137   *It stands your grace upon* it is incumbent upon your grace

138   *his endowments* the possessions with which he has (involuntarily) endowed them

        are (presumably this is accented; that is, 'it is true that . . .')

142   *kind* manner

143   *Be his own carver.* The phrase seems to have been proverbial – 'help himself'. It gains point from the double sense of carving with a table-knife and a sword.

144   *find out right with wrong* achieve your rights by doing
       wrong

150   *never* (probably to be pronounced 'ne'er')

153   *power* army
       ill-left 'left ill-equipped' or 'left in disorder'

155   *attach* arrest

158   *as neuter* neutral

164   *Bagot.* At II.2.140 (see Commentary) he had declared
       his intention of going to Ireland.

165   *caterpillars of the commonwealth* parasites on society

166   *weed.* The word could be used of the removal of
       harmful creatures as well as plants. It is part of the
       recurrent image of England as a garden.

170   *Things past redress are now with me past care.* York
       gives vent to his divided feelings in a semi-proverbial
       expression.

II.4   This scene is based on Holinshed, who explains that
       because of storms Richard was late in hearing that
       Bolingbroke had landed in England, and that Richard
       did not set out immediately on hearing the news, but
       was persuaded to delay till his preparations were
       complete.
       (stage direction) *Earl of Salisbury.* John de Montacute
       (or Montagu), 1350–1400.
       Welsh Captain. In Holinshed the Welsh captain
       is Owen Glendower, who figures prominently in
       1 Henry IV. The fact that the Welsh Captain speaks of
       omens and portents (lines 8–15), as Glendower does
       in the later play, gives some colour to the suggestion
       that Shakespeare identified the two. But he seems to
       have preferred not to give the captain a name. He is im-
       portant rather for his representative quality than for any
       personal characteristics. See Commentary to III. 1.43.

1   *ten days.* According to Holinshed the Welshmen
       waited for fourteen days.

2   *hardly* with difficulty

3   *yet* still, so far

5–6   *thou trusty Welshman.* | *The King reposeth all his con-*
        fidence in thee. Holinshed records that Richard 'had
        also no small affiance [confidence] in the Welshmen,
        and Cheshire men'.

8 ff.   The expression of superstitious fear in these lines is
        the main point of the scene. Glendower in *1 Henry IV*
        (III.1) speaks similarly. Whether or not the Welsh
        Captain is Glendower, Shakespeare may have felt that
        such sentiments were specially appropriate in the
        mouth of a Welshman. According to Holinshed the
        withering of the bay trees happened in England, not
        Wales: 'In this year in a manner throughout all the
        realm of England old bay trees withered, and after-
        wards, contrary to all men's thinking, grew green
        again, a strange sight, and supposed to import some un-
        known event.' This passage occurs first in the second
        (1587) edition of Holinshed, and the parallel is part of
        the evidence for Shakespeare's use of this edition. The
        bay tree was symbolical of victory and immortality;
        its withering was thus a particularly bad omen.

9   *meteors . . . fixèd stars.* Meteors, of course, are 'un-
        fixed' stars.

10   *The pale-faced moon looks bloody on the earth. Looks*
        used of planets and stars implies influence as well as
        appearance. This line may mean that the normally
        pale-faced moon appears bloody to earthly watchers,
        or that it exerts a bloody influence.

11   *lean-looked* lean-looking
        prophets soothsayers (rather than religiously inspired
        men)

14   *to enjoy* in hope of profiting

19–21   *I see thy glory . . . west.* These lines anticipate Richard's
        imagery at III.3.178–83.

22   *Witnessing* betokening

24   *crossly* adversely

III.1 The basis of the scene is Holinshed's statement that 'the foresaid dukes with their power went towards Bristol where, at their coming, they showed themselves before the town and castle, being an huge multitude of people. There were enclosed within the castle the Lord William Scroop Earl of Wiltshire and Treasurer of England, Sir Henry Green, and Sir John Bushy, knights, who prepared to make resistance. But when it would not prevail they were taken and brought forth bound as prisoners into the camp before the Duke of Lancaster. On the morrow next ensuing they were arraigned before the Constable and Marshal and found guilty of treason for misgoverning the King and realm, and forthwith had their heads smit off.' Shakespeare omits Wiltshire, who makes no appearance in the play though at II.2.135 he is said to be at Bristol, and at III.2.141–2 and III.4.53 he is mentioned as having been executed along with Bushy and Green. It is possible that Shakespeare wrongly identified him with Bagot – see Commentary to III.2.122.

(stage direction) F directs Ross, Percy, and Willoughby also to enter. They are not required by the action; but it may have been the custom to bring them on to dress the stage.

3   *presently* immediately
      part leave

4   *urging* stressing

5–6   *to wash your blood | From off my hands* to justify my condemning you. The phrase inevitably recalls Pontius Pilate's action, directly referred to by Richard at IV.1.238–41.

9   *A happy gentleman in* a gentleman fortunate in
      blood and lineaments birth and personal appearance

10   *clean* utterly

11–12   *You have in manner with your sinful hours | Made a divorce betwixt his Queen and him.* This accusation does not appear to be borne out by the relations between

Richard and his Queen in the rest of the play. It may have been suggested by Holinshed's 'there reigned abundantly the filthy sin of lechery, and fornication, with abominable adultery, specially in the King . . .'. Shakespeare may also have been influenced by the clearly homosexual relationship of Edward and Gaveston in Marlowe's *Edward II*, though he does not necessarily imply sexual opposition between the King's favourites and the Queen. In *Woodstock* Richard displays intense affection for Greene. Perhaps the principal point in *Richard II* is simply that the Queen stands at this point in the play as a symbol of the virtue from which Richard's favourites are diverting him.

11   *in manner* as it were

12   *divorce* (used metaphorically)

13   *possession* joint rights

20   *in* into (adding to them as well as mixing breath among them. So in *Romeo and Juliet*, I.1.133: 'Adding to clouds more clouds with his deep sighs.')

22   *signories* estates, manors

23   *Disparked* (converted to other, less aristocratic, uses land in which game had been kept)

24   *From my own windows torn my household coat* broken the windows in which my coat-of-arms was emblazoned ('tear' could mean 'break')

25   *imprese* crest, heraldic device (this is the Italian plural of the singular *impresa*)

27   *gentleman* nobleman

36   *your house* (Langley)

37   *intreated* treated

41   *at large* in full (or 'in general terms')

43   *Glendower*. Owen Glendower is not mentioned elsewhere in this play (but see Commentary to II.4, opening stage direction), though he is important in *1 Henry IV*. Holinshed says that Glendower 'served King Richard at Flint Castle when he [Richard] was

taken by Henry, Duke of Lancaster'. Probably
Shakespeare's main reason for the choice of name
here was its obvious Welshness, though he may have
been thinking ahead to the events of the reign of
Henry IV.

III.2   The basis of this scene is Holinshed, who reports that
the King 'landed near the castle of Barkloughly in
Wales ... and stayed a while in the same castle,
being advertised of the great forces which the Duke of
Lancaster had got together against him, wherewith he
was marvellously amazed, knowing certainly that those
which were thus in arms with the Duke of Lancaster
against him would rather die than give place, as well
for the hatred as fear which they had conceived at
him.' He went to Conway, 'but when he understood
as he went thus forward that all the castles even from
the borders of Scotland unto Bristol were delivered
unto the Duke of Lancaster, and that likewise the
nobles and commons as well of the south parts as
the north were fully bent to take part with the same
Duke against him; and further, hearing how his
trusty councillors had lost their heads at Bristol,
he became so greatly discomforted that, sorrowfully
lamenting his miserable state, he utterly despaired
of his own safety and, calling his army together,
which was not small, licensed every man to depart
to his home.' Holinshed's later comment is interesting as an expression of the kind of sympathy which
Shakespeare too begins to evoke; he writes how re-
markable it is that Bolingbroke should have been
advanced to the throne, 'and that King Richard
should thus be left desolate, void, and in despair of all
hope and comfort, in whom if there were any offence
it ought rather to be imputed to the frailty of wanton
youth than to the malice of his heart; but such is the

deceivable judgement of man which, not regarding things present with due consideration, thinketh ever that things to come shall have good success, with a pleasant and delightful end'.

(stage direction) *colours* banners

Bishop of Carlisle. He was Thomas Merke, a friend and follower of King Richard. The Pope appointed him Bishop in 1397, at Richard's request. He was arrested in 1399 and pardoned in 1400, after which he became a country vicar, and died in 1409. Holinshed reports that he died 'shortly after' 1400.

1   *Barkloughly*. The name derives from Holinshed, where it seems to be an error for a form of Harlech.

2   *brooks* enjoys

6-7   *I . . . rebels*. The two words are contrasted.

6   *salute* greet. Richard bends to touch the ground.

8   *long-parted mother with* mother long parted from

9   *fondly*. The word implies a mixture of affection and slight folly. Shakespeare often uses the image of tears and smiles at once, as in the description of Cordelia hearing news of King Lear: 'You have seen | Sunshine and rain at once: her smiles and tears | Were like a better way' (*King Lear*, IV.3.17-19). See also V.2.32.

14   *spiders that suck up thy venom*. It was believed that spiders were dangerously poisonous, and that they sucked their poison from the earth.

15   *heavy-gaited* (referring to the toad's clumsy movements)

     toads. Like spiders, they were thought to be poisonous.

21   *double* forked

23   *senseless* (addressed to things which lack the sense of hearing)

24-5   *stones* | *Prove armèd soldiers*. This seems like a reference to the myth of Cadmus, who sowed dragons' teeth which sprang up as soldiers. Gospel echoes are also possible: Luke 19.40: 'I tell you that if these would hold their peace then shall the stones cry immediately', and 3.8: 'God is able of these stones to raise up children unto Abraham.'

27   *Fear not* do not doubt that. Or perhaps *Fear not, my lord* should form a complete sentence.

29–32 These lines were omitted from F, perhaps because they are obscure. Perhaps they mean 'We must accept, not neglect, the means that the heavens offer; otherwise we run counter to heaven's wish – we refuse heaven's offer . . .'. The sentiment is common, e.g. Prospero in *The Tempest*, I.2.181–4:

> my zenith doth depend upon
> A most auspicious star, whose influence
> If now I court not, but omit, my fortunes
> Will ever after droop.

34   *security* over-confidence

36   *Discomfortable* disheartening. Shakespeare does not use the negative form elsewhere; it may have been suggested by Holinshed's statement that Richard became 'greatly discomforted'.

37–8 *when the searching eye of heaven is hid | Behind the globe, that lights the lower world.* Richard again compares himself with the sun; his absence in Ireland is like the nightly departure of the sun to light the other side of the world (*the lower world*). The notion that robberies are liable to take place at night is commonplace enough, but it may be worth comparing Falstaff's 'we that take purses go by the moon and the seven stars, and not "by Phoebus, he, that wandering knight so fair"' (*1 Henry IV*, I.2.13–15). The syntax of Richard's lines is obscure, and the sense difficult for the actor to convey, but this is probably what Shakespeare wrote. A common emendation alters *that* to 'and', which simplifies the sentence and makes the meaning clearer.

41   *this terrestrial ball* (the earth)

42   *He* (the sun)

215

42   *fires* (metaphorically) sets on fire

46   *at themselves* (at the revelation of their own wickedness)

49   *the Antipodes* (the people living on the opposite side of the earth. Richard has only been as far as Ireland, but the metaphor is continued from line 38.)

54   *rude* rough, stormy

55   *balm* consecrated oil

57   *elected* chosen

58   *pressed* conscripted

59   *shrewd* harmful

59–61   *crown ... angel*. These were both coins, on the names of which Shakespeare often puns. *In heavenly pay* establishes the wordplay which leads to the curious notion of wage-earning angels.

62   *still* always

63   *power* army (though Salisbury takes it in the more abstract sense)

64   *nea'er*. Q prints 'neare', which in Elizabethan English could mean 'nearer'. 'Nearer' is required by the sense, and in speaking could be elided to form one syllable.

67–74   For Richard in relation to time, see Introduction, page 36.

76–81   Here the verse takes the form of the sestet of a sonnet.

76   *But now* just now

         twenty. Perhaps the requirements of metre are responsible for the discrepancy with *twelve* (line 70).

79   *dead* death-like

80   *fly*. This may be indicative – 'do fly'; imperative – 'fly!'; or subjunctive – 'let [them] fly!'

90   *power* (including the sense of 'army')

         (stage direction) *Scroop*. Sir Stephen Scroop was a famous warrior, and was among the few who remained faithful to King Richard after his arrest. He died in 1408.

91   *betide* (subjunctive: 'may [they] betide . . .')

92   *care-tuned* tuned to the key of sorrow

93   *Mine ear is open.* Dr Johnson comments: 'It seems to
be the design of the poet to raise Richard to esteem in
his fall, and consequently to interest the reader in his
favour. He gives him only passive fortitude, the virtue
of a confessor rather than of a king. In his prosperity
we saw him imperious and oppressive, but in his
distress he is wise, patient, and pious.'

95   *care* trouble

99   *his fellow* (Bolingbroke's equal)

101   *They break their faith to God as well as us* (because the
King is God's deputy)

102   *Cry* (even if you) proclaim

109   *his limits* its banks

110   *fearful* filled with fear

111   *steel* (of arms and armour)

112   *Whitebeards* old men

114   *speak big* imitate men's tones
       female womanish

115   *stiff unwieldy* (perhaps because new, or because the
boys are not strong enough to wear it properly)
       arms armour

116   *beadsmen* almsmen, pensioners (with the duty of
offering prayers or 'beads' on behalf of their benefactors)

117   *double-fatal yew* (fatal both because the tree's berries
are poisonous and because its wood is used to make
bows)

118   *distaff-women* women normally occupied in spinning
       manage wield
       bills bill-hooks, halberds. These are *rusty* from long
disuse.

119   *seat* throne

122   *Where is Bagot?* He appears again in IV.1. It has been
thought odd that Richard, at line 132, in referring to
Three Judases, and again at line 141, when he names all
but Bagot, should seem to know without being told that
Bagot has survived. This may be the result of imper-

fect revision on Shakespeare's part. Ure comments: 'I suggest that Shakespeare, when he wrote l. 132, was already thinking ahead to ll. 141–2 and IV.1; he was planning to have one of the four men alive for IV.1, but forgot that Richard could not yet know, when he breaks out at l. 132, what Shakespeare was arranging to have him told at ll. 141–2: Shakespeare carelessly anticipated but did not grossly resurrect.' He may, however, have recalled that according to Holinshed Bagot 'escaped into Ireland', which probably means to join the King there. See Commentary to II.2.122.

125 *Measure* pass through
peaceful unopposed

128 *Peace have they made with him indeed.* The quibble on 'making peace' is not uncommon, and Scroop's line should carry a sombre irony. Compare *Macbeth*, IV.3.178–9:

MACDUFF
The tyrant has not battered at their peace?
ROSS
No. They were well at peace when I did leave 'em.

129 *vipers, damned without redemption.* The viper was traditionally treacherous. Shakespeare may have been influenced by Matthew 23.33: 'Ye serpents, ye generation of vipers, how will ye escape the damnation of hell?' (*without*, beyond hope of)

131 *Snakes in my heart-blood warmed, that sting my heart.* The image was common. Shakespeare uses it again at V.3.57 (*A serpent that will sting thee to the heart*), and in *2 Henry VI*, III.1.343–4: 'I fear me you but warmed the starvèd snake | Who, cherished in your breasts, will sting your hearts.' There was a well-known fable about a farmer bitten by a snake which he found nearly dead from cold and warmed in his breast.

132 *Judases.* Richard elsewhere (for example, IV.1.170)

218

compares himself to Christ; but Judas was a common word for a traitor.

133 *Would they make peace? Terrible hell.* The line is metrically short. This may be intended to invite emphasis on Richard's outburst. *They* is emphatic. F reads:

> Would they make peace? terrible Hell make warre
> Vpon their spotted Soules for this Offence.

This is probably an unauthentic attempt to regularize the metre.

134 *spotted* stained, sinful. There may also be a hint of the spotted skin of the viper.

135 *his property* its distinctive quality

138 *hands* (for signing treaties, or shaking in amity, or lifting in submission)

138-40 *Those . . . ground.* The inflated expression gives weight to the statement of a fact which has been in suspense since line 122.

140 *graved* buried

141 Richard's failure – or inability – to speak here may give a cue to the actor. As often in Shakespeare, affliction does not find immediate expression.

150 *deposèd.* Richard already sees himself as deposed from the throne. The word may also carry the sense of 'deposited'.

153-4 *that small model of the barren earth | Which serves as paste and cover to our bones.* Probably a reference to the flesh as microcosm, corresponding on a small scale to the earth. But *model* might also mean 'mould' or 'something that envelops closely'. According to this interpretation Richard says that all we finally possess is the earth that surrounds our body.

154 *paste* pastry (alluding to the pastry cover, sometimes called a coffin, in which meat was baked)

156 *stories of the death of kings.* The most famous collection of such stories was *A Mirror for Magistrates* (1559

etc.) but there were others. The lines that follow recall Shakespeare's *Richard III*, V.3, in which the ghosts of his dead enemies appear to Richard.

158   *ghosts they have deposed* ghosts of those whom they have deprived of life

162   *antic* buffoon, jester. Dr Johnson commented 'Here is an allusion to the *antick* or *fool* of old farces, whose chief part is to deride and disturb the graver and more splendid personages'; the image is continued in *little scene* (line 164). Death was frequently portrayed as a skeleton grinning at the futile pretensions of mankind.

163   *Scoffing his state* scoffing at his (the king's) splendour

164   *scene*. The image of life as a play enacted upon the stage of the world was common; see Introduction, page 46.

165   *monarchize* play a king's part. This is the first known use of the word.

        kill with looks (an image of kingly power, able to order execution with a glance)

166   *self and vain conceit* vain conceit of himself. *Self* is adjectival.

167-8   *As if this flesh which walls about our life | Were brass impregnable*. This may be influenced by Job 6.12: 'Is my strength the strength of stones? or is my flesh of brass?' But brass was a common symbol of imperishability. In the story of Friar Bacon and Friar Bungay, well known to Shakespeare and his audience through Robert Greene's play, one of Friar Bacon's aims is to surround Britain with a wall of brass; and Marlowe's Doctor Faustus says 'I'll have them wall all Germany with brass' (I.1).

168   *humoured thus*. Either 'death having thus amused himself'; or 'death having thus indulged the king'; or 'while the king is in this humour (mood)'. All three meanings may well be present.

169-70   *pin | Bores through his castle wall*. The image changes, and becomes that of an attack on a besieged castle.

171   *Cover your heads* replace your hats. Richard tells his subjects not to treat him with the reverence due to kingship. He is stressing his humanity.

175–6   The short lines invite the actor to use pauses for emphasis. There is no need to assume textual corruption.

176   *Subjected*. The King is a 'subject' – to human needs.

179   *presently* promptly
    prevent the ways to wail. An odd expression: *prevent* is used in the now obsolete sense 'avoid by prompt action'; *the ways to wail* seems to mean 'paths to grief'. The desire for alliteration probably played its part in the choice of words.

183   *to fight* in fighting; if you fight

184–5   *fight and die is death destroying death, | Where fearing dying pays death servile breath* to die fighting is to destroy death's power by means of death, whereas to live in fear of death is to pay it undeserved homage

186   *of* from (or perhaps, since at line 192 Richard inquires about York's whereabouts, 'about')

187   *make a body of a limb* make a single troop as effective as an entire army

189   *change* exchange
    our day of doom day that decides our fate

190   *overblown* blown over, passed away

194   *complexion* general appearance

196–7   *eye | My* eye that my. Q has a colon following *eye*. An alternative reading is that line 196 is a separate sentence.

198   *by small and small* little by little

199   *To lengthen out the worst* lengthening, stretching out the worst news. The metaphor is of the rack.

202   *gentlemen* men of rank
    gentlemen in arms (perhaps both 'gentlemen-in-arms', that is 'gentlemen bearing coats-of-arms', and 'gentlemen are up in arms')

203   *Upon his party* on his side

204   *Beshrew* (a mild oath) confound

204–5   *forth | Of* out of, away from

207–8   Dr Johnson comments 'This sentiment is drawn from
         nature. Nothing is more offensive to a mind convinced
         that his distress is without a remedy, and preparing to
         submit quietly to irresistible calamity, than these
         petty and conjectured comforts which unskilful
         officiousness thinks it virtue to administer.'

212   *ear* plough, till
         the land (metaphorically for Bolingbroke's cause)

213   *none* no hope (of growing, or prospering)

214   *counsel is but vain* advice (to the contrary) will be
         ineffectual

215   *double wrong* (in thinking to deceive me and in increas-
         ing my grief by again leading me into false hope. The
         notion of the *double* or forked *tongue* of a snake may be
         present.)

III.3   This scene takes place outside the walls of Flint
         Castle, on the estuary of the River Dee. It is based on
         Holinshed, though Shakespeare has omitted an episode
         in which King Richard, having arrived in Wales, is
         kidnapped and forcibly taken to Flint.
         Staging
         The staging of this scene presents problems. The first
         episode takes place outside the castle (lines 20, 26).
         Bolingbroke sends Northumberland towards the castle
         in order to deliver his message (line 32). In the mean-
         time he and those with him will *march | Upon the
         grassy carpet of this plain* (lines 49–50), and he gives the
         command to do so. Some stylization of movement
         seems inevitable. Perhaps on the Elizabethan stage
         Bolingbroke and his men would have conversed at the
         front of one side of the platform, and marched across
         to the other. Richard's entry at line 61 must be on an
         upper level and therefore at the back of the stage. For

the staging of the rest of the scene, see Commentary to line 61, stage direction, and line 183, stage direction.

(stage direction) *colours* banners

1   *So that by this intelligence.* . . . The scene begins in the middle of a conversation. Presumably Bolingbroke enters with a written message that he has been reading.

    intelligence information

6   *hid his head* taken shelter

6–11 On the significance of this quibbling, see Introduction, pages 23–4.

13 *so brief . . . to* so brief as to

14 *taking . . . the head* acting without restraint *and* omitting the title

15 *Mistake* misunderstand

17 *mistake the heavens are* 'fail to remember that the heavens are' or 'transgress against the heavens which . . .' (though this does not suit well with Bolingbroke's response). Some editors break the sentence after *mistake*.

25 *lies* resides, dwells

31 *Noble lord* (probably Northumberland)

32 *rude ribs* rough walls

33 *breath of parley* call (of a trumpet) inviting opponents to conference

34 *his* its. This is the normal form; but the *ears* may be the King's as well as the castle's. Coleridge commented: 'I have no doubt that Shakespeare purposely used the personal pronoun, "his", to shew, that although Bolingbroke was only speaking of the castle, his thoughts dwelt on the king.'

35 *Henry Bolingbroke.* Coleridge commented: 'almost the only instance in which a name forms the whole line; Shakespeare meant it to convey Bolingbroke's opinion of his own importance'.

40 *banishment repealed* the revoking of my banishment

42 *advantage of my power* superiority of my forces

43   *summer's dust*. Historically it was August 1399.

45   Coleridge's comment may afford a hint to the actor: 'At this point Bolingbroke seems to have been checked by the eye of York. . . . He passes suddenly from insolence to humility, owing to the silent reproof he received from his uncle.' But Bolingbroke could be hypocritical rather than humble. Coleridge suggests that 'York again checks him' at the end of line 57.

46   *is such* is that such

48   *stooping duty* submissive kneeling

52   *tattered* 'having pointed projections' or 'dilapidated' (in contrast with *Our fair appointments*). The word does not necessarily imply that the castle is easily to be taken, though *ruined ears* (line 34) might support such an interpretation.

53–61   *fair appointments . . . on the walls*. Holinshed reports that Northumberland 'mustered his army before the King's presence, which undoubtedly made a passing fair show', and that the King 'was walking aloft on the brayes [outworks] of the walls to behold the coming of the Duke afar off'. His companions here seem to derive from a later stage in Holinshed's account, corresponding to Shakespeare's line 176: 'The King accompanied with the Bishop of Carlisle, the Earl of Salisbury, and Sir Stephen Scroop, knight, who bare the sword before him, and a few other, came forth into the outer ward and sat down in a place prepared for him.'

53   *appointments may be well perused* equipment may be well observed. The silence of the drums will make this a peaceable show of strength.

56   *fire and water* (in the form of lightning and rain or cloud)

56–7   *shock | At meeting tears the cloudy cheeks of heaven*. Bolingbroke alludes to the belief that thunder was caused by a clash between the opposed elements of fire and water in the form of lightning and rain.

57   *cheeks of heaven.* This may allude to the puffing cheeks of cherubs often represented in maps.

58   *fire ... yielding water.* In the traditional 'chain of being' fire was dominant among the elements, so water would 'yield' to it. Similarly Richard is seen in line 63 as the sun, dominant among planets, in line 68 as the king, dominant among men, and in line 69 as the eagle, dominant among birds. Bolingbroke is not obviously yielding to Richard. He may be claiming that while Richard rages, Bolingbroke will drop tears of sorrow on the ground. There may also be the implication that this is the more fruitful thing to do.

59–60 *I rain | My waters – on the earth, and not on him.* This is a difficult passage. Q prints:

            I raigne.
    My water's on the earth, and not on him.

If the second of these lines is intended to be a separate sentence, it may mean 'My (beneficent) water falls on the earth, not on Richard'. This would also mean that a strong pun would be felt in line 59 ('rain', 'reign'). On the other hand the full stop after 'raigne' in Q may be accidental – it comes at the end of a page. If so, Bolingbroke must mean 'Let him rage in anger while I scatter my blessings on the earth, though not on Richard.'

61   (stage direction) King Richard's appearance on the walls is an impressive moment. When he speaks, at line 72, he explains why he has not spoken before. This strongly suggests that his entry should be made in silence, to be commented on by Bolingbroke and York only when he has taken up his position. Formality of staging seems essential. Probably Northumberland and the other lords should be with the trumpeters, as Bolingbroke has instructed them to speak on his behalf, and King Richard's amazement (line 72) should be addressed directly to them.

Bolingbroke and York should stand somewhat aside (line 91).

The trumpets sound parley without, and answer within. This presumably means that the stage trumpets (those *without*) sound and are answered by the backstage ones (those *within*), imagined to be inside the castle.

the walls (the upper level of the stage)

63   *blushing, discontented sun.* This passage may be referring to the proverb 'A red morning foretells a stormy day'. The rising sun is *discontented* because the day is to be one of bad weather.

65   *he* (the sun)

        envious. In Shakespeare's time this word had the stronger sense of 'hostile', 'harmful', rather than simply 'jealous'.

68   *Yet* 'still' as well as 'nevertheless'

68–9   *eye, | As bright as is the eagle's.* The eagle, king of birds, was believed to be able to look into the sun, chief of the heavenly bodies, without coming to harm.

69   *lightens forth* sends down as lightning, flashes out

71   *stain* (compare line 66)

        show sight

72 ff.   *We.* Richard repeatedly uses the royal plural.

72–3   *stood | To watch* stood in expectation of seeing

76   *awful duty* duty of showing awe or reverence

77   *hand* signature

79–81   *hand . . . he.* The hand is representative of the person.

81   *profane* commit sacrilege

83   *torn their souls* (sinned by turning their allegiance from Richard to Bolingbroke. The jingle with *turning* is deliberate.)

85   *my.* Here and later in the speech Richard lapses from the plural form as he speaks of himself as an individual rather than a king.

88–9   *Your children . . . | That lift your* the children . . . of you who lift your

89   *vassal* subject

91   *yon methinks he stands.* King Richard has not so far
       addressed Bolingbroke since he returned from exile,
       and now does not deign to address him directly.

93–4   *open | The purple testament open* the blood-coloured will
       (– in which war is bequeathed – preparatory to putting
       it into operation)

95   *ere the crown he looks for live in peace* before the English
       crown, which Bolingbroke hopes for (or 'expects'),
       may be worn in peace

95–6   *crown . . . crowns* crown (of kingship) . . . heads

97   *the flower of England's face.* Three senses are felt.
       England is likened to a flower; so is the human face;
       and *the flower* suggests brave young men.

100   *pastor's* shepherd's (Richard's). Many editors read
       'pasture's' or 'pastures' '.

102   *civil and uncivil arms. Civil,* used in civil war; *uncivil,*
       barbarous.

103   *thrice-noble* (by descent from Edward III; by descent
       from John of Gaunt; and on his own account, as the
       following lines make plain)

106   *your royal grandsire* (King Edward III)

108   *head* source (as of a spring)

112   *scope* aim

113   *lineal royalties* hereditary rights of royalty

114   *Enfranchisement* freedom from banishment (and
       restoration of rights)

115   *thy royal party* your majesty's part

116   *commend* hand over

117   *barbèd* armoured with barbs (coverings for the breasts
       and flanks of war-horses)

121–2 *returns | His* replies that his

128   *look so poorly* seem so abject
       speak so fair speak so courteously

136   *sooth* blandishment, flattery

140   *Swellest thou, proud heart? I'll.* Q has 'Swellst thou
       (prowd heart) Ile' which might suggest the meaning
       'If thou swellest, I'll . . .', but the interrogative form

227

seems more actable. Presumably the King's excited state of mind has a physical effect; the actor would naturally put his hand to his heart.

140–41   *scope* ... *scope* room, space ... permission, opportunity (and compare line 112)

143–54   This passage may have been suggested by Hall's *Chronicle*, where it is said that Richard 'with a lamentable voice and a sorrowful countenance delivered his sceptre and crown to the Duke of Lancaster, requiring every person severally by their names to grant and assent that he might live a private and a solitary life, with the sweetness whereof he would be so well pleased that it should be a pain and punishment to him to go abroad'.

143   *the King ... he.* Richard begins by referring to himself in the third person, as if conscious of the division between the man and the office.

146   *A* in

147   *a set of beads* a rosary

149   *gay apparel.* Richard was known for his extravagance in dress. Holinshed records that 'he was in his time exceeding sumptuous in apparel, insomuch as he had one coat which he caused to be made for him of gold and stone, valued at 30,000 marks'. See also Commentary to II.1.21.

       almsman (beggar who prayed for those who gave him alms). *Gown* suggests one who wore the uniform of a particular institution.

150   *figured* decorated

       dish of wood (alms-dish)

151   *palmer* pilgrim

152   *carvèd saints* (wooden figures of saints such as might be in a monk's cell)

154   *obscure* (accented on the first syllable)

155   *I'll be buried in the King's highway.* There is obvious irony in the suggestion that the King will be buried, not in a sanctified place, but under his own highway.

156   *trade* traffic (quibbling with *tread*, in line 158)

159   *buried once* once I am buried

162   *Our sighs and they* (like wind and rain)
        lodge beat down

163   *revolting* rebelling

164   *play the wantons* play a game, amuse ourselves

165   *make some pretty match* play a clever game

166   *still* continually

167   *fretted us* worn out for us

168–9   *there lies | Two kinsmen digged their graves with weeping eyes.* The rhyme helps to give this the quality of an imaginary epitaph.

171   *idly* foolishly

173–4   *Will his majesty | Give Richard leave to live till Richard die?* (a trick question, showing Richard's distrust)

175   *make a leg* make an obeisance, a bend of the knee. Addressing Northumberland, Richard seems ironically to be saying that if Northumberland gives assent, Bolingbroke is sure to say yes.

176   *base-court* (lower or outer court of the castle, occupied by servants)

177   *may it please you to come down.* This may mean 'if it please you to come down', or may be an independent question.

178   *glistering Phaethon.* Phaethon (three syllables) was the mythical son of Apollo, the sun-god. He borrowed his father's sun-chariot but was too weak to control it and drove dangerously close to the earth. Zeus prevented the destruction of the earth by killing Phaethon with a thunderbolt. The story was a common image of rash failure. It is especially appropriate to Richard in this play because of his frequent association with the sun (which was his own badge). 'Phaethon' is the Greek for 'shining' (or 'glistering').

179   *Wanting the manage of* lacking the power to control. *Manage* was a technical term in horsemanship.
        unruly jades (compared with the rebellious nobles.

Jades is a contemptuous term for horses.)

181   *do them grace* favour them

182   *base-court ... court*. Richard plays on the ideas of 'courtyard' and the King's 'court', and also puns on 'base'.

183   *night-owls shriek where mounting larks should sing* instead of the lark's song we hear the cries of owls, foreboding evil

    (stage direction) Probably on the Elizabethan stage the King and his followers left the upper stage and descended out of view of the audience. On the modern stage a stairway is sometimes used so that he is in view throughout.

185   *fondly* foolishly

187   *Stand all apart*. Probably he instructs his men to stand at a respectful distance from Richard.

188   (stage direction) *He kneels down*. This is one of the rare directions for action in Q.

188   *He kneels down ... force will have us do*. Holinshed has:
–207   'Forthwith as the Duke got sight of the King he showed a reverend duty, as became him in bowing his knee, and coming forward did so likewise the second and third time, till the King took him by the hand and lift [*sic*] him up, saying "Dear cousin, ye are welcome." The Duke humbly thanking him said "My sovereign lord and king, the cause of my coming at this present is, your honour saved, to have again restitution of my person, my lands and heritage, through your favourable licence." The King hereunto answered "Dear cousin, I am ready to accomplish your will, so that ye may enjoy all that is yours without exception."'

192   *Me rather had* I had rather

193   *courtesy* (combining the modern, general meaning with the sense of an obeisance)

195   *Thus high at least*. Richard touches his head to indicate the crown.

202   *hands*. F's 'Hand' may well be correct.

203   *want their remedies* lack the capacity to cure the misfortunes with which they show sympathy

204–5   *I am too young to be your father | Though you are old enough to be my heir.* Historically both Richard and Bolingbroke were thirty-three.

III.4   This scene has no historical basis. It is apparently set in the Duke of York's garden (see II.2.116–17 and III.4.70). In Q the direction refers to the Queen 'with her attendants', who are not distinguished in the speech prefixes. F has 'and two Ladies'. Shakespeare may have thought of more than two ladies, one perhaps suggesting each type of diversion; but the Folio probably reflects the stage practice of Shakespeare's time. The division of speeches in the present edition is arbitrary, and may be varied at will by a producer. On the significance of the scene, see Introduction, pages 26–7.

1   *here in this garden.* This phrase sets the scene economically.

3   *bowls.* This was a common Elizabethan game. Bowling greens were often found in gardens.

4   *rubs.* A *rub* in bowls was a technical term for anything which impeded the course of the bowl. It was often used metaphorically of a difficulty – 'Ay, there's the rub' (*Hamlet*, III.1.65).

5   *runs against the bias.* In bowls, *bias* is a weight inserted in the side of the bowl to make it run in a certain way. The Queen feels that her fortune is going against its natural inclination.

7–8   *can keep no measure ... no measure keeps* cannot dance (*measure*, dance step) ... knows no bounds

10   *tell tales.* See Introduction, pages 44–6.

13   *wanting* lacking, absent

14   *remember* remind

15   *being altogether had* since I possess it completely

18   *boots* helps

22–3   *And I could sing would weeping do me good, | And never
            borrow any tear of thee.* The Queen probably means
            that she herself has already wept so much that if this
            could have done her any good all would now be well,
            and she would feel like singing.

23   (stage direction) *Gardeners.* Q has 'Enter Gardeners',
            F 'Enter a Gardiner and two Seruants'. The Garden-
            er's first speech makes it clear that there are two
            under-gardeners. The fact that the Gardener has two
            men under him may make it less surprising that he
            should speak as formally as he does. The gardens of
            great Elizabethan estates were internationally famous,
            and their Head Gardeners had heavy responsibility.
            Admittedly Shakespeare's Gardener is not a pure
            administrator – he is going to *root away | The noisome
            weeds* – but he is a man of authority. More to the
            purpose, dramatically he is a symbolic rather than
            naturalistic character, and it is more important for
            the actor to concentrate attention on what he says than
            to entertain by his manner of saying it. See Introduc-
            tion, pages 26–7.

26   *My wretchedness unto a row of pins* I will wager my
            misery against something very trivial that . . .

27   *They will.* The metre seems to demand elision:
            'They'll.'

28   *Against a change* when a change is about to happen

29   *young.* Q1 has 'yong'; Q2–5, 'yon'; F, 'yond'. Q1 has
            superior authority and this looks like a simple case of
            progressive textual corruption. A. W. Pollard com-
            ments: 'it is the word "yong" that suggested the
            comparison of the fruit to "vnruly children" in the
            next line' (*King Richard II: A New Quarto*, 1916,
            page 56).
            apricocks apricots

31   *Stoop* (punning on the bending of the boughs and of
            the back of an old man)

31   *prodigal* (punning on 'excessive' and 'prodigal' or 'unruly' children; *weight* thus has both literal and metaphorical force)

32   *bending* (with the weight of the fruit)

35   *lofty* 'tall' and 'overweening'

36   *even* equal

38   *noisome* harmful

40, 54 (*first part*), 67   (speech prefixes) Neither Q nor F differentiates between the two men. The present arrangement is arbitrary.

40   *compass of a pale* (small area – in contrast to the kingdom)
    pale fence (and 'national boundary')

42   *firm* stable

43   *sea-wallèd.* Compare II.1.46–7.

46   *knots* (flower-beds laid out in intricate designs)

47   *caterpillars* (echoing Bolingbroke's word for the traitors, II.3.165)

48   *suffered* permitted

49   *fall of leaf* autumn

57   *at time of year* in season

58   *skin* (introduced to stress the metaphor)

59   *overproud in* excessively swollen with

65   *crown* (the king's, and the crown of a tree)

67   Editors have sometimes padded out the short line, but the rhythmical irregularity emphasizes the exclamation.

68   *Depressed* brought low

69   *'Tis doubt* there is a risk

72   *pressed to death.* An allusion to *la peine forte et dure*, a punishment of pressing to death inflicted by English law on those accused of felony or petty treason who refused to plead either guilty or not guilty: who, that is, like the Queen here, stood silent.

73   *old Adam's likeness.* Adam was the first gardener.

75   *suggested* tempted

79   *Divine* predict

82   *To breathe* in speaking

84–9   *Their fortunes both are weighed . . . King Richard down.*
        The Gardener's imagery anticipates the symbol of the
        buckets in IV.1.183–8.

84   *weighed* balanced against each other

86   *vanities* 'follies'; or specifically, 'Richard's favourites'
        (opposed to the *peers* of line 88)
        light (in the balance, and also 'of little value')

89   *odds* advantage, superiority

90   *Post* hasten

93   *Doth not thy embassage belong to me* does your message
        not concern me

95   *serve me* serve (your message) on me

96   *Thy sorrow* the sorrow that you report

98   *What* (perhaps 'why' rather than an exclamation)

104   *fall* let fall

105   *rue, sour herb of grace.* The herb 'rue' was known as
        'herb of grace' because 'rue' means 'repentance',
        which comes by the grace of God. Here it is associated
        especially with pity.

106   *for ruth* as a symbol of pity

IV.1   The place is Westminster Hall; Richard himself had
        caused it to be splendidly rebuilt. The material of the
        scene derives from Holinshed, but Shakespeare com-
        presses the time-scheme and rearranges the order of
        events. He begins with accusations against Aumerle by
        Bagot, Fitzwater, and others. According to Holinshed
        Bagot made his accusation on Thursday, 16 October
        1399, and Fitzwater two days later. Bolingbroke's
        proposal (line 87) that Mowbray be recalled from
        exile was made on 27 October. After Carlisle has
        reported Mowbray's death York enters with news of
        Richard's abdication. His brief speech reports the
        events of 30 September, when the commissioners who
        had witnessed the abdication reported to Parliament.

Bolingbroke's acceptance of the throne is resisted by
Carlisle, who speaks in defence of Richard. According
to Holinshed the Bishop made such a speech on 22
October, and it was directed, not against the deposition, but against the proposal that Richard 'might
have judgement decreed against him so as the realm
were not troubled by him'. Shakespeare then turns to
the account of the abdication, which happened in the
Tower of London on 29 September. In Holinshed
Richard signs an instrument of abdication, represented
in the play by his great speech of renunciation (lines
200–221). The scene's closing episode shows the
beginning of the Abbot of Westminster's plot against
King Henry. In Holinshed this was planned at the
Abbot's house some three months later.

(stage direction) *Fitzwater*. Walter, Baron Fitzwalter,
1368–1406 or 1407. *Fitzwater* is the form of the name
in Holinshed, representing the old pronunciation.

Surrey. The son of Richard's half-brother, Sir
Thomas Holland, he lived from 1374 to 1400, when
he was executed. He is the Earl of Kent referred to in
V.6.8, he and Aumerle both having been deprived of
their dukedoms for their parts in the conspiracy
against Bolingbroke – see Commentary to V.2.41. See
also the note on the Lord Marshal, I.1, opening stage
direction.

Abbot of Westminster. The Abbot at the time of the
events shown in the play was William of Colchester.

to Parliament. This (as in Q) and F's '*as to the Parliament*' suggest a processional entry.

2   *speak thy mind* (probably this is felt as a single,
      transitive verb – 'tell')

4   *wrought it with the King* 'persuaded Richard to have
      Gloucester killed' or 'collaborated with him in the
      plan to have him killed' (*wrought it*, 'worked' it,
      brought it about)

5   *timeless* untimely

235

6   *Aumerle.* Holinshed has: 'there was no man in the
       realm to whom King Richard was so much beholden
       as to the Duke of Aumerle; for he was the man that,
       to fulfil his mind, had set him in hand with all that
       was done against the said duke'.

10–17 *In that dead time when Gloucester's death was plotted ...*
       Than Bolingbroke's return to England. This is his-
       torically inaccurate, as Gloucester was killed before
       Bolingbroke's banishment.

10   *dead time* past (with all the overtones of 'dead')

11   *of length* long

12   *restful* quiet (untroubled by Gloucester's plots)

13   *Calais* (where Gloucester was killed)

15–19 *I heard ... cousin's death.* Holinshed says that in
       Bagot's bill read to the Parliament of 16 October 1399
       it was stated 'that Bagot had heard the Duke of
       Aumerle say that he had rather than twenty thousand
       pounds that the Duke of Hereford were dead, not for
       any fear he had of him, but for the trouble and mis-
       chief that he was like to procure within the realm'.

17   *Than Bolingbroke's return* (that is, than that Boling-
       broke should return – an elliptical construction)

18   *withal* as well

21   *fair stars* noble birth. Dr Johnson comments: 'The
       birth is supposed to be influenced by the *stars*, there-
       fore our author with his usual licence takes *stars* for
       birth.'

22   *On equal terms.* Aumerle, being of higher rank than
       Bagot, could refuse to fight him.

24   *attainder* accusation

25   *gage ... manual seal.* See Commentary to I.1.69.
       manual seal (or 'sign manual')

28   *being* it (the blood) is

29   *temper* quality (especially the bright surface of a well-
       tempered sword)

31–2   *Excepting one ... moved me so.* Though he despises
       Bagot as his inferior, Aumerle has challenged him.

Now he says that, for his own greater honour, he wishes his accuser were the noblest of all present except Bolingbroke, whom he would prefer to fight.

31 *best* highest in rank

32 *moved* angered

33–90 Holinshed's account of the examination of Bagot includes the statement that 'The Lord Fitzwater herewith rose up and said to the King that where the Duke of Aumerle excuseth himself of the Duke of Gloucester's death, "I say" quoth he "that he was the very cause of his death," and so he appealed him of treason, offering by throwing down his hood as a gage to prove it with his body. There were twenty other lords also that threw down their hoods as pledges to prove the like matter against the Duke of Aumerle.'

33 *thy valour* (possibly ironical: 'thy valorous self')

stand on insist on, raise difficulties about (as in 'stand on ceremony')

sympathy correspondence (in rank). Fitzwater sneeringly asserts his equality with Aumerle.

34 *in gage* in pledge

40 *rapier*. This could be either a long or a short sword, used for thrusting. It was in use in Shakespeare's time, but not in Richard II's. Dr Johnson sternly commented: 'The edge of a sword had served his purpose as well as the point of a rapier, and he had then escaped the impropriety of giving the English nobles a weapon which was not seen in England till two centuries afterwards.'

45 *appeal* accusation

all entirely

47–8 *to the extremest point | Of mortal breathing* to the death

49 *And if* (perhaps *An if*, if)

50 *more* again

52–9 F omits these lines, perhaps simply to economize on actors, perhaps because the number of challenges seemed excessive. See Introduction, page 28.

52   *task the earth to the like* charge the earth in similar fashion (perhaps by throwing down another gage)

53   *lies* accusations of lying

54   *hollowed* shouted loudly, 'hollered'

55   *From sun to sun* from sunrise to sunset. This was the prescribed time-limit for single combat. Q reads 'sinne to sinne', which could conceivably be defended.

56   *Engage it* take up the gage, accept the challenge

57   *Who sets me else?* who else challenges me, puts up stakes against me? *Sets* and *throw* are both dicing metaphors.

62   *in presence* present

65   *boy* (a strong insult here; the word was used of a menial servant)

66   *That lie* (both the accusation of lying, and the lie that the accusation is. These lines are full of quibbles on the word.)

67   *it shall render* my sword will give back in return (for the accusation)

72   *How fondly dost thou spur a forward horse* (related to the proverb 'Do not spur a free horse')
       fondly foolishly, unnecessarily
       forward willing

74   *in a wilderness* (that is, even in a wilderness, where they would fight uninterrupted to the bitter end. Compare I.1.64–6.)

76   *There is my bond of faith* there is my gage (or *honour's pawn*, line 70). Either he throws down a second gage or points to the one he threw at line 34.

77   *tie thee to my strong correction* engage you to undergo severe punishment at my hands

78   *in this new world* (under the new order, with a new king)

79   *appeal* accusation

80   *Norfolk* (Mowbray)

83–4   *Some honest Christian trust me with a gage. | That Norfolk lies.* Q and F have a comma after *gage*.

Aumerle is asking to borrow a gage, either because he has thrown down both his gloves (at lines 25 and 57) or because Shakespeare is now thinking of the gages as hoods not gloves (see Commentary to I.1.69). It may be that he asks specially to be trusted with a gage with which to prove *That Norfolk lies*. If so he receives it after *lies*. Otherwise he receives it after *gage* and then says 'Now I throw down this to prove that . . .'.

85   *repealed* called back (from banishment)
     to try his honour. This may modify *repealed* ('called back in order to put his honour to the test') or *throw* ('I throw this down . . . as a test of his honour').

86–9   *These differences . . . signories*. Holinshed: 'The King licensed the Duke of Norfolk to return, that he might arraign his appeal.' Holinshed also reports that 'This year Thomas Mowbray, Duke of Norfolk, died in exile at Venice, whose death might have been worthily bewailed of all the realm if he had not been consenting to the death of the Duke of Gloucester.'

86   *rest under gage* remain as challenges

89   *he is*. This is printed as 'he's' in F, and elision seems necessary; but the line is long in any case.

90   *we*. Bolingbroke begins to use the royal plural.
     his trial (either 'Aumerle's testing of Mowbray's honour', or 'Mowbray's proving of his honour in opposition to Aumerle' – in either case, in trial by combat)

91   *never*. So Q; 'ne're' F, which may indicate the correct pronunciation.

93   *field* (of battle)

96   *toiled* exhausted
     retired himself withdrew

103–4   *bosom | Of good old Abraham* (a biblical – and pro-verbial – way of saying 'heavenly rest')

108   *plume-plucked* humbled (possibly in reference to the fable attributed to Aesop about the crow that dressed

239

itself in stolen feathers and was shamed when other
birds took them away)

112   *fourth of that name.* The metre seems defective, and
F's version – 'of that name, the fourth' – is attractive.

113–35   Holinshed reports that Carlisle 'boldly showed forth
his opinion concerning that demand' (that Richard,
having abdicated, should be tried), 'affirming that
there was none amongst them worthy or meet to give
judgement upon so noble a prince as King Richard
was, whom they had taken for their sovereign and
liege lord by the space of two-and-twenty years and
more. "And I assure you," said he, "there is not so
rank a traitor nor so arrant a thief nor yet so cruel a
murderer apprehended or detained in prison for his
offence but he shall be brought before the justice to
hear his judgement; and will ye proceed to the judgement of an anointed king, hearing neither his answer
nor excuse? I say that the Duke of Lancaster, whom
ye call king, hath more trespassed to King Richard and
his realm than King Richard hath done either to him
or us.'

115–16   *Worst in this royal presence may I speak, | Yet best
beseeming me to speak the truth* though in the presence
of royalty it is as the lowest in rank that I speak, still
it is fitting that I even more than anyone else should
speak the truth (as I am a bishop). It is interesting that
the Bishop modifies *royal* to *noble* two lines later,
perhaps as he is about to deny Bolingbroke's regality.

119   *noblesse* nobility

120   *Learn him forbearance* teach him to refrain
foul a wrong (as presuming to sit in judgement on his
King)

123   *but* except when

124   *apparent* obvious

125   *figure* image

126   *elect* chosen

129   *forfend it God* may God forbid

130   *souls refined* civilized, or Christianized, people

134   *My Lord of Hereford.* The Bishop uses the least of
       Bolingbroke's titles.

136–49 *let me prophesy.* The Bishop's prophecy recalls John of
       Gaunt's (II.1.33–68), though this is spoken in favour
       of Richard, whereas that criticized him. The two thus
       reflect a central problem of the play: that England,
       which has suffered under Richard's irresponsible
       reign, will suffer too if his right to the crown is
       usurped. Carlisle looks forward to the state of affairs
       to be portrayed in *1* and *2 Henry IV*. His sentiments
       reflect those of the 'Homily against Disobedience and
       Wilful Rebellion', which was familiar through being
       regularly read aloud in church.

141   *kin with kin, and kind with kind, confound* destroy
       kinsmen and fellow-countrymen by their own actions.
       The killing of each other by members of the same
       family, and especially of son by father or father by
       son, is a common symbol in Shakespeare for the
       worst kind of disorder such as is brought about by
       civil war.

144   *field of Golgotha and dead men's skulls.* Golgotha, or
       Calvary, where Jesus Christ was crucified, means 'the
       place of skulls'. Carlisle anticipates Richard's com-
       parisons of himself with Christ (lines 169–71, 238–41).
       In the Bishops' Bible Golgotha is called 'a place of a
       skull' (Mark 15.22, etc.), and the Prayer Book Gospel
       for Good Friday includes John 19.17: 'and went forth
       into a place which is called the place of dead men's
       skulls; but in Hebrew Golgotha'.

145   *this house against this house.* Carlisle foresees the Wars
       of the Roses, with an echo of biblical phraseology as in
       Mark 3.25: 'And if a house be divided against itself
       that house cannot continue.'

149   *cry against you woe* (woe probably has adverbial rather
       than exclamatory force)

150–53 *Well ... day of trial.* Holinshed: 'As soon as the

241

Bishop had ended this tale he was attached by the Earl Marshal and committed to ward in the abbey of Saint Albans.'

151   *Of* on a charge of

154   This passage is not in Q1–3. See 'An Account of the
–319   Text', page 269, and Introduction, page 12.

154   *commons' suit.* Holinshed: 'On Wednesday [22 October 1399] following, request was made by the commons that sith King Richard had resigned and was lawfully deposed from his royal dignity, he might have judgement decreed against him, so as the realm were not troubled by him, and that the causes of his deposing might be published through the realm for satisfying of the people; which demand was granted.'

156   *surrender* (his throne); abdicate

157   *conduct* escort

159   *sureties* men who will be responsible for your appearance

       your days of answer the time when you must appear to stand trial

161   *looked for* expected

       (stage direction) From this point onwards F ceases to use 'King' for Richard in speech prefixes and stage directions. Q continues to do so till the end of V.1.

163   *shook* shaken (a common Elizabethan form)

167   *Yet I well remember....* Holinshed: 'Which renunciation to the deposed king was a redoubling of his grief, insomuch as thereby it came to his mind how in former times he was acknowledged and taken for their liege lord and sovereign, who now – whether in contempt or in malice, God knoweth – to his face forsware him to be their king.'

168   *favours* 'faces' and 'friendly acts'

170   *Judas did to Christ.* Matthew 26.49: 'And forthwith when he came to Jesus, he said "Hail, master"; and kissed him.'

171   (an alexandrine)

173   *clerk* altar-server (who makes the responses – *Amen* being the most frequent – at the end of each prayer read by the priest)

176   *service* (punning on the ecclesiastical and the general sense)

180   *Give me the crown.* Presumably it has been carried in by Richard's attendants.

183   *Now is this golden crown like a deep well.* In stage practice it is most effective if the crown is held upside-down between Richard and Bolingbroke. The notion of Fortune's buckets is not uncommon in medieval and Elizabethan literature. There was a proverbial expression 'Like two buckets of a well, if one go up the other must go down.'

184   *owes* owns, has

       filling one another (because when the full bucket is raised it causes the other to descend and be filled in turn)

194–6   *Your cares ... new care won.* These lines include elaborate wordplay on *care*. First it means 'grief', then 'responsibility', then 'diligence', then 'anxiety'. We may paraphrase: 'The cause of my grief is my loss of responsibility, brought about by my former lack of diligence; the cause of your trouble is the access of responsibility achieved by your recent pains.'

198   *'tend* are attendant upon

200   *Ay, no. No, ay.* Both 'Yes, no. No, yes' and 'I, no. No I'. M. M. Mahood comments: 'besides suggesting in one meaning (Aye, no; no, aye) his tormenting indecision, and in another (Aye – no; no I) the over-wrought mind that finds an outlet in punning, also represents in the meaning "I know no I" Richard's pathetic play-acting, his attempt to conjure with a magic he no longer believes. Can he exist if he no longer bears his right name of King? The mirror shows him the question is rhetorical but he dashes it to the ground, only to have Bolingbroke expose the self-

deception of this histrionic gesture: "The shadow..." '
(*Shakespeare's Wordplay*, page 87).

200 *nothing* (and '*no* thing')

201 *no no, for I resign to thee* (I cannot say 'no', because in fact I *do* resign in your favour)

202 *undo* ('undress', as he removes the emblems of kingship, 'unmake', and 'ruin')

203 *heavy weight* (the crown: *heavy* also meaning 'sad')

206 *balm* consecrated oil (with which he had been anointed at his coronation)

209 *release all duteous oaths* release my subjects from all the oaths of allegiance to me that they have sworn

211 *revenues* (accented on the second syllable)

214 *are made* (that) are made

215 *Make me* (God) make me

 with nothing grieved. There is deliberate paradox here. Richard asks to be grieved by having nothing, but also to be grieved by nothing. The ambiguity is highly expressive of the delicate balance of Richard's state of mind, wishing to be relieved of his care yet reluctant to give up his crown.

221–2 *that you read | These accusations*. In Holinshed Richard himself 'read the scroll of resignation', though 'for the articles which before ye have heard were drawn and engrossed up ... the reading of those articles at that season was deferred'. Shakespeare chooses not to remind us of Richard's sins.

221 *read* (aloud, as an admission of guilt)

227 *ravel out* unravel; expose

229 *record* (accented on the second syllable)

231 *read a lecture* (read aloud, as a warning)

232 *heinous article*. Holinshed reports that Parliament considered the thirty-three articles 'heinous to the ears of all men'.

 article item

234 *oath* (Bolingbroke's oath of loyalty)

237 *bait* torment

238   *with* like

        with Pilate. Bolingbroke had implicitly compared himself to Pilate at III.1.5–6. The image occurs in Holinshed where, in the Flint Castle episode, the Archbishop of Canterbury promises that Richard shall not be hurt, 'but he prophesied not as a prelate, but as a Pilate'.

240   *delivered*. This may create a quibble on *Pilate* as 'pilot'. Christ was 'delivered' to Pilate and by him back to the Jews.

        sour bitter

245   *sort* pack, gang (contemptuous). Perhaps there is a pun on *salt*.

248–9   *soul's . . . body*. In this antithesis, frequent in the play, Richard asserts his right to the crown while renouncing its attributes.

249   *pompous* magnificent, splendid

251   *state* stateliness

253   *haught* haughty

256   *'tis usurped* (possibly an allusion to the Lancastrian rumour that Richard was illegitimate. Or he may mean that now he is unkinged, he has no identity. Either he admits that he himself usurps a name to which he has no right, or he claims that others usurp his name from him.)

260   *sun of Bolingbroke*. Now the image of the sun is transferred from Richard to Bolingbroke.

261   *water-drops* tears

263   *An if* if

        sterling valid currency. The image is continued in *bankrupt* (line 266).

264   *straight* immediately

266   *his* its

267   *some* (could mean 'some one')

269   *torments* (a form of 'tormentest')

280   *Was this face. . . .* It is difficult not to associate these lines with Marlowe's *Doctor Faustus*, V.1.99: 'Was

this the face that launched a thousand ships . . .', and Shakespeare's audience, too, may well have noticed the resemblance. Marlowe's play was written a few years before Shakespeare's.

281–2 *under his household roof | Did keep ten thousand men.* Holinshed, summarizing Richard's character, says that 'there resorted daily to his court above ten thousand persons that had meat and drink there allowed them'.

283 *wink* close their eyes

284 *Is this the face which.* This is the reading of F, the most authoritative text for this section of the play. But Q4 repeats 'Was . . . that', as in lines 280 and 282. We cannot say for certain which is right, and an actor would be justified in following Q 4 if he preferred to do so.

284–5 *faced . . . outfaced* countenanced . . . discountenanced, superseded

285 *That.* Q 4 has 'And'. The situation is the same as that referred to in the note to line 284. An actor might prefer 'And'.

288 *an.* Q 4's reading, 'a', is also possible. See the note to line 284.

291–3 *shadow of your sorrow . . . 'shadow of my sorrow'.* Bolingbroke speaks contemptuously: 'the (mere) shadow cast by your sorrow', the action provoked by it, or *external manner of laments* (line 295) has destroyed the shadow of your face simply by passing across it, as one shadow obliterates another. Richard takes up the phrase with a suggestion of greater reality: 'the shadowing forth, or embodiment, of my sorrow'.

295 *these external manner* (an archaic construction comparable with 'all manner of', or the modern colloquial 'these kind of . . .'. Q 4's 'manners', followed by many editors, is probably a sophistication.)

296 *to* compared to

298 *substance* (opposed to *shadow*; compare II.2.14: *Each substance of a grief hath twenty shadows*)

299   *thy . . . that* of you . . . who

307   *to* as

312   *Then give me leave to go.* Richard's request seems anti-
       climactic. It may represent a calculated deflation of
       Bolingbroke, Richard having led him to expect a more
       taxing request.

314   *sights* (the sight of each one of you)

316   '*convey*'. The word was slang for 'steal', and Richard
       picks it up in this sense.

317   *nimbly* (also associated with thieving. Compare *The
       Winter's Tale*, IV.4.667–8: 'a nimble hand is necessary
       for a cutpurse'.)

320   *pageant* spectacle. (The line would have been in-
       appropriate when the deposition scene was omitted.)

321 *to*   Holinshed reports on 'the conspiracy which was
end of   contrived by the Abbot of Westminster as chief
scene   instrument thereof'. The Abbot 'highly feasted these
          lords his special friends' and they devised the plot
          referred to at V.2.52, 96–9, and V.3.14–19.

328   *bury mine intents* conceal my plans

332   *supper*. The sentence is sometimes made to end here,
       but probably *Come* is subjunctive: 'If you will
       come . . .'.

V.1   The material of this scene is not derived from
       Holinshed (except for lines 51–2). In portraying a
       final meeting between Richard and his Queen Shake-
       speare may have been influenced by Samuel Daniel's
       Civil Wars, though his treatment is different; see
       Commentary to lines 40–50, and Introduction, page
       15.
       (stage direction) *attendants* (presumably the Ladies of
       III.4)

2   *Julius Caesar's ill-erected Tower* (the Tower of London.
       There was an old tradition that it had originally been
       built by Julius Caesar.)

2   *ill-erected* built for evil purposes or with evil results. The Queen is thinking especially of its present use, for imprisoning Richard.

3   *flint* flinty, merciless

6   (stage direction) *guard* (perhaps implying more than one man)

8   *rose.* In *1 Henry IV*, I.3.173, Hotspur calls Richard 'that sweet lovely rose'.

11   *the model where old Troy did stand.* She addresses Richard, and finds that in his present condition he is to his former self as the ruins of Troy were to the city in its greatness.
        model ground plan
        old Troy. London was known as 'Troia novans', or 'new Troy', because of a legend that after the Trojan war Aeneas led a party of Trojans to Britain and that his great-grandson, Brut, founded London and called it Troia-Nova.

12   *map* image, outline of former glory

15   *triumph is become an alehouse guest.* Triumph is entertained in the *alehouse* Bolingbroke, opposed to the more beautiful and stately *inn*.

18   *state* stateliness, splendour

22   *Hie* go, hasten

24–5   *Our holy lives must win a new world's crown | Which our profane hours here have thrown down* by leading holy lives we must win in heaven the crown that our worldly lives here have cast away

25   *thrown* (probably to be pronounced 'throwen'. F's 'stricken' could be correct)

29–31   *The lion dying thrusteth forth his paw | And wounds the earth, if nothing else, with rage | To be o'erpowered.* The comparison between a monarch and lion is commonplace, but Shakespeare may have been influenced here by Marlowe's *Edward II*, V.1.11–15, where Edward says of himself:

248

But when the imperial lion's flesh is gored
He rends and tears it with his wrathful paw,
And, highly scorning that the lowly earth
Should drink his blood, mounts up to the air.

32   *correction, mildly kiss.* F has 'correction mildly, kiss', which is as plausible a reading.

37   *sometimes* sometime, former

38   *even* (probably to be pronounced 'e'en')

40–50   *In winter's tedious nights ... a rightful king.* These lines seem to show the verbal influence of Daniel's *Civil Wars*, III, stanza 65. Richard soliloquizes on the difference between himself in prison and a peasant:

> Thou sitt'st at home safe by thy quiet fire,
> And hearest of others' harms, but feelest none;
> And there thou tellest of kings and who aspire,
> Who fall, who rise, who triumphs, who do moan.
> Perhaps thou talkest of me, and dost inquire
> Of my restraint, why I live here alone.
> O, know 'tis others' sin, not my desert,
> And I could wish I were but as thou art.

41   *tales.* See Introduction, page 45.

42   *betid* past

43   *quite* (or 'quit') requite, cap

44   *lamentable tale of me.* The phrase resembles one used by Sidney in *Astrophil and Stella* (published in 1591), in which the lover complains that his beloved wept to hear a sad tale of love but does not pity his real plight. So he says:

> Then think, my dear, that you in me do read
> Of lover's suit some sad tragedy.
> I am not I; pity the tale of me.

46   *For why* because (that is, 'weeping because')
       senseless inanimate, without feeling
       sympathize respond to

48   *weep the fire out.* There is an allusion to the 'weeping'
       of resin from burning wood, as in *The Tempest*,
       III.1.18–19, when Miranda says to Ferdinand 'When
       this burns, | 'Twill weep for having wearied you.'

49   *some* (of the brands)

52   *Pomfret* (Pontefract, in Yorkshire. Holinshed: 'For
       shortly after his resignation he was conveyed to the
       castle of Leeds in Kent, and from thence to Pomfret.')

53   *there is order ta'en* arrangements have been made

55–9   *Northumberland, thou ladder . . . into corruption.* These
       lines are recalled by King Henry in *2 Henry IV*,
       III.1.65–79:

              But which of you was by –
       You, cousin Nevil, as I may remember –
       When Richard, with his eye brimful of tears,
       Then checked and rated by Northumberland,
       Did speak these words, now proved a prophecy?
       'Northumberland, thou ladder by the which
       My cousin Bolingbroke ascends my throne' –
       Though then, God knows, I had no such intent
       But that necessity so bowed the state
       That I and greatness were compelled to kiss –
       'The time shall come,' thus did he follow it,
       'The time will come that foul sin, gathering head,
       Shall break into corruption'; so went on,
       Foretelling this same time's condition
       And the division of our amity.

58–9   *foul sin, gathering head, | Shall break into corruption* (like
       an ulcer or boil)

61   *helping him to all* as you have helped him to get it all

68   *worthy* deserved

69   *and there an end* (a common tag meaning 'and let that
       be the end of it')

70   *part . . . part* part (from your Queen) . . . depart

74   *unkiss the oath* (unseal with a kiss the marriage vow that
       had been ratified by a kiss)

75   *And yet not so* 'yet let us not kiss, since it was with a kiss that the vow was made', or 'yet the oath cannot be kissed away, as it was made with a kiss'

77   *pines the clime* afflicts the land

78   *pomp* splendour. Holinshed describes the great splendour of the wedding.

79   The scene moves into couplets for the grave, stylized parting of Richard and his Queen.

80   *Hallowmas.* All Saints' Day, 1 November; because of the change in calendar it corresponded in Shakespeare's time to our 12 November, so was closer to the shortest day.
      shortest of day (the winter solstice)

84   *That were . . . policy.* F, followed by most editors, gives this line to Northumberland, but this breaks the rhythm of the speeches and has no special authority.
      little policy hardly politic, poor statesmanship

86–96 These lines bring together many of the words in the play's vocabulary of grief – *weeping, woe, sighs, groans, moans, sorrow,* and *grief.* See Introduction, pages 41–2.

86   *So* (tantamount to 'No; for if so . . .')

88   *Better far off than, near, be ne'er the nea'er* it is better to be far apart than, being near to each other, be no closer to being together. Dr Johnson comments: 'To be *never the nigher,* or as it is commonly spoken in the midland counties, *ne'er the ne'er,* is, *to make no advance towards the good desired.*' The final word is a comparative form which has become contracted.

92   *piece the way out* make the journey seem longer

96   *mine* my heart. The conceit that lovers exchanged hearts was commonplace.

97   *Give me mine own again* (in a second kiss)

97–8 *'Twere no good part | To take on me to keep and kill thy heart* it would not be a good action for me to undertake to look after your heart and then to kill it (as my grief would kill me and therefore also it)

101   *make woe wanton* play verbal games with grief. The characters show consciousness of the dramatist's wordplay, as Gaunt and Richard had at II.1.84–8.
   fond loving yet also pointless

V.2   The first part (to line 40) is probably indebted to Daniel's *Civil Wars*, II, stanzas 66–70, which describe the triumphal entry of Bolingbroke into London, with the humbled Richard behind him. Holinshed too has a description of Bolingbroke's triumphal progress and reception. The remainder of the scene is based on Holinshed (see Commentary to line 52 *to end*).
   (stage direction) *the Duchess*. Historically, York's wife at this time was Aumerle's stepmother. Aumerle's mother, Isabella of Castile, had died in 1394. Shakespeare was mainly interested in providing a wife for York and a mother for Aumerle.

2   *story*. The Duchess's words recall Richard's prophecy that the Queen, by telling *the lamentable tale of me*, would *send the hearers weeping to their beds* (V.1.44–5).

3   *cousins* (Richard and Bolingbroke)

5–6   This episode is recalled by the Archbishop of York in *2 Henry IV*, I.3.103–7, speaking of Richard:

> Thou that threwest dust upon his goodly head,
> When through proud London he came sighing on
> After the admirèd heels of Bolingbroke,
> Criest now 'O earth, yield us that king again,
> And take thou this!'

5   *rude* (stronger in Shakespeare's time than now: 'brutal')
   windows' tops upper windows

6   *King Richard*. The Duchess still refers to Richard as the King.

9   *his aspiring rider seemed to know* seemed to know how aspiring its rider was

15–16   *that all the walls | With painted imagery*. This refers to the painted cloths common in Elizabethan houses, on which figures were portrayed with sentences issuing from their mouths, as in a strip cartoon. York imagines that the walls were covered with such cloths.

16   *at once* all together

19   *lower* (bowing lower, deferentially addressing the crowd)

21   *still* continually, all the time

24   *well graced* 'graceful' and 'popular'

25   *idly* listlessly, indifferently

27   *Even* (probably to be pronounced 'e'en')

28   *gentle*. This word is omitted in F. Since it is extrametrical and comes again in line 31, its presence in Q may be accidental.

33   *badges* outward signs (*tears* of grief, *smiles* of patience)

36   *barbarism itself* even savages

38   *bound our calm contents* submit ourselves in calm content

41   *Aumerle that was*. Holinshed: 'it was finally enacted that such as were appellants in the last Parliament against the Duke of Gloucester and other, should in this wise following be ordered: the Dukes of Aumerle, Surrey, and Exeter there present were judged to lose their names of Dukes, together with the honours, titles, and dignities thereunto belonging.'

42   *that* (that title)

43   *Rutland*. Aumerle had been made Earl of Rutland in 1390, and after the Duke of Gloucester's arrest was given the Dukedom of Aumerle.

44   *in Parliament*. See Commentary to line 52 *to end*.

46–7   *the violets now | That strew the green lap of the new-come spring* (those who are in favour in the new court)

52 to   *What news from Oxford? Do these justs and triumphs*
end of   *hold?* Holinshed reports that the Abbot of West-
scene   minster and his confederates 'devised that they should take upon them a solemn justs to be enter-

prised between him [the Earl of Huntingdon] and twenty on his part, and the Earl of Salisbury and twenty with him at Oxford, to the which triumph King Henry should be desired, and when he should be most busily marking the martial pastime he suddenly should be slain and destroyed, and so by that means King Richard, who as yet lived, might be restored to liberty and have his former estate and dignity.' When Huntingdon arrived at Oxford 'he found all his mates and confederates there, well appointed for their purpose, except the Earl of Rutland, by whose folly their practised conspiracy was brought to light and disclosed to King Henry. For this Earl of Rutland departing before from Westminster to see his father the Duke of York as he sat at dinner had his counterpane of the indenture of the confederacy in his bosom.

'The father espying it would needs see what it was; and though the son humbly denied to show it, the father being more earnest to see it by force took it out of his bosom, and, perceiving the contents thereof, in a great rage caused his horses to be saddled out of hand and, spitefully reproving his son of treason for whom he was become surety and mainpernor for his good a-bearing in open Parliament, he incontinently mounted on horseback to ride towards Windsor to the King to declare unto him the malicious intent of his complices.' (The remainder of the episode is represented in V.3.23 *to end.*)

52 *Do these justs and triumphs hold?* F reads 'Hold those jousts and triumphs?' This improves the metre; but the line may be deliberately irregular in preparation for the short ones that follow.

Do . . . hold will (they) be held

justs and triumphs tournaments and processional shows

55 *If God prevent not, I purpose so* (with sinister overtones)

56   *seal* (the wax seal, usually red, hanging from the document)

        without outside

57   *lookest.* The metre demands elision.

66   *'gainst* in preparation for

67   *Bound to himself?* York points out that if, as his wife suggests, Aumerle had borrowed money on a bond, the document would be in his creditor's possession, not his own.

74   Many editors add 'Enter a Servant' after *there.* This is unnecessary. York calls impatiently, and is not answered till line 84.

79   *I will appeach the villain* (*appeach*, inform against, denounce). York's vehemence against his son may be explained partly by the fact that he has entered into surety for Aumerle's loyalty (lines 44–5). Aumerle has thus let him down personally, as well as endangered him.

85–7   The reactions of the silent servant are a likely source of comedy in the staging of this episode.

85   *Strike him, Aumerle! Poor boy, thou art amazed.* Presumably the Duchess instructs her son to strike the servant so as to obstruct York's preparations for departure. But he is too *amazed* ('bewildered') to do so.

87   (stage direction) The servant's exit is not marked in the early editions. He could remain on stage as a bewildered, perhaps amused, observer of the quarrel between his master and mistress.

90   *Have we more sons?* Historically the answer was yes; York had another son, Richard, who is the Earl of Cambridge in *Henry V.*

91   *my teeming-date* the time during which I may have children

95   *fond* foolish

98   *interchangeably set down their hands* signed reciprocally (so that each had a record of the other's oath)

99   *He shall be none* he shall not be one of them

100   *that* what they do

103   *groaned* (in childbirth)

104   *Thou wouldst* (probably to be pronounced 'thou'dst')

113   Holinshed: 'Rutland, seeing in what danger he stood, took his horse and rode another way to Windsor in post, so that he got thither before his father.'

        post hasten

117-18   *never will I rise up from the ground | Till Bolingbroke have pardoned thee.* She fulfils this threat.

V.3   The first part of the scene looks forward to the plays about Prince Hal, and may have been written for this purpose. Legends about the young prince's dissolute behaviour were common. For the remainder of the scene, see Commentary to line 23 *to end*.

1   *unthrifty* prodigal, profligate

       son (Prince Hal, later Henry V; historically he was only twelve years old at this time)

3   *plague* calamity (as prophesied by Richard, III.3.85–90, and Carlisle, IV.1.137–47)

       hang over (because plague was believed to come from the clouds)

9   *watch* night-watchmen, civic guard

       passengers wayfarers, travellers

10   *Which*. The construction seems clumsy. Many editors emend to 'While'.

       wanton (probably the noun, meaning 'spoiled child')

11   *Takes on the* takes as a

15   *gallant* (accented on the second syllable) fine young gentleman (ironically)

16   *would* would go

       stews 'brothels' or 'disreputable area'

18   *with that* (with the glove as a favour)

20   *both* (both his *dissolute* and his *desperate* characteristics)

22   *happily* 'perhaps' and 'happily'

22   (stage direction) *amazed* (this is Q's word) distraught

23 *to*   Here Shakespeare resumes the episode begun at
end of   V.2.52 (see Commentary). Holinshed's narration con-
scene   tinues: 'The Earl of Rutland, seeing in what danger
he stood, took his horse and rode another way to
Windsor in post, so that he got thither before his
father, and when he was alighted at the castle gate he
caused the gates to be shut, saying that he must needs
deliver the keys to the King. When he came before the
King's presence he kneeled down on his knees, be-
seeching him of mercy and forgiveness, and, declaring
the whole matter unto him in order as everything had
passed, obtained pardon. Therewith came his father,
and, being let in, delivered the indenture which he
had taken from his son unto the King, who, thereby
perceiving his son's words to be true, changed his
purpose for his going to Oxenford and dispatched
messengers forth to signify unto the Earl of Northumberland his High Constable, and to the Earl of
Westmorland his High Marshal, and to other his
assured friends, of all the doubtful danger and
perilous jeopardy.' The conspirators rose in open
rebellion and were defeated at Cirencester.

25   *God save your grace.* Aumerle kneels, probably here,
and remains kneeling till line 37.

26   *To have* that I may have

30   *My tongue cleave to my roof within my mouth.* Compare
Psalm 137.6: 'let my tongue cleave to the roof of my
mouth'.

33   *on the first* (*Intended*, not *committed*)

34   *after-love* gratitude and future loyalty

35   *turn the key* (of one of the doors on the stage)

38–46   There are metrical irregularities in these lines – 41 and
45 are alexandrines, and 38, 40, and 46 are short lines –
but this is not uncommon in the play.

40   *safe* harmless (probably he draws his sword)

42   *secure* over-confident

257

43   *Shall I for love speak treason to thy face?* must I because of my love and loyalty speak treason (call you foolhardy) to your face?

49   *my haste forbids me show* (through lack of breath)

50   *thy promise passed* the promise you have passed (or 'given')

52   *hand* handwriting

56   *Forget* forget your promise

60   *sheer* pure

63   *converts to bad* changes to bad (in Aumerle)

65   *digressing* (continuing the metaphor of the stream) transgressing

66   *be his vice's bawd* serve his wickedness

67   *An* if. Q2 and later editions, as well as modern editors, read 'And'. But Q1 is the authoritative text, 'and' was in any case a common form of 'an' meaning 'if', and the sense is at least as good if we read *An* – York says 'if he consumes my honourable reputation in his shameful one, then my virtue . . .'.

69   *his dishonour dies* (that is, he dies himself)

79   *'The Beggar and the King'* (a reference to the title of an old ballad about King Cophetua and a beggar-maid. King Henry suggests that the *scene* has changed from that of a serious play to a frivolity.)

84–5   *This festered joint cut off, the rest rest sound; | This let alone will all the rest confound* if this diseased limb (Aumerle) is amputated, the others will remain healthy; otherwise it will contaminate and destroy all the others

87   *Love loving not itself, none other can.* Probably the Duchess means 'If York does not love himself (in his son), he can love no other', that is, his advice to Bolingbroke cannot be trusted. But the line could be a more private plea, addressed either to York or uttered as a generalization: 'If York does not love his own son, who else can be expected to do so?'

88   *make* do

89 *Shall thy old dugs once more a traitor rear?* are you, old as you are, going to rear this traitor anew (by redeeming him from death)?

92 *walk upon my knees* (a traditional form of penance)

96 *Unto* in support of

97 *true* loyal

101 *from our breast* (from the heart)

102 *would be denied* wishes to be refused

105 *still kneel* will kneel perpetually ('shall' in F and some editions)

112 *An if* if, supposing that

116 *short as sweet.* The saying 'short and sweet' was current in Shakespeare's time.

118 *'Pardonne-moi'* excuse me; forgive me for refusing you. *Moi* rhymes with *destroy*.

121 *sets the word itself against the word* makes the word contradict itself

123 *chopping* (a contemptuous word, perhaps meaning 'affected', or perhaps 'chopping and changing' with reference to the wordplay that has just been heard)

124 *to speak. Set thy tongue there* to show pity. Let your tongue express it.

125 *in thy piteous heart plant thou thine ear* (an exceptionally strained image) let there be no division between your ear and your piteous heart

126 *pierce* (pronounced to rhyme with *rehearse*, as in *Love's Labour's Lost*, IV.2.79: 'Master Person – quasi Pierce-one')

127 *rehearse* pronounce, repeat

129 *suit* (as in a card game – 'in hand' – as well as 'plea')

131 *happy vantage of* fortunate gain from

133 *Twice saying pardon doth not pardon twain.* Either the Duchess assures the King that to say 'pardon' again will not pardon someone else as well, or else *twain* means 'divide in two' in which case she must mean 'to say "pardon" again will not weaken the pardon (as a second negative weakens the first)'.

136 *But* but as for

trusty (ironically)

brother-in-law (John Holland, Duke of Exeter and Earl of Huntingdon, Richard II's half-brother on his mother's side). He had married Bolingbroke's sister, Elizabeth, and was deprived of his dukedom at the same time as Aumerle (see Commentary to V.2.41). He is referred to at II.1.281, but the reference here is not likely to mean much to the audience.

the Abbot (of Westminster, who appears at the end of IV.1)

137 *consorted crew* conspiring gang (there were about a dozen altogether; see V.2.96-9)

138 *straight* immediately

139 *powers* forces

145 *old* unregenerate. She refers to his character thus far, which she wishes to be changed. In fact Aumerle did 'prove true'. He died heroically at the Battle of Agincourt. Shakespeare describes his death in *Henry V*, IV.6.3-32.

old . . . I pray God make thee new. The biblical 'Therefore if any man be in Christ he is a new creature; old things are passed away; behold, all things are become new' (2 Corinthians 5.17) had passed into proverbial use.

V.4 This scene is based on Holinshed: 'One writer which seemeth to have great knowledge of King Richard's doings saith that King Henry, sitting on a day at his table, sore sighing, said "Have I no faithful friend which will deliver me of him, whose life will be my death, and whose death will be the preservation of my life?" This saying was much noted of them which were present, and especially of one called Sir Piers of Exton. This knight incontinently departed from the court with eight strong persons in his company, and

came to Pomfret. . . .' Shakespeare's indebtedness to
this episode resumes at V.5.98.

(stage direction) Q has no scene divisions, and its
direction here is '*Manet sir Pierce Exton, etc.*' Exton
may have been among the nobles on stage at the
beginning of the previous scene, but it seems unlikely
that he would remain throughout the interview with
York and his family: see V.3.27: *Withdraw yourselves,
and leave us here alone.*

Sir Piers of Exton. Nothing is known of him except
that he is said to have been the murderer of King
Richard.

Man servant (Q has '*Man*' as the speech prefix; F has
'*Enter Exton and Servants*'. Only one servant is
necessary, but there may be others.)

2   *will* who will
5   *urged it* insisted on it
7   *wishtly.* The context makes it clear that this word
means 'intently' or 'significantly', but the exact form
and meaning of the word are doubtful. It may be a
variant form of 'wistly' (as it is printed in Q 3–5 and F),
meaning 'intently', or of 'whistly', meaning 'silently',
or of the later dialectical 'wisht' meaning 'melancholy'.
11 *rid* get rid of

V.5   Most of the first part is invented. Later Shakespeare
uses Holinshed; see Commentary to line 98.
3   *for because* because
5   *hammer it out* puzzle it out
8   *generation* progeny, offspring
still-breeding thoughts thoughts which will continually
produce other thoughts
9   *this little world* (the prison; also perhaps his *little
world* of man – itself a prison)
10 *In humours like the people of this world* in their tem-
peraments like the people of this real world

13 *scruples* doubts

13-14 *do set the word itself | Against the word* set one passage of Scripture against another, contradictory one (the expression is also used at V.3.121)

14-17 *'Come, little ones'; | And then again, | 'It is as hard to come as for a camel | To thread the postern of a small needle's eye.'* The texts referred to here come together in Matthew 19.14, 24, Mark 10.14, 25, and Luke 18.16, 25. The second presents difficulties of interpretation of which Shakespeare may have been aware. *Camel* may mean 'cable-rope' rather than the animal; and *needle* the entrance for pedestrians in a large citygate. Shakespeare's *thread* and *postern* seem to hint at both possibilities.

17 *needle* (pronounced 'neele' or 'neeld')

20 *ribs* (framework of the castle, as the ribs are of a man's chest)

21 *ragged* rugged

25 *seely* simple-minded

26-7 *refuge their shame | That* take shelter from their shame in the thought that

33 *treasons* (the thought of them)

40-41 *With nothing shall be pleased till he be eased | With being nothing.* The first *nothing* may be part of a double negative: 'shall be pleased by anything till he has been granted the "ease" of death'; or it may mean the opposite: 'shall be pleased by having nothing (or losing everything) till . . .'.

41 *Music do I hear.* This may be either a statement or a question.

42 *Ha, ha* (an exclamation as he catches out the musician in a rhythmical error; not a laugh)

43 *time is broke, and no proportion kept* the rhythm is faulty, and the correct note values are not observed

46 *check* rebuke

46-8 *disordered string . . . true time broke.* E. W. Naylor (*Shakespeare and Music*, 1931, page 32) explains: 'The "disorder'd string" is himself, who has been playing his part "out of time" ("disorder'd" simply means "out of its place" – i.e. as we now say, "a bar wrong"), and this has resulted in breaking the "concord" – i.e. the harmony of the various parts which compose the state.'

46   *string* stringed instrument

47   *my* (emphatic)

48   *my true time broke* the discord in my own affairs

49   *waste* (including the sense of 'cause to waste away')

50   *numbering clock* (one on which the hours are numbered, not an hourglass)

51–4   *My thoughts are minutes, and with sighs they jar | Their watches on unto mine eyes, the outward watch | Whereto my finger, like a dial's point, | Is pointing still in cleansing them from tears.* This is a difficult passage. It may be paraphrased: 'each of my sad thoughts is like a minute, and the sighs that they cause impel the intervals of time forward to my eyes, which are the point on the outer edge of the watch to which my finger, like a hand on a dial, continually points in wiping tears from them'.

58   *times* quarters and halves

59   *posting* hastening

60   *jack of the clock* (a small figure of a man which struck the bell of a clock every quarter or every hour). The general meaning is that for Bolingbroke time now passes with joyful rapidity, while Richard languishes in prison, counting the hours away.

62   *though it have holp madmen to their wits* (*have holp*, may have helped). The idea that music could help to restore sanity was accepted in Shakespeare's day. He makes notable use of it in *King Lear*, IV.7.25 ff.

66   *strange brooch* rare jewel

67–8   *royal . . . noble . . . groats.* These were all coins. A royal was ten shillings, a noble six-and-eightpence, and a groat fourpence. The difference between a royal and a noble was thus ten groats. Richard is *the cheapest* of those present; to call him royal is to price him ten groats too high. A similar witticism is recorded of Queen Elizabeth. An eighteenth-century anecdote about a clergyman called John Blower runs: ''Tis said that he never preached but one sermon in his life, which was before Queen Elizabeth; and that as he was going about to caress the Queen, he first said "My royal Queen", and a little after "My noble Queen". Upon which says the Queen "What, am I ten groats worse than I was?" At which words being baulked (for he was a man of modesty) he could not be prevailed with to preach any more, but he said he would always read the Homilies for the future; which accordingly he did' (from Thomas Hearne's 'A letter containing an Account of some Antiquities between Windsor and Oxford' in his edition of *The Itinerary of John Leland the Antiquary*, 1711).

67   *peer* 'lord' and 'equal'
70   *sad dog* dismal fellow
75   *sometimes* once
76   *earned* grieved
78   *roan* of mixed colour
      Barbary (an exceptionally good breed of horse, here also used as the name of a particular one)
80   *dressed* tended, groomed
85   *jade* worthless horse
      eat (pronounced 'et') eaten
86   *clapping* patting
88   *pride must have a fall.* The proverb is biblical (Proverbs 16.18: 'Pride goeth before destruction; and an high mind before the fall').
94   *galled* made sore
      jauncing moving up and down (with the horse's motion)
      (stage direction) *meat* food
95   The change to couplets heightens the tension.
98   Here Shakespeare resumes the episode from Holinshed quoted in the preliminary note to V.4 (page 260). Sir

Piers, arrived at Pomfret, commanded 'the esquire that was accustomed to sew [serve] and take the assay before King Richard to do so no more, saying "Let him eat now, for he shall not long eat." King Richard sat down to dinner and was served without courtesy or assay; whereupon much marvelling at the sudden change he demanded of the esquire why he did not his duty. "Sir," said he, "I am otherwise commanded by Sir Piers of Exton, which is newly come from King Henry." When King Richard heard that word he took the carving knife in his hand and strake the esquire on the head, saying "The devil take Henry of Lancaster and thee together." And with that word Sir Piers entered the chamber, well armed, with eight tall men likewise armed, every of them having a bill in his hand.

'King Richard, perceiving this, put the table from him, and, stepping to the foremost man, wrung the bill out of his hands and so valiantly defended himself that he slew four of those that thus came to assail him. Sir Piers being half dismayed herewith leapt into the chair where King Richard was wont to sit, while the other four persons fought with him and chased him about the chamber. And in conclusion, as King Richard traversed his ground from one side of the chamber to another, and coming by the chair where Sir Piers stood he was felled with a stroke of a poleaxe which Sir Piers gave him upon the head, and therewith rid him out of life, without giving him respite once to call to God for mercy of his past offences. It is said that Sir Piers of Exton, after he had thus slain him, wept right bitterly as one stricken with the prick of a guilty conscience for murdering him whom he had so long time obeyed as king.'

99 *Taste of it first, as thou art wont to do.* It was a customary precaution for the king's food to be tasted before he ate it.

105 *What means death in this rude assault?* This line has

been variously explained. It may mean 'what does death mean by assaulting me so violently?' or *means* may be equivalent to 'meanest': 'What do you mean, death, by ...?' or 'What – do you [the murderers] mean death ...?' Or the line may be taken along with the next as an expression of the paradox that though death apparently means to kill him, yet he is able to wrest a weapon from one of his attackers and kill him with it.

107 *room* place

109 *staggers* causes to stagger

my person (a last assertion of royalty)

111-12 C. E. Montague writes of F. R. Benson that, having uttered these lines 'much as any other man might utter them under the first shock of the imminence of death, he half rises from the ground with a brightened face and repeats the two last words with a sudden return of animation and interest, the eager spirit leaping up, with a last flicker before it goes quite out, to seize on this new "idea of" the death of the body'.

V.6 The material of the final scene is compressed from Holinshed. See Commentary to line 30.

3 *Ciceter*. The town now known as Cirencester, spelt here as in the early editions. The name is still often pronounced like this, or as 'Cicester'.

7-8 *The next news is, I have to London sent | The heads of Salisbury, Spencer, Blunt, and Kent.* The reason is given in Holinshed: 'the heads of the chief conspirators were set on poles over London Bridge, to the terror of others'. The baldness of the couplet is not altogether happy. Dover Wilson says of it and the following one: 'Is not this the very accent of Quince himself? The immortal lines

The actors are at hand and by their show
You shall know all that you are like to know,

go on like rhyming stilts, and to the identical jog-trot in metre' (New Cambridge edition, Introduction, page lxx).

8   *Salisbury, Spencer, Blunt*. Q has *Oxford, Salisbury, Blunt*. *Oxford* is historically wrong; he was not implicated in the plot against Henry. This may well have been Shakespeare's error, though it is sometimes blamed on the printer. But the fact that the statement is corrected in F, which may transmit an alteration made or approved by Shakespeare, justifies the emendation.

10   *At large discoursèd* related in full

14   *Brocas and Sir Bennet Seely*. This is based on Holinshed: 'Many other that were privy to this conspiracy were taken and put to death, some at Oxford, as Sir Thomas Blunt, Sir Bennet Cilie, knight ... but Sir Leonard Brokas and [others] ... were drawn, hanged, and beheaded at London.'

15   *consorted* conspiring

18   *wot* know

19–21 *The grand conspirator ... to the grave*. Holinshed has: 'the Abbot of Westminster, in whose house the conspiracy was begun, as is said, going between his monastery and mansion, for thought fell into a sudden palsy, and shortly after, without speech, ended his life'.

20   *clog* burden

      sour bitter

      melancholy (thought of as a physical substance, black bile, causing disease when present in excess)

22–9 Holinshed has: 'The Bishop of Carlisle was impeached, and condemned of the same conspiracy; but the King of his merciful clemency pardoned him of that offence, although he died shortly after, more through fear than force of sickness, as some have written.'

23   *doom* judgement

25   *reverent room* place of religious retirement (*reverent*, worthy of respect)

26   *More than thou hast* (perhaps 'bigger than you have', that is, your prison cell)

    joy 'enjoy', or 'add joy to'. Probably Bolingbroke is (whether ironically or not) proposing to Carlisle the pleasures of monastic retirement.

30   Shakespeare takes up again Holinshed's episode of the murder of Richard: 'After he was thus dead, his body was embalmed and cered and covered with lead, all save the face, to the intent that all men might see him and perceive that he was departed this life; for as the corpse was conveyed from Pomfret to London, in all the towns and places where those that had the conveyance of it did stay with it all night, they caused dirge to be sung in the evening, and mass of Requiem in the morning; and as well after the one service as the other, his face, discovered, was showed to all that coveted to behold it.' Holinshed records King Henry's presence at the solemn obsequies at Saint Paul's and Westminster.

38   *They love not poison that do poison need* (recalling the proverbial expression 'A king loves the treason but hates the traitor')

43   *With Cain* like Cain (who killed his own brother. Compare I.1.104.)

48   *incontinent* immediately

49   *I'll make a voyage to the Holy Land.* Henry's intention of undertaking a crusade in expiation of his sin is several times referred to in *1* and *2 Henry IV*.

51   *Grace* honour with your presence

AN ACCOUNT OF THE TEXT

Richard II was first printed in 1597, in the edition known as the first Quarto (Q1). It is described on the title-page as *The Tragedy of King Richard the Second. As it hath been publicly acted by the Right Honourable the Lord Chamberlain his Servants.* The Lord Chamberlain's was the acting company to which Shakespeare belonged. The play seems to have been printed from his own manuscript, and with an unusually high standard of accuracy. As no manuscript has survived, modern editions must be based on the quarto. But it lacks one important episode – that portraying Richard's abdication (IV.1.154–319). This was omitted most probably for political reasons, perhaps out of tact, or because the printers feared prosecution, or because they had been instructed to omit it. It contains nothing obviously inflammatory, but was certainly considered dangerous at a time of anxiety about the succession (see Introduction, pages 11–14). A little tinkering was done to bridge the gap but there was no real revision, and the fact that the Abbot's line 'A woeful pageant have we here beheld' (IV.1.320) was retained though the 'pageant' had disappeared is a good reason for believing that the cut was not theatrical.

Richard II was popular, and the quarto was reprinted twice in 1598 (Q2 and Q3). The abdication scene continued to be omitted. The fourth edition (Q4) appeared in 1608. By this time the succession problem had been resolved, and the printer was able to announce on the title-page *The Tragedy of King Richard the Second: With new additions of the Parliament Scene, and the deposing of King Richard, as it hath been lately acted by the King's Majesty's Servants at the Globe. By William Shakespeare.* Unfortunately the text of the added passages contains many obvious mistakes, and was printed probably from an unauthorized source. The next edition appeared in 1615, and is a reprint of the previous one.

The other important text is the one in the collected edition of Shakespeare's plays, the first Folio (F), of 1623. The printers seem to have worked from a copy of Q 3 with the substitution of a few leaves from Q 5. There are two main reasons why this text is important. One is that the quarto from which it was printed had been altered from a source that was obviously theatrical in origin. The natural assumption is that it had been checked against the theatre prompt-book, which would be a manuscript or printed copy annotated and marked in accordance with theatre practice. It would, for example, indicate trumpet calls that Shakespeare had not noted in the manuscript, and might mark cuts. The stage directions in F are notably more precise and businesslike than those in the quartos. They obviously reflect the stage practice of Shakespeare's company and are our main source of information about how the play was put on the stage in his time. They have been incorporated in the present edition. Other alterations were made, some of which may be considered improvements on Q1. We have no reason to suppose that F presents an authoritatively corrected text, and the present edition is conservative in adopting Folio readings where Quarto ones are acceptable. The Collations, however, record plausible readings from F among the Rejected Emendations.

The other main reason for F's importance is that it includes a good text of the abdication episode omitted from the early quartos. Modern editors therefore use F as their basic text for this passage, while adopting some readings from Q4. The present edition is closer to F than most modern ones.

Fifty-one lines of the play were omitted from F. They are: I.3.129–33; I.3.239–42; I.3.268–93; II.2.77; III.2.29–32, 49, 182; IV.1.52–9; V.3.98. Some of these omissions may be accidental, some may represent theatrical cutting.

In the present edition spelling and punctuation have been modernized, speech prefixes have been made consistent, and stage directions have been regularized and amplified where necessary. The Collations that follow record departures from Q1 (F for the abdication episode); places where the present edition preserves original readings that other editors have often altered; and the more important modifications of the original stage directions. Quotations from early editions are given in the original spelling, but long 's' [ʃ] has been replaced by the modern form. 'Q' indicates a reading common to all the early quartos (Q1–5). The more interesting textual points are discussed in the Commentary.

COLLATIONS

I

The following list indicates readings in the present edition of *Richard II* which depart from the first edition (Q1) or, in the abdication episode (IV.1.154–319), from the first Folio (F1). It does not list corrections of simple misprints. Alterations of punctuation are recorded when a decision affecting the sense has had to be made. When the emendation derives from a later quarto or the Folio, this is indicated. Most of the other emendations were first made by eighteenth-century editors.

THE CHARACTERS IN THE PLAY] *not in* Q, F

I.1.   3 Hereford] Q1 *often, but by no means regularly, spells* Herford
        15 presence. *Exit Attendant* Face] presence face
       118 my] F; *not in* Q
       122 subject, Mowbray. So] subiect Mowbray so
       152 gentlemen] F; gentleman Q
     162–3 When, Harry, when? | Obedience bids] When Harry? when obedience bids, | Obedience bids Q1; When *Harrie* when? Obedience bids, | Obedience bids Q2–5, F

I.2.   47 sit] F; set Q

I.3.   33 comest] Q5, F; comes
       172 then] F; *not in* Q
       180 you owe] F; y'owe Q
       193 far as] fare as Q; fare, as F (*see Commentary*)
       222 night] Q4–5, F; nightes Q1–3
       239 had it] had't

I.4.   20 cousin, cousin] F; Coosens Coosin Q
      52–3 *Enter Bushy* | Bushy, what news?] F; *Enter
            Bushie with newes.* Q
        65 ALL] *not in* Q, F (*which also omits* 'Amen')

II.1.   18 fond] found Q1
        48 as a moat] Q4–5, F; as moate Q1–3
       102 encagèd] F (incaged); inraged Q
       124 brother] Q2–5; brothers Q1, F
       177 the] F; a Q
       257 King's] Q3–5, F; King Q1
       280 The son of Richard Earl of Arundel] *not in* Q, F
       284 Coint] Coines Q; *Quoint* F

II.2.   16 eye] F; eyes
       147 BAGOT] *not in* Q (F *gives the line to Bushy*)

II.3.   9 Cotswold] Cotshall Q; Cottshold F
        36 Hereford, boy?] Q3; Herefords boy? Q1
       163 Bristol] Bristow

III.2. 31 not – heaven's offer we] not, heauens offer, we
            Q1
        32 succour] succors
        40 boldly] bouldy Q1
        72 O'erthrows] F; Ouerthrowes Q

III.3. 12–13 Would you have been so brief with him, he
            would | Have been so brief with you to shorten
            you] F; would you haue beene so briefe with
            him, | He would haue bin so briefe to shorten
            you Q
        31 lord] F; Lords Q
     59–60 rain | My waters – on] raigne. | My water's on
            Q1–2; raine | My water's on Q3–5; raine | My
            Waters on F

272

III.3. 119 a prince and] (Sisson) princesse Q1–2; a Prince
Q 3–5; a Prince, is F

140 Swellest thou, proud heart? I'll] F; Swellst thou
(prowd heart) Ile

III.4. *Speech prefixes to* 3, 6, 10, 11 (second part), 19 (first part),
21] *Lady* Q.; *La.* F

11 joy] griefe

21 weep, . . . good.] Q2; weep; . . . good? Q1

34 too] F; two

Speech prefixes to 40, 54 (first part), 67] *Man.* Q.; *Ser.* F

57 garden! We at] garden at

80 Camest] Q2; Canst

IV.1. 22 him] Q 3 (my Q2); them

43 Fitzwater] F; Fitzwaters

54 As may] As it may

55 sun to sun] sinne to sinne

62 true.] true (true, Q2; true: F)

76 my] Q 3; *not in* Q1 (the Q2)

83–4 gage. | That] gage, | That

154–319 *This passage is not in* Q1–3. *See 'An Account of the
Text', page* 269. *In its place,* Q1 *has:* Bull. Let it
be so, and loe on wednesday next, | We solemnly
proclaime our Coronation, | Lords be ready
all.

182 and] (Q 4, 5) *not in* F

250 and] (Q 4) a F

253 haught, insulting] (haught insulting Q4–5)
haught-insulting F

254 Nor] (Q 4) No, nor F

259 mockery king] (Q 4) Mockerie, King F

318 proclaim | Our coronation. Lords, be ready, all.]
Q1; set downe | Our Coronation: Lords, prepare
your selues. F

332 I will] Ile

V.1. 20 this.] this: Q1 (*where the colon could be the
equivalent of a modern fullstop*)

41 thee] Q2; the

V.1.   88 off than, near,] (*unpunctuated*, Q) off, then
             neere, F
V.2. 11, 17 thee] F; the Q (*where however 'thee' is often spelt
             thus*)
V.3.   35 that I may] Q2; that May
         74 shrill-voiced] Q3; shril voice
        110 KING HENRY] Q2; *yorke*
     134-5 With all my heart | I pardon him] I pardon him
             with al my heart
V.5.   27 sit] Q3; set
V.6.   8 Salisbury, Spencer] F; Oxford, Salisbury Q
         43 thorough shades] through shades Q1; through
             the shade Q2-5, F

2

Rejected emendations
The list printed below gives readings of the authoritative
editions (Q1, and F1 for the abdication scene) which have been
preserved in the present edition but which are often emended.
The common emendations are given to the right of the square
bracket. The aim has been to list alterations affecting the sense,
especially those that are to be found in some of the editions still
current. Most of them derive from the Folio, which until the
early years of this century was generally considered the most
authoritative early text. As the Folio has a special interest in
spite of its generally inferior authority, some of its more
interesting variants are noted even when they have been
generally rejected. When a reading derives from an early
edition (Q1-5, F) this is indicated. Most of the unattributed
emendations were first made by eighteenth-century editors,
many of them in an attempt to regularize the metre. The temptation to do this is strong, but Shakespeare may not have had the
precise rhythmic sense that many of his editors assume in him.

I.1.   97 Fetch] Fetcht Q3-5, Fetch'd F
        186 up] downe F

I.1.	187	deep] foule F
I.2.	62	thy] my F
I.3.	15	As] And
	20	my succeeding] his succeeding F
	26	ask] demand of
	84	innocence] innocency
	193	far as] fare as (*see Commentary*)
I.4.	23	Ourself and Bushy] Ourself and Bushy, Bagot here, and Green
	59	the] his F
II.1.	70	raged] ragged; reined
	115	And thou – | KING RICHARD – a lunatic] And thou. | *King*. Ah lunatick Q 3–5; And – | *Rich*. And thou, a lunaticke F
	254	noble] *omitted in* F *and by many editors*
	278, 285	Brittaine] Britain; Brittany; Bretagne
II.2.	12	trembles. At something] (trembles, at something Q1) trembles, yet at something
	25	more is] more's F
	31	on thinking] in thinking
	88	The nobles they are fled. The commons they are cold] The nobles they are fled, the commons cold
	110	disorderly thrust] thrust disorderly
	112	T'one] (Q: Tone) Th'one F
	113	T'other] (Q: tother) th'other F
	118	Berkeley] Barkley Castle F
	128	that is] that's F
	137	Will the hateful commons] The hateful commons will
II.3.	65	thank's] thankes F
	80	self-borne] self-born
	98	lord] the Lord F
	122	in] of Q2–5, F
	150	never] ne'er (ne're Q 3–5; neu'r F)
	157	unto] to Q2–5, F
II.4.	8	are all] all are Q2–5, F

III.2. 30 neglected; else heaven] (Q1: neglected. Else heauen) neglected; else, if heaven
       38 that] and
       40 boldly] (bouldy Q1) bloudy Q2, bloody F
    133–4 Would they make peace? Terrible hell | Make war upon their spotted souls for this.] Would they make peace? terrible Hell make warre | Vpon their spotted Soules for this Offence. F

III.3. 17 mistake the] mistake; the; mistake. The; mistake: the
   100 pastor's] (pastors Q1) pasture's; pastures'
   121 thus. The King returns] thus the King returns:
   168 laid there] (laide; there Q1) laid – there
   177 you,] you;
   182 base-court. Come down – down] (Q1: base court come downe: downe) base court? Come down? Down
   202 hands] hand F

III.4. 27 They will] They'le F
    29 young] yon Q2
    67 you the] you then the
    80 this] these

IV.1. 13 mine] my F
    49 And if] An if
    89 he is] hee's F
    91 never] ne're F
   112 fourth of that name] of that Name the Fourth F
   165 knee] limbes? Q4
   182 thine] yours Q4
   209 duteous oaths] duties rites Q4
   214 are made] that sweare Q4
   219 Henry] Harry Q4
   275 that] the Q4
   284 Is this the face which] Was . . . that Q4
   285 That] And Q4
   288 an] a Q4

IV.1.   295 manner] manners Q4
              laments] lament
      318–19 proclaim | Our coronation. Lords, be ready, all.]
              set downe | Our Coronation: Lords, prepare your
              selues. F

V.1.   25   thrown] stricken F
         32   the correction] thy correction Q2
              correction, mildly] Correction mildly, F
         34   the king] a King Q2, F
         37   sometimes] sometime Q3, F
         43   quite] quit F
         44   tale] fall F
         62   He] And he
         64   urged another way,] urged, another way,,; urged,
              another way; urged another way
         66   men] friends F
         71   Doubly divorced! Bad] (Doubly diuorst (bad)
              Q1; Doubly diuorc'd? (bad F
         84   RICHARD] North. F

V.2.   18   the one] one F
         28   gentle] not in F
         52   Do these justs and triumphs hold?] Hold those
              Iusts & Triumphs? F
         55   prevent not] prevent me not; prevent it not
         74   Some editors add the direction: Enter a Servant.
              See Commentary.
         78   by my life, by my troth] my life, my troth Q2,
              F; by my life, my troth
        113   Spur, post] Spurre post F

V.3.   10   Which] While
         20   Yet] But yet [with relineation, lines ending yet,
              hope, forth, means] (Harold Brooks, in Ure's
              edition)
         30   my roof] the roof
         40   Villain] omitted (Ure)
         45   What is the matter,] omitted (Ure)
         67   An] And F and editors

V.3.   105 still] shall F
         143 cousin,] Cosin too, Q6
V.4.   7 wishtly] wistly Q3, F
V.5.   56 which] that F
          70 never] euer Q5, F
         105 means] meanest

3

Stage directions

Stage directions in the present edition are based on those of
Q1. The original directions have been normalized and clarified.
They are often inadequate, failing for instance to indicate
many obvious entrances and exits. Additional directions have
been made from F, which is much more precise in its instruc-
tions to the performers, and often indicates the practice of
Shakespeare's company. Further directions have been added
where necessary to clarify the action. All directions for speeches
to be given aside or addressed to a particular character are
editorial. Below are listed some of the other additions and
alterations to Q's stage directions. When these derive in
whole or part from F, this is noted. Minor alterations such as
the addition of a character's name to *Exit*, the change of *Exit*
to *Exeunt*, the normalization of character names, and the provision of exits and entrances where these are obviously demanded
by the context are not listed here.

I.1.   0 *Enter King Richard and John of Gaunt, with other*
              nobles, including the Lord Marshal, and at-
              tendants] Enter King Richard, Iohn of Gaunt, with
              other Nobles and attendants. Q, F
          15 *not in* Q, F
          69 *not in* Q, F
          78 *not in* Q, F
         149 *not in* Q, F
         165 *not in* Q, F
         195 F; *not in* Q

278

I.3.   6   *The trumpets sound and the King enters with his nobles, including Gaunt, and Bushy, Bagot, and Green. When they are set, enter Mowbray, Duke of Norfolk, in arms, defendant; and a Herald]* The trumpets sound and the King enters with his nobles, when they are set, enter the Duke of Norfolke in armes defendant. Q; *Flourish. Enter King, Gaunt, Bushy, Bagot, Greene, & others: Then Mowbray in Armor, and Harrold.* F

         25   *The trumpets sound. Enter Bolingbroke, Duke of Hereford, appellant, in armour; and a Herald]* The trumpets sound. Enter Duke of Hereford appellant in armour. Q; *Tucket. Enter Hereford, and Harold.* F

         54   *not in* Q, F

       117   *A charge sounded. King Richard throws his warder into the lists]* not in Q. *A charge sounded* F

       122   *A long flourish. King Richard consults his nobles, then addresses the combatants]* not in Q. *A long Flourish.* F

       248   *Flourish. Exit King Richard with his train]* not in Q. *Exit. Flourish.* F

I.4.   0   *Enter the King with Bagot and Green at one door, and the Lord Aumerle at another]* Enter the King with Bushie, &c at one dore, and the Lord Aumarle at another. Q; *Enter King, Aumerle, Greene, and Bagot.* F

        52   (see Commentary)

II.1.   0   *Enter John of Gaunt sick, with the Duke of York, the Earl of Northumberland, attendants, and others]* Enter Iohn of Gaunt sicke, with the duke of Yorke, &c. Q; *Enter Gaunt, sicke with Yorke.* F

        68   *Enter King Richard, Queen Isabel, Aumerle, Bushy, Green, Bagot, Ross, and Willoughby]* F; Enter king and Queene, & c. Q

      223   *Flourish. Exeunt King Richard and Queen Isabel.*

Northumberland, Willoughby, and Ross remain] *Exeunt King and Queene: Manet North.* Q ; *Flourish. Manet North. Willoughby, & Ross.* F

II.3.   82   *not in* Q, F

III.1.   0   *Enter Bolingbroke, York, Northumberland, with Bushy and Green, prisoners*] *Enter Duke of Hereford, Yorke, Northumberland, Bushie and Greene prisoners.* Q ; *Enter Bullingbrooke, Yorke, Northumberland, Rosse, Percie, Willoughby, with Bushie and Greene Prisoners.* F

III.2.   0   *Drums ; flourish and colours. Enter King Richard, Aumerle, the Bishop of Carlisle, and soldiers*] *Enter the King Aumerle, Carleil, &c.* Q ; *Drums : Flourish, and Colours. Enter Richard, Aumerle, Carlile, and Souldiers.* F

III.3.   0   *Enter with drum and colours Bolingbroke, York, Northumberland, attendants, and soldiers*] *Enter Bull. Yorke, North.* Q ; *Enter with Drum and Colours, Bullingbrooke, Yorke, Northumberland, Attendants.* F

       61   *The trumpets sound parley without, and answer within ; then a flourish. King Richard appeareth on the walls with the Bishop of Carlisle, Aumerle, Scroop, and Salisbury*] *The trumpets sound, Richard appeareth on the walls.* Q ; *Parle without, and answere within : then a Flourish. Enter on the Walls, Richard, Carlile, Aumerle, Scroop, Salisbury.* F

      183   *not in* Q, F

      186   *not in* Q, F

      209   F; *not in* Q

III.4.   0   *Enter the Queen with two Ladies, her attendants*] *Enter the Queene with her attendants* Q ; *Enter the Queene, and two Ladies.* F

      23   *Enter Gardeners, one the master, the other two his men*] *Enter Gardeners.* Q ; *Enter a Gardiner, and two Seruants.* F

III.4.   28 *not in* Q, F

72 *not in* Q, F

101 *Exit Queen with her Ladies*] *Exit* Q, F

IV.1.   0 *Enter Bolingbroke with the Lords Aumerle,
Northumberland, Harry Percy, Fitzwater, Surrey,
the Bishop of Carlisle, the Abbot of Westminster,
another Lord, Herald, and officer, to Parliament*]
Enter Bullingbrooke with the Lords tᵣ parliament.
Q; *Enter as to the Parliament, Bullingbrooke,
Aumerle, Northumberland, Percie, Fitz-Water,
Surrey, Carlile, Abbot of Westminster. Herauld,
Officers, and Bagot.* F

1 *Enter Bagot with officers*] *Enter Bagot.* Q; *not in*
F

24 *not in* Q, F

34 *not in* Q, F

48 *not in* Q, F

55 *not in* Q, F

70 *not in* Q, F

83 *not in* Q, F

157 F; *not in* Q4

161 *Enter Richard and York*] F; *Enter king Richard.*
Q4

267 *not in* F, Q4

274 *Enter attendant with a glass*] *Enter one with a
Glasse.* F; *not in* Q4

287 *not in* F, Q4

319 *Exeunt all except the Abbot of Westminster, the
Bishop of Carlisle, Aumerle*] *Exeunt. Manent
West. Caleil, Aumerle.* Q1; *Exeunt.* F

V.1.   6 *Enter Richard and guard*] F; *Enter Ric.* Q

96 *not in* Q, F

98 *not in* Q, F

V.2.   71 *He plucks it out of his bosom, and reads it*] Q;
Snatches it F

87 *not in* Q, F

V.3.   0 *Enter Bolingbroke, now King Henry, with Harry*

Percy and other lords] Enter the King with his nobles. Q ; *Enter Bullingbrooke, Percie, and other Lords.* F

V.3. 37 *Aumerle locks the door. The Duke of York knocks at the door and crieth] The Duke of Yorke knokes at the doore and crieth.* Q ; *not in* F

38 YORK (*within*)] *Yor.* Q ; *Yorke within.* | *Yor.* F

44 *King Henry opens the door. Enter York] not in* Q ; *Enter Yorke.* F

73 DUCHESS OF YORK (*within*)] *Du.* Q ; *Dutchesse within.* | *Dut.* F

81 *Aumerle admits the Duchess. She kneels] not in* Q ; *Enter Dutchesse.* F (*after line* 85)

96, 97 *not in* Q, F

135 *not in* Q, F

V.3.145–V.4.0 *Exeunt | Enter Sir Piers of Exton and a Man] Exeunt. Manet sir Pierce Exton, &c.* Q ; *Exeunt.* | *Enter Exton and Seruants.* F

V.4. 11 *Exeunt] not in* Q ; *Exit.* F

V.5. 41 *The music plays]* Q ; *Musick (at end of line* 38) F

94 *Enter Keeper to Richard with meat] Enter one to Richard with meate.* Q ;*Enter Keeper with a Dish.* F

102 *not in* Q, F

104 *The murderers, Exton and servants, rush in] The murderers rush in.* Q ; *Enter Exton and Seruants.* F

106 *not in* Q, F

107 *He kills another servant. Here Exton strikes him down] Here Exton strikes him downe.* Q ; *Exton strikes him downe.* F

112 *not in* Q, F

118 *Exeunt with the bodies] not in* Q ; *Exit.* F

V.6. 0 *Flourish. Enter King Henry with the Duke of York, other lords, and attendants] Enter Bullingbrooke with the duke of Yorke.* Q ; *Flourish. Enter Bullingbrooke, Yorke, with other Lords & attendants.* F

V.6.   18 *Enter Harry Percy with the Bishop of Carlisle,*
       guarded] *Enter H Percie.* Q; *Enter Percy and*
       Carlile. F
       44 *not in* Q, F

Genealogical Table

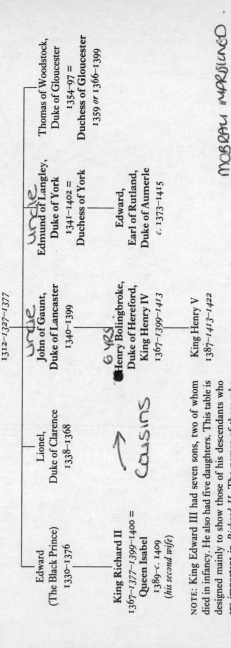

King Edward III
1312–1327–1377

Edward (The Black Prince) 1330–1376

Lionel, Duke of Clarence 1338–1368

John of Gaunt, Duke of Lancaster 1340–1399

Edmund of Langley, Duke of York 1341–1402 = Duchess of York

Thomas of Woodstock, Duke of Gloucester 1354–97 = Duchess of Gloucester 1359 or 1366–1399

King Richard II 1367–1377–1399–1400 = Queen Isabel 1389–c. 1409 (his second wife)

Henry Bolingbroke, Duke of Hereford, King Henry IV 1367–1399–1413

Edward, Earl of Rutland, Duke of Aumerle c. 1373–1415

King Henry V 1387–1413–1422

NOTE: King Edward III had seven sons, two of whom died in infancy. He also had five daughters. This table is designed mainly to show those of his descendants who are important in *Richard II*. The names of those who appear in the play are printed in heavy type. Italicized dates are those of reigns; other dates are those of births and deaths.

Act 3 scene 3. Pg 95.

- The King is in Ireland
- Takes place after Bol returns
  after being banished by Rich
- The King has taken Bol possessions
- Bol returns to reclaim his inheritance
- The population has gone onto Bol's side
- YORK has been left in charge of the
  country
- JOG has died.

ACT 2 scene 1.
Opens with a conversation between
JOG and York, Gaunt hopes that Rich
will listen to his advice as he is a
dying man, York says he is wasting
his time and criticises his bad
habbits eg fashion etc (Rich)
King arrives very offhand will
not listen to advice, Gaunt dies
Rich convis cates goods and prepares
to go to IRELAND at the end of the
scene there is a converstain between
NORTH, willoe and ROSS. Initially
they discuss the bad state of the country
as soon NORTH realises they are
all anti Rich - Reveals Bol and his
supporters are returning to the country
NORTH - sees BOL AS poss King

READ MORE IN PENGUIN

In every corner of the world, on every subject under the sun, Penguin represents quality and variety – the very best in publishing today.

For complete information about books available from Penguin – including Puffins, Penguin Classics and Arkana – and how to order them, write to us at the appropriate address below. Please note that for copyright reasons the selection of books varies from country to country.

In the United Kingdom: Please write to *Dept. EP, Penguin Books Ltd, Bath Road, Harmondsworth, West Drayton, Middlesex UB7 0DA*

In the United States: Please write to *Consumer Sales, Penguin USA, P.O. Box 999, Dept. 17109, Bergenfield, New Jersey 07621-0120*. VISA and MasterCard holders call 1-800-253-6476 to order Penguin titles

In Canada: Please write to *Penguin Books Canada Ltd, 10 Alcorn Avenue, Suite 300, Toronto, Ontario M4V 3B2*

In Australia: Please write to *Penguin Books Australia Ltd, P.O. Box 257, Ringwood, Victoria 3134*

In New Zealand: Please write to *Penguin Books (NZ) Ltd, Private Bag 102902, North Shore Mail Centre, Auckland 10*

In India: Please write to *Penguin Books India Pvt Ltd, 706 Eros Apartments, 56 Nehru Place, New Delhi 110 019*

In the Netherlands: Please write to *Penguin Books Netherlands bv, Postbus 3507, NL-1001 AH Amsterdam*

In Germany: Please write to *Penguin Books Deutschland GmbH, Metzlerstrasse 26, 60594 Frankfurt am Main*

In Spain: Please write to *Penguin Books S. A., Bravo Murillo 19, 1° B, 28015 Madrid*

In Italy: Please write to *Penguin Italia s.r.l., Via Felice Casati 20, I–20124 Milano*

In France: Please write to *Penguin France S. A., 17 rue Lejeune, F–31000 Toulouse*

In Japan: Please write to *Penguin Books Japan, Ishikiribashi Building, 2–5–4, Suido, Bunkyo-ku, Tokyo 112*

In South Africa: Please write to *Longman Penguin Southern Africa (Pty) Ltd, Private Bag X08, Bertsham 2013*

READ MORE IN PENGUIN

THE NEW PENGUIN SHAKESPEARE

All's Well That Ends Well	Barbara Everett
Antony and Cleopatra	Emrys Jones
As You Like It	H. J. Oliver
The Comedy of Errors	Stanley Wells
Coriolanus	G. R. Hibbard
Hamlet	T. J. B. Spencer
Henry IV, Part 1	P. H. Davison
Henry IV, Part 2	P. H. Davison
Henry V	A. R. Humphreys
Henry VI, Parts 1–3	Norman Sanders
(three volumes)	
Henry VIII	A. R. Humphreys
Julius Caesar	Norman Sanders
King John	R. L. Smallwood
King Lear	G. K. Hunter
Love's Labour's Lost	John Kerrigan
Macbeth	G. K. Hunter
Measure for Measure	J. M. Nosworthy
The Merchant of Venice	W. Moelwyn Merchant
The Merry Wives of Windsor	G. R. Hibbard
A Midsummer Night's Dream	Stanley Wells
Much Ado About Nothing	R. A. Foakes
The Narrative Poems	Maurice Evans
Othello	Kenneth Muir
Pericles	Philip Edwards
Richard II	Stanley Wells
Richard III	E. A. J. Honigmann
Romeo and Juliet	T. J. B. Spencer
The Sonnets *and* **A Lover's Complaint**	John Kerrigan
The Taming of the Shrew	G. R. Hibbard
The Tempest	Anne Barton
Timon of Athens	G. R. Hibbard
Troilus and Cressida	R. A. Foakes
Twelfth Night	M. M. Mahood
The Two Gentlemen of Verona	Norman Sanders
The Two Noble Kinsmen	N. W. Bawcutt
The Winter's Tale	Ernest Schanzer